JERUSALEM

Selma Lagerlöf 1858-1940

Cover Painting:

"View Of Jerusalem" by Pierre Tetar Van Elven (1828-1908).

Cover Design Copyright © 2008 by Vera Nazarian

ISBN-13: 978-1-934648-47-6
ISBN-10: 1-934648-47-7

Original Swedish Language Publication: 1901-1902

Reprint Trade Paperback Edition

March 2008

A Publication of
Norilana Books
P. O. Box 2188
Winnetka, CA 91396
www.norilana.com

Printed in the United States of America

Jerusalem

Norilana Books

Classics

www.norilana.com

Jerusalem

A Novel

❧

SELMA LAGERLÖF

❧

Translated from the Swedish
by
Velma Swanston Howard

With an Introduction
by
Henry Goddard Leach

Contents

Introduction 9

BOOK ONE 15

The Ingmarssons 16

I 16

II 26

III 30

IV 36

BOOK TWO 49

At The Schoolmaster's 50

"And They Saw Heaven Open" 59

Karin, Daughter Of Ingmar 66

In Zion 86

The Wild Hunt 95

Hellgum 112

The New Way 129

BOOK THREE 151

Loss Of "L'Univers" 152

Hellgum's Letter 165

The Big Log 178

The Ingmar Farm 180

Hök Matts Ericsson 184

The Auction 190

Gertrude 204

The Dean's Widow 219

The Departure Of The Pilgrims 223

renunciation of her lover for her religion, the brother who buys the old farmstead so that his brother's wife may have a home if she should ever return from the Holy Land. As for the closing pages that describe the departure of the Jerusalem-farers, they are difficult to read aloud without a sob and a lump in the throat.

The underlying spiritual action of *Jerusalem* is the conflict of idealism with that impulse which is deep rooted in the rural communities of the old world, the love of home and the home soil. It is a virtue unfortunately too dimly appreciated in restless America, though felt in some measure in the old communities of Massachusetts and Virginia, and Quaker homesteads near Philadelphia. Among the peasant aristocracy of Dalecarlia attachment to the homestead is life itself. In *Jerusalem* this emotion is pitted on the one hand against religion, on the other against *love*. Hearts are broken in the struggle *which* permits Karin to sacrifice the Ingmar Farm to obey the inner voice that summons her on her religious pilgrimage, and *which* leads her brother, on the other hand, to abandon the girl of his heart and his life's personal happiness in order to win back the farm.

The tragic intensity of *Jerusalem* is happily relieved by the undercurrent of Miss Lagerlöf's sympathetic humour. When she has almost succeeded in transporting us into a state of religious fervour, we suddenly catch her smile through the lines and realize that no one more than she feels the futility of fanaticism. The stupid blunders of humankind do not escape her; neither do they arouse her contempt. She accepts human nature as it is with a warm fondness for all its types. We laugh and weep simultaneously at the children of the departing pilgrims, who cry out in vain: "We don't want to go to Jerusalem; we want to go home."

To the translator of *Jerusalem,* Mrs. Velma Swanston Howard, author and reader alike must feel indebted. Mrs. Howard has already received generous praise for her translation of *Nils* and other works of Selma Lagerlöf. Although born in Sweden she has achieved remarkable mastery of English diction. As a friend of Miss Lagerlöf and an artist she is enabled herself to pass through the temperament of creation and to reproduce the original in essence as well as sufficient verisimilitude. Mrs.

Howard is no mere artisan translator. She goes over her page not but a dozen times, and the result is not a labored performance, but a work of real art in strong and confident prose.

HENRY GODDARD LEACH.
Villa Nova, Pennsylvania.
June 28, 1915.

BOOK ONE

The Ingmarssons

I

A young farmer was plowing his field one summer morning. The sun shone, the grass sparkled with dew, and the air was so light and bracing that no words can describe it. The horses were frisky from the morning air, and pulled the plow along as if in play. They were going at a pace quite different from their usual gait; the man had fairly to run to keep up with them.

The earth, as it was turned by the plow, lay black, and shone with moisture and fatness, and the man at the plow was happy in the thought of soon being able to sow his rye. "Why is it that I feel so discouraged at times and think life so hard?" he wondered. "What more does one want than sunshine and fair weather to be as happy as a child of Heaven?"

A long and rather broad valley, with stretches of green and yellow grain fields, with mowed clover meadows, potato patches in flower, and little fields of flax with their tiny blue flowers, above which fluttered great swarms of white butterflies—this was the setting. At the very heart of the valley, as if to complete the picture, lay a big old-fashioned farmstead, with many gray outhouses and a large red dwelling-house. At the gables stood two tall, spreading pear trees; at the gate were a couple of young birches; in the grass-covered yard were great piles of firewood; and behind the barn were several huge haystacks. The farmhouse rising above the low fields was as pretty a sight as a ship, with masts and sails, towering above the broad surface of the sea.

The man at the plow was thinking: "What a farm you've got! Many well-timbered houses, fine cattle and horses, and servants who are as good as gold. At least you are as well-to-do as any one in these parts, so you'll never have to face poverty.

"But it's not poverty that I fear," he said, as if in answer to his own thought. "I should be satisfied were I only as good a man as my father or my father's father. What could have put such silly nonsense into your head?" he wondered. "And a moment ago you were feeling so happy. Ponder well this one thing: in father's time all the neighbours were guided by him in all their undertakings. The morning he began haymaking they did likewise and the day we started in to plow our fallow field at the Ingmar Farm, plows were put in the earth the length and breadth of the valley. Yet here I've been plowing now for two hours and more without any one having so much as ground a plowshare.

"I believe I have managed this farm as well as any one who has borne the name of Ingmar Ingmarsson," he mused. "I can get more for my hay than father ever got for his, and I'm not satisfied to let the weed-choked ditches which crossed the farm in his time remain. What's more, no one can say that I misuse the woodlands as he did by converting them into burn-beaten land.

"There are times when all this seems hard to bear," said the young man. "I can't always take it as lightly as I do to-day. When father and grandfather lived, folks used to say that the Ingmarssons had been on earth such a long time that they must know what was pleasing to our Lord. Therefore the people fairly begged them to rule over the parish. They appointed both parson and sexton; they determined when the river should be dredged, and where gaols should be built. But me no one consults, nor have I a say in anything.

"It's wonderful, all the same, that troubles can be so easily borne on a morning like this. I could almost laugh at them. And still I fear that matters will be worse than ever for me in the fall. If I should do what I'm now thinking of doing, neither the parson nor the judge will shake hands with me when we meet at

the church on a Sunday, which is something they have always
done up to the present. I could never hope to be made a guardian
of the poor, nor could I even think of becoming a
churchwarden."

Thinking is never so easy as when one follows a plow up
a furrow and down a furrow. You are quite alone, and there is
nothing to distract you but the crows hopping about picking up
worms. The thoughts seemed to come to the man as readily as if
some one had whispered them into his ear. Only on rare
occasions had he been able to think as quickly and clearly as on
that day, and the thought of it gladdened and encouraged him. It
occurred to him that he was giving himself needless anxiety; that
no one expected him to plunge headlong into misery. He thought
that if his father were only living now, he would ask his advice
in this matter, as he had always done in the old days when grave
questions had come up.

"If I only knew the way, I'd go to him," he said, quite
pleased at the idea. "I wonder what big Ingmar would say if
some fine day I should come wandering up to him? I fancy him
settled on a big farm, with many fields and meadows, a large
house and barns galore, with lots of red cattle and not a black or
spotted beast among them, just exactly as he wanted it when he
was on earth. Then as I step into the farmhouse—"

The plowman suddenly stopped in the middle of a furrow
and glanced up, laughing. These thoughts seemed to amuse him
greatly, and he was so carried away by them that he hardly knew
whether or not he was still upon earth. It seemed to him that in a
twinkling he had been lifted all the way up to his old father in
heaven.

"And now as I come into the living-room," he went on,
"I see many peasants seated on benches along the walls. All
have sandy hair, white eyebrows, and thick underlips. They are
all of them as like father as one pea is like another. At the sight
of so many people I become shy and linger at the door. Father
sits at the head of the table, and the instant he sees me he says;
'Welcome, little Ingmar Ingmarsson!' Then father gets up and
comes over to me. 'I'd like to have a word with you, father,' I
say, 'but there are so many strangers here.' 'Oh, these are only
relatives!' says father. 'All these men have lived at the Ingmar

Farm, and the oldest among them is from way back in heathen times.' 'But I want to speak to you in private,' I say.

"Then father looks round and wonders whether he ought to step into the next room, but since it's just I he walks out into the kitchen instead. There he seats himself in the fireplace, while I sit down on the chopping block.

"'You've got a fine farm here, father,' I say. 'It's not so bad,' says father, 'but how's everything back home?' 'Oh, everything is all right there; last year we got twelve kroner for a ton of hay.' 'What!' says father. 'Are you here to poke fun at me, little Ingmar?'

"'But with me everything goes wrong' I say. 'They forever telling me that you were as wise as our Lord himself, but no one cares a straw for me.' 'Aren't you one of the district councillors?' the old man asks. 'I'm not on the School Board, or in the vestry, nor am I a councillor.' 'What have you done that's wrong, little Ingmar?' 'Well, they say that he who would direct the affairs of others, first show that he can manage his own properly.'

"Then I seem to see the old man lower his eyes and sit pondering. In a little while he says: 'Ingmar, you ought to marry some nice girl who will make you a good wife.' 'But that's exactly what I can't do, father,' I reply. 'There is not a farmer in the parish, even among the poor and lowly, who would give me his daughter.' 'Now tell me straight out what's back of all this, little Ingmar,' says father, with such a tender note in his voice.

"'Well, you see, father, four years ago—the same year that I took over the farm—I was courting Brita of Bergskog.' 'Let me see'—says father, 'do any of our folks live at Bergskog?' He seems to have lost all remembrance of how things are down on earth. 'No, but they are well-to-do people, and you must surely remember that Brita's father is a member of Parliament?' 'Yes, of course; but you should have married one of our people, then you would have had a wife who knew about our old customs and habits.' 'You're right, father, and I wasn't long finding that out!'

"Now both father and I are silent a moment; then the old man continues: 'She was good-looking, of course?' 'Yes,' I reply. 'She had dark hair and bright eyes and rosy cheeks. And she was clever, too, so that mother was pleased with my choice. All might have turned out well but, you see, the mistake of it was that she didn't want me.' 'It's of no consequence what such a slip of a girl wants or doesn't want.' 'But her parents forced her to say "yes."' 'How do you know she was forced? It's my candid opinion that she was glad to get a rich husband like you, Ingmar Ingmarsson.'

"'Oh, no! She was anything but glad. All the same, the banns were published and the wedding day was fixed. So Brita came down to the Ingmar Farm to help mother. I say, mother is getting old and feeble.' 'I see nothing wrong in all that, little Ingmar,' says father, as if to cheer me up.

"'But that year nothing seemed to thrive on the farm; the potato crop was a failure, and the cows got sick; so mother I decided it was best to put off the wedding a year. You see, I thought it didn't matter so much about the wedding as long as the banns had been read. But perhaps it was old-fashioned to think that way.'

"'Had you chosen one of our kind she would have exercised patience,' says father. 'Well, yes,' I say. 'I could see that Brita didn't like the idea of a postponement; but, you see, I felt that I couldn't afford a wedding just then. There had been the funeral in the spring, and we didn't want to take the money out of the bank.' 'You did quite right in waiting,' says father. 'But I was a little afraid that Brita would not care to have the christening come before the wedding.' 'One must first make sure that one has the means,' says father.

"'Every day Brita became more and more quiet and strange. I used to wonder what was wrong with her and fancied she was homesick, for she had always loved her home and her parents. This will blow over, I thought, when she gets used to us; she'll soon feel at home on the Ingmar Farm. I put up with it for a time; then, one day, I asked mother why Brita was looking so pale and wild eyed. Mother said it was because she was with child, and she would surely be her old self again once that was over with. I had a faint suspicion that Brita was brooding over my putting off the wedding, but I was afraid to ask her about it. You know, father, you always said that the year I married, the house was to have a fresh coat of red paint. That year I simply couldn't afford it. By next year everything will be all right, I thought then.'"

The plowman walked along, his lips moving all the while. He actually imagined that he saw before him the face of his father. "I shall have to lay the whole case before the old man, frankly and clearly," he remarked to himself, "so he can advise me."

"'Winter had come and gone, yet nothing was changed. I felt at times that if Brita were to keep on being unhappy I might better give her up and send her home. However, it was too late to think of that. Then, one evening, early in May, we discovered that she had quietly slipped away. We searched for her all through the night, and in the morning one of the housemaids found her.'

"I find it hard now to continue, and take refuge in silence. Then father exclaims: 'In God's name, she wasn't dead, was she?' 'No, not she,' I say, and father notes the tremor in my voice. 'Was the child born?' asks father. 'Yes,' I reply, 'and she had strangled it. It was lying dead beside her.' 'But she couldn't have been in her right mind.' 'Oh, she knew well enough what she vas about!' I say. 'She did it to get even with me for forcing myself upon her. Still she would never have done this thing had I married her. She said she had been thinking that since I did not want my child honourably born, I should have no child.' Father is dumb with grief, but by and by he says to me: 'Would you have been glad of the child, little Ingmar?' 'Yes,' I answer. 'Poor boy! It's a shame that you should have fallen in with a bad woman! She is in prison, of course,' says father. 'She was sent up for three years.' 'And it's because of this that no man will let you marry a daughter of his?' 'Yes, but I haven't asked anyone, either.' 'And this is why you have no standing in the parish?' 'They all think it ought not to have gone that way for Brita. Folks say that if I had been a sensible man, like yourself, I would have talked to her and found out what was troubling her.' 'It's not so easy for a man to understand a bad woman!' says father. 'No, father, Brita was not bad, but she was a proud one!' 'It comes to the same thing,' says father.

"Now that father seems to side with me, I say: 'There are many who think I should have managed it in such a way that no one would have known but that the child was born dead.' 'Why shouldn't she take her punishment?' says father. 'They say if this had happened in your time, you would have made the servant who found her keep her tongue in her head so that nothing could have leaked out.' 'And in that case would you have married her?' 'Why then there would have been no need of my marrying her. I would have sent her back to her parents in a week or so and the banns annulled, on the grounds that she was not happy with us.' 'That's all very well, but no one can expect a young chap like you to have an old man's head on him.' 'The whole parish thinks that I behaved badly toward Brita.' 'She has done worse in bringing disgrace upon honest folk.' 'But I made her take me.' 'She ought to be mighty glad of it,' says father. 'But, father, don't you think it is my fault her being in prison?' 'She put herself there, I'm thinking.' Then I get up and say very slowly: 'So you don't think, father, that I have to do anything for her when she comes out in the fall?' 'What should you do? Marry her?' 'That's just what I ought to do.' Father looks at me a moment, then asks: 'Do you love her?' 'No! She has killed my love.' Father closes his eyes and begins to meditate. 'You see, father, I can't get away from this: that I have brought misfortune upon some one.'

"The old man sits quite still and does not answer.

"'The last time I saw her was in the courtroom. Then she was so gentle, and longed so for her child. Not one harsh word did she say against me. She took all the blame to herself. Many in that courtroom were moved to tears, and the judge himself had to swallow hard. He didn't give her more than three years, either.'

"But father does not say a word.

"'It will be hard for her when fall comes, and she's sent home. They won't be glad to have her again at Bergskog. Her folks all feel that she has brought shame upon them, and they're pretty sure to let her know it, too! There will be nothing for her but to sit at home all the while; she won't even dare to go to church. It's going to be hard for her in every way.'

"But father doesn't answer.

"'It is not such an easy thing for me to marry her! To have a wife that menservants and maidservants will look down upon is not a pleasant prospect for a man with a big farmstead. Nor would mother like it. We never invite people to the house, either to weddings or funerals.'

"Meanwhile, not a word out of father.

"Of course at the trial I tried to help her as much as I could. I told the judge that I was entirely to blame, as I took the girl against her will. I also said that I considered her so innocent of any wrong that I would marry her then and there, if she could only think better of me. I said that so the judge would give her a lighter sentence. Although I've had two letters from her, there's nothing in them to show any changed feeling toward me. So you see, father, I'm not obliged to marry her because of that speech.'

"Father sits and ponders, but he doesn't speak.

"'I know that this is simply looking at the thing from the viewpoint of men, and we Ingmars have always wanted to stand well in the sight of God. And yet sometimes I think that maybe our Lord wouldn't like it if we honoured a murderess.'

"And father doesn't utter a sound.

"'Think, father, how one must feel who lets another suffer without giving a helping hand. I have passed through too much these last few years not to try to do something for her when she gets out.

"Father sits there immovable.

"Now I can hardly keep back the tears. 'You see, father, I'm a young man and will lose much if I marry her. Every one seems to think I've already made a mess of my life; they will think still worse of me after this!'

"But I can't make father say a word.

"'I have often wondered why it is that we Ingmars have been allowed to remain on our farm for hundreds of years, while the other farms have all changed hands. And the thought comes to me that it may be because the Ingmars have always tried to walk in the ways of God. We Ingmars need not fear man; we have only to walk in God's ways.'

"Then the old man looks up and says: 'This is a difficult problem, my son. I guess I'll go in and talk it over with the other Ingmarssons.'

"So father goes back to the living-room, while I remain in the kitchen. There I sit waiting and waiting, but father does

not return. Then, after hours and hours of this, I get cross and go
to him. 'You must have patience, little Ingmar,' says father.
'This is a difficult question.' And I see all the old yeomen sitting
there with closed eyes, deep in thought. So I wait and wait and,
for aught I know, must go on waiting."

Smiling, he followed the plow, which was now moving along
very slowly, as if the horses were tired out and could scarcely
drag it. When he came to the end of the furrow he pulled up the
plow and rested. He had become very serious.

"Strange, when you ask anyone's advice you see yourself
what is right. Even while you are asking, you discover all at
once what you hadn't been able to find out in three whole years.
Now it shall be as God wills."

He felt that this thing must be done, but at the same time
it seemed so hard to him that the mere thought of it took away
his courage. "Help me, Lord!" he said.

Ingmar Ingmarsson was, however, not the only person
abroad at that hour. An old man came trudging along the
winding path that crossed the fields. It was not difficult to guess
his occupation, for he carried on his shoulder a long-handled
paint brush and was spattered with red paint from his cap to his
shoe tips. He kept glancing round-about, after the manner of
journeymen painters, to find an unpainted farmhouse or one that
needed repainting. He had seen, here and there, one and another
which he thought might answer his purpose, but he could not
seem to fix upon any special one. Then, finally, from the top of a
hillock he caught sight of the big Ingmar Farm down in the
valley. "Great Caesar!" he exclaimed, and stopped short. "That
farmhouse hasn't been painted in a hundred years. Why, it's
black with age, and the barns have never seen a drop of point.
Here there's work enough to keep me busy till fall."

A little farther on he came upon a man plowing. "Why,
there's a farmer who belongs here and knows all about this
neighbourhood," thought the painter. "He can tell me all I need
know about that homestead yonder." Whereupon he crossed the
path into the field, stepped up to Ingmar, and asked him if he
thought the folks living over there wanted any painting done.

Ingmar Ingmarsson was startled, and stood staring at the

man as though he were a ghost.

"Lord, as I live, it's a painter!" he remarked to himself. "And to think of his coming just now!" He was so dumbfounded that he could not answer the man. He distinctly recalled that every time any one had said to his father: "You ought to have that big, ugly house of yours painted, Father Ingmar," the old man had always replied that he would have it done the year Ingmar married.

The painter put the question a second time, and a third, but Ingmar stood there, dazed, as if he had not understood him.

"Are they ready at last with their answer?" he wondered. "Is this a message from father to say that he wishes me to marry this year?"

He was so overwhelmed by the thought that he hired the man on the spot. Then he went on with his plowing, deeply moved and almost happy.

"You'll see it won't be so very hard to do this now that you know for certain it is father's wish," he said.

II

A fortnight later Ingmar Ingmarsson stood polishing some harness. He seemed to be in a bad humour, and found the work rather irksome. "Were I in our Lord's place," he thought, then put in another rub or two and beg again: "Were I in our Lord's place, I'd see to it that a thing was done the instant your mind was made up. I shouldn't allow folks such a long time to think it over, and ponder all the obstacles. I shouldn't give them time to polish harness and paint wagons; I'd take them straight from the plow."

He caught the sound of wagon wheels from the road, and looked out. He knew at once whose rig it was. "The senator from Bergskog is coming!" he shouted into the kitchen, where his mother was at work. Instantly fresh wood was laid on the fire and the coffee mill was set going.

The senator drove into the yard, where he pulled up without alighting. "No, I'm not going into the house," he said, "I only want a word or two with you, Ingmar. I'm rather pressed for time as I am due at the parish meeting."

"Mother is just making some fresh coffee," said Ingmar.

"Thank you, but I must not be late."

"It's a good while now since you were here, Senator," said Ingmar pressingly.

Then Ingmar's mother appeared in the doorway, and protested:

"Surely you're not thinking of going without first coming in for a drop of coffee?"

Ingmar unbuttoned the carriage apron, and the senator began to move. "Seeing it's Mother Martha herself that commands me I suppose I shall have to obey," he said.

The senator was a tall man of striking appearance, with a certain ease of manner. He was of a totally different stamp from Ingmar or his mother, who were very plain looking, with sleepy faces and clumsy bodies. But all the same, the senator had a profound respect for the old family of Ingmars, and would gladly have sacrificed his own active exterior to be like Ingmar, and to become one of the Ingmassons. He had always taken Ingmar's part against his own daughter, so felt rather light of heart at being so well received.

In a while, when Mother Martha had brought the coffee, he began to state his errand.

"I thought," he said, and cleared his throat. "I thought you had best be told what we intend to do with Brita." The cup which Mother Martha held in her hand shook a little, and the teaspoon rattled in the saucer. Then there was a painful silence. "We have been thinking that the best thing we could do would be to send her to America." He made another pause, only to be met by the same ominous silence. He sighed at the thought of these unresponsive people. "Her ticket has already been purchased."

"She will come home first, of course," said Ingmar.

"No; what would she be doing there?"

Again Ingmar was silent. He sat with his eyes nearly closed, as if he were half asleep.

Then Mother Martha took a turn at asking questions. "She'll be needing clothes, won't she?"

"All that has been attended to; there is a trunk, ready packed, at Lövberg's place, where we always stop when we come to town."

"Her mother will be there to meet her, I suppose?"

"Well, no. She would like to, but I think it best that they be spared a meeting."

"Maybe so."

"The ticket and some money are waiting for her at Lövberg's, so that she will have everything she needs. I felt that Ingmar ought to know of it, so he won't have this burden on his mind any longer," said the senator.

Then Mother Martha kept still, too. Her headkerchief had slipped back, and she sat gazing down at her apron.

"Ingmar should be looking about for a new wife."

Both mother and son persistently held their peace.

"Mother Martha needs a helper in this big household. Ingmar should see to it that she has some comfort in her old age." The senator paused a moment, wondering if they could have heard what he said. "My wife and I wanted to make everything right again," he declared finally.

In the meantime, a sense of great relief had come to Ingmar. Brita was going to America, and he would not have to marry her. After all a murderess was not to become the mistress of the old Ingmar home. He had kept still, thinking it was not the thing to show at once how pleased he was, but now he began to feel that it would be only right and proper for him to say something.

The senator quietly bided his time. He knew that he had to give these old-fashioned people time to consider. Presently Ingmar's mother said:

"Brita has paid her penalty; now it's our turn." By this the old woman meant that if the senator wanted any help from the Ingmarssons, in return for his having smoothed the way for them, they would not withhold it. But Ingmar interpreted her utterance differently. He gave a start, as if suddenly awakened from sleep. "What would father say of this?" he wondered. "If I were to lay the whole matter before him, what would he be likely to say? 'You must not think that you can make a mockery of God's judgment,' he would say. 'And don't imagine that He will let it go unpunished if you allow Brita to shoulder all the blame. If her father wants to cast her off just to get into your good graces, so that he can borrow money from you, you must nevertheless follow God's leading, little Ingmar Ingmarsson.'

"I verily believe the old man is keeping close watch of me in this matter," he thought. "He must have sent Brita's father here to show me how mean it is to try to shift everything on to her, poor girl! I guess he must have noticed that I haven't had any great desire to take that journey these last few days."

Ingmar got up, poured some brandy into his coffee, and

raised the cup.

"Here's a thank you to the senator for coming here today," he said, and clinked cups with him.

III

Ingmar had been busy all the morning, working around the birches down by the gate. First he had put up a scaffolding, then he had bent the tops of the trees toward each other so that they formed an arch.

"What's all that for?" asked Mother Martha.

"Oh, it suits my fancy to have them grow that way for a change," said Ingmar.

Along came the noon hour, and the men folks stopped their work; after the midday meal the farm hands went out into the yard and lay down in the grass to sleep. Ingmar Ingmarsson slept, too, but he was lying in a broad bed in the chamber off the living-room. The only person not asleep was the old mistress, who sat in the big room, knitting.

The door to the entrance hall was cautiously opened, and in came an old woman carrying two large baskets on a yoke. After passing the time of day, she sat down on a chair by the door and took the lids off the baskets, one of which was filled with rusks and buns, the other with newly baked loaves of spiced bread. The housewife at once went over to the old woman and began to bargain. Ordinarily she kept a tight fist on the pennies, but she never could resist a temptation to indulge her weakness for sweets to dip in her coffee.

While selecting her cakes she began to chat with the old woman, who, like most persons that go from place to place and know many people, was a ready talker. "Kaisa, you're a sensible person," said Mother Martha, "and one can rely on you."

"Yes, indeed," said the other. "If I didn't know enough to keep mum about most of the things I hear, there'd be some fine hair-pulling matches, I'm thinking!"

"But sometimes you are altogether too close-mouthed, Kaisa."

The old woman looked up; the inference was quite plain to her.

"May the Lord forgive me!" she said tearfully, "but I talked to the senator's wife at Bergskog when I should have come straight to you."

"So you have been talking to the senator's wife!" And the emphasis given to the last two words spoke volumes.

Ingmar had been startled from his sleep by the opening of the outside door. No one had come in, apparently; still the door stood ajar. He did not know whether it had sprung open or whether some one had opened it. Too sleepy to get up, he settled back in bed. And then he heard talking in the outer room.

"Now tell me, Kaisa, what makes you think that Brita doesn't care for Ingmar."

"From the very start folks have been saying that her parents made her take him," returned the old woman, evasively.

"Speak right out, Kaisa, for when I question you, you don't have to beat about the bush. I guess I'm able to bear anything you may have to tell me."

"I must say that every time I was at Bergskog Brit always looked as if she'd been crying. Once, when she and I were alone in the kitchen, I said to her: 'It's a fine husband you'll be getting, Brita.' She looked at me as if she thought I was making fun of her. Then she came at me with this: 'You may well say it, Kaisa. Fine, indeed!' She said it in such a way that I seemed to see Ingmar Ingmarsson standing there before my face and eyes, and he's no beauty! As I've always had a great respect for all the Ingmarssons, that thought had never before entered my mind. I couldn't help smiling a little. Then Brita gave me a look and said once more: 'Fine, indeed'' With that she turned on her heel and ran into her room, crying as if her heart would break. As I was leaving I said to myself: 'It will all come out right; everything always comes out right for the Ingmarssons.' I didn't wonder at her parents doing what they did. If Ingmar Ingmarsson had proposed to a daughter of mine, I shouldn't have given myself a moment's peace till she said yes."

Ingmar from his bedroom could hear every word that was spoken.

"Mother is doing this on purpose," he thought. "She's been wondering about that trip to town to-morrow. Mother fancies I'm going after Brita, to fetch her home. She doesn't suspect that I'm too big a coward to do it."

"The next time I saw Brita," the old woman went on, "was after she had come here to you. I couldn't ask her just then how she liked it here, seeing the house was full of visitors; but when I had gone a ways into the grove she came running after me.

"'Kaisa!' she called, 'have you been up at Bergskog lately?'

"'I was there day before yesterday,' I replied.

"'Gracious me! were you there day before yesterday? And I feel as if I hadn't been at home in years!' It wasn't easy to know just what to say to her, for she looked as if she couldn't bear the least little thing and would be ready to cry at whatever I might say. 'You can surely go home for a visit?' I said. 'No; I don't think I shall ever go home again.' 'Oh, do go,' I urged. 'It's beautiful up there now; the woods are full of berries; the bushes are thick with red whortleberries.' 'Dear me!' she said, her eyes growing big with surprise, 'are there whortleberries already?' 'Yes, indeed. Surely you can get off a day, just to go home and eat your fill of berries?' 'No, I hardly think I want to,' she said. 'My going home would make it all the harder to come back to this place.' 'I've always heard that the Ingmars are the best kind of folks to be with,' I told her. 'They are honest people.' 'Oh, yes,' she said, 'they are good in their way.' 'They are the best people in the parish,' I said, 'and so fair-minded.' 'It is not considered unfair then to take a wife by force.' 'They are also very wise.' 'But they keep all they know to themselves.' 'Do they never say anything?' 'No one ever says a word more than what is absolutely necessary.'

"I was just about to go my way, when it came to me to ask her where the wedding was going to be held—here or at her home. 'We're thinking of having it here, where there is plenty of room.' 'Then see to it that the wedding day isn't put off too long,' I warned. 'We are to be married in a month,' she answered.

"But before Brita and I parted company, it struck me that the Ingmarssons had had a poor harvest, so I said it was not likely that they would have a wedding that year. 'In that case I shall have to jump into the river,' she declared.

"A month later I was told that the wedding had been put off and, fearing that this would not end well, I went straight to Bergskog and had a talk with Brita's mother. 'They are certainly making a stupid blunder down at the Ingmar Farm,' I told her. 'We are satisfied with their way of doing things,' she said. 'Every day we thank God that our daughter has been so well provided for.'"

"Mother needn't have given herself all this bother," Ingmar was thinking, "for no one from this farm is going to fetch Brita. There was no reason for her being so upset at the sight of the arch: that is only one of those things a man does so that he can turn to our Lord and say: 'I wanted to do it. Surely you must see that I meant to do it.' But doing it is another matter." "The last time I saw Brita," Kaisa vent on, "was in the middle of the winter after a big snowfall. I had come to a narrow path in the wild forest, where it was heavy walking. Soon I came upon some one who was sitting in the snow, resting. It was Brita. 'Are you all by yourself up here?' I asked. 'Yes, I'm out for a walk.' she said. I stood stock-still and stared at her; I couldn't imagine what she was doing there. 'I'm looking round to see if there are any steep hills hereabout,' she then said. 'Dear heart! are you thinking of casting yourself from a cliff?' I gasped, for she looked as if she was tired of life.

"'Yes,' she said. 'If I could only find a hill that was high and steep I'd certainly throw myself down.' 'You ought to be ashamed to talk like that, and you so well cared for.' 'You see, Kaisa, I'm a bad lot.' 'I'm afraid you are.' 'I am likely to do something dreadful, therefore I might better be dead.' 'That's only silly gabble, child.' 'I turned bad as soon as I went to live with those people.' Then, coming quite close to me, with the wildest look in her eyes, she shrieked: 'All they think about is how they can torture me, and I think only of how I can torture them in return.' 'No, no, Brita; they are good people.' 'All they care about is to bring shame upon me.' 'Have you said so to them?' 'I never speak to them. I only think and wonder how I'm going to get even with them. I'm thinking of setting fire to the farm, for I know he loves it. How I'd like to poison the cows! they are so old and ugly and white around the eyes that one would think they were related to him.' 'Barking dogs never bite,' I said. 'I've got to do something to him, or I'll never have any peace of mind.' 'You don't know what you are saying, child,' I protested. 'What you are thinking of doing would forever destroy your peace of mind.'

"All at once she began to cry. Then, after a little, she became very meek and said that she had suffered so from the bad thoughts that came to her. I then walked home with her and, as we parted company, she promised me that she would do nothing rash if I would only keep a close mouth.

"Still I couldn't help thinking that I ought to talk to some one about this," said Kaisa. "But to whom? I felt kind of backward about going to big folk like yourselves—"

Just then the bell above the stable rang. The midday rest was over. Mother Martha suddenly interrupted the old woman: "I say, Kaisa, do you think things can ever be right again between Ingmar and Brita?"

"What?" gasped the old woman in astonishment.

"I mean, if by chance she were not going to America, do you suppose she would have him?"

"Well, I should say not!"

"Then you are quite sure she would give him no for an answer."

"Of course she would."

Ingmar sat on the edge of the bed, his legs dangling over the side.

"Now you got just what you needed, Ingmar," he thought; "and now I guess you'll take that journey to-morrow," he said, pounding the edge of the bed with his fist. "How can mother think she'll get me to stay at home by showing me that Brita doesn't like me!"

He kept pounding the side of the bed, as if in thought he were knocking down something that was resisting him.

"Anyway, I'm going to chance it once more," he decided. "We Ingmars begin all over again when things go wrong. No man that is a man can sit back calmly and let a woman fret herself insane over his conduct."

Never had he felt so keenly his utter defeat, and he was determined to put himself right.

"I'd be a hell of a man if I couldn't make Brita happy here!" he said.

He dealt the bedpost a last blow before getting up to go back to his work.

"As sure as you're born it was Big Ingmar that sent old Kaisa here, in order to make me tale that trip to the city."

IV

Ingmar Ingmarsson had arrived in the city, and was walking slowly toward the big prison house, which was beautifully situated on the crest of a hill overlooking the public park. He did not glance about him, but went with eyes downcast, dragging himself along with as much difficulty as though he were some feeble old man. He had left off his usual picturesque peasant garb on this occasion, and was wearing a black cloth suit and a starched shirt which he had already crumpled. He felt very solemn, yet all the while he was anxious and reluctant.

On coming to the gravelled yard in front of the jail he saw a guard on duty and asked him if this was not the day that Brita Ericsson was to be discharged.

"Yes, I think there is a woman coming out to-day," the guard answered.

"One who has been in for infanticide," Ingmar explained.

"Oh, that one! Yes, she'll be out this forenoon."

Ingmar stationed himself under a tree, to wait. Not for a second did he take his eyes off the prison gate. "I dare say there are some among those who have gone in there that haven't fared any too well," he thought. "I don't want to brag, but maybe there's many a one on the inside that has suffered less than I who am outside. Well, I declare, Big Ingmar has brought me here to fetch my bride from the prison house," he remarked to himself. "But I can't say that little Ingmar is overpleased at the thought; he would have liked seeing her pass through a gate of honour instead, with her mother standing by her side, to give her to the bridegroom. And then they should have driven to the church in a flower-trimmed chaise, followed by a big bridal procession, and she should have sat beside him dressed as a bride, and smiling under her bridal crown."

The gate opened several times. First, a chaplain come out, then it was the wife of the governor of the prison, and then some servants who were going to town. Finally Brita came. When the gate opened he felt a cramp at the heart. "It is she," he thought. His eyes dropped. He was as if paralyzed, and could not move. When he had recovered himself, he looked up; she was then standing on the steps outside the gate.

She stood there a moment, quite still; she had pushed back her headshawl and, with eyes that were clear and open, she looked out across the landscape. The prison stood on high ground, and beyond the town and the stretches of forest she could see her native hills.

Suddenly she seemed to be shaken by some unseen force; she covered her face with her hands and sank down upon the stone step. Ingmar could hear her sobs from where he stood.

Presently he went over to her, and waited. She was crying so hard that she seemed deaf to every other sound; and he had to stand there a long time. At last he said:

"Don't cry like that, Brita!"

She looked up. "O God in Heaven!" she exclaimed, "are you here?"

Instantly all that she had done to him flashed across her mind—and what it must have cost him to come. With a cry of joy she threw her arms around his neck and began to sob again.

"How I have longed that you might come!" she said.

Ingmar's heart began to beat faster at the thought of her being so pleased with him. "Why, Brita, have you really been longing for me?" he said, quite moved.

"I have wanted so much to ask your forgiveness."

Ingmar drew himself up to his full height and said very coldly:

"There will be plenty of time for that I don't think we ought to stop here any longer."

"No, this is no place to stop at," she answered meekly.

"I have put up at Lövberg's," he said as they walked

along the road.

"That's where my trunk is."

"I have seen it there," said Ingmar. "It's too big for the back of the cart, so it will have to be left there till we can send for it."

Brita stopped and looked up at him. This was the first time he had intimated that he meant to take her home.

"I had a letter from father to-day. He says that you also think that I ought to go to America."

"I thought there was no harm in our having a second choice. It wasn't so certain that you would care to come back with me."

She noticed that he said nothing about wanting her to come, but maybe it was because he did not wish to force himself upon her a second time. She grew very reluctant. It couldn't be an enviable task to take one of her kind to the Ingmar Farm. Then something seemed to say:

"Tell him that you will go to America; it is the only service you can render him. Tell him that, tell him that!" urged something within her. And while this thought was still in her mind she heard some one say: "I'm afraid that I am not strong enough to go to America. They tell me that you have to work very hard over there." It was as if another had spoken, and not she herself.

"So they say," Ingmar said indifferently.

She was ashamed of her weakness and thought of how only that morning she had told the prison chaplain that she was going out into the world a new and a better woman. Thoroughly displeased with herself, she walked silently for some time, wondering how she should take back her words. But as soon as she tried to speak, she was held back by the thought that if he still cared for her it would be the basest kind of ingratitude to repulse him again. "If I could only read his thoughts!" she said herself.

Presently she stopped and leaned against a wall. "All this noise and the sight of so many people makes my bead go round," she said. He put out his hand, which she took; then they went along, hand in hand. Ingmar was thinking, "Now we look like sweethearts." All the same he wondered how it would be when he got home, how his mother and the rest of the folks would take it.

When they came to Lövberg's place, Ingmar said that his horse was now thoroughly rested, and if she had no objection they might as well cover the first few stations that day. Then she thought: "Now is the time to tell him that you won't go. Thank him first, then tell him that you don't want to go with him." She prayed God that she might be shown if he had come for her only out of pity. In the meantime Ingmar had drawn the cart out of the shed. The cart had been newly painted, the dasher shone, and the cushions had fresh covering. To the buckboard was attached a little half-withered bouquet of wild flowers. The sight of the flowers made her stop and think. Ingmar, meanwhile, had gone back to the stable and harnessed the horse, and was now leading him out. Then she discovered another bouquet of the same sort between the harness, and began to feel that after all he must like her. So it seemed best not to say anything. Otherwise he might think she was ungrateful and that she did not understand how big a thing he was offering her.

For a time they drove along without exchanging a word. Then, in order to break the silence, she began to question him about various home matters. With every question he was reminded of some one or other whose judgment he feared. How so and so will wonder and how so and so will laugh at me, he thought.

He answered only in monosyllables. Time and again she felt like begging him to turn back. "He doesn't want me," she thought. "He doesn't care for me; he is doing this only out of charity."

She soon stopped asking questions. They drove on for miles in deep silence. When they came to their first stopping place, which was an inn, there were coffee and hot biscuits in readiness for them; and on the tray were some more flowers. She knew then that he had ordered this the day before, when passing. Was that, too, done only out of kindness and pity? Was he happy yesterday? Was it only to-day that he had lost heart, after seeing her come out of prison? To-morrow, when he had forgotten this, perhaps all would be well again.

Sorrow and remorse had softened Brita: she did not grant

to cause him any more unhappiness. Perhaps, after all, he really—

They stayed at the inn overnight and left early the next morning. By ten o'clock they were already within sight of their parish church. As they drove along the road leading to the church it was thronged with people, and the bells were ringing.

"Why, it's Sunday!" Brita exclaimed, instinctively folding her hands. She forgot everything else in the thought of going to church and praising God. She wanted to begin her new life with a service in the old church.

"I should love to go to church," she said to Ingmar, never thinking that it might be embarrassing for him be seen there with her. She was all devotion and gratitude! Ingmar's first impulse was to say that she couldn't; he felt somehow that he had not the courage to face the curious glances and gossiping tongues of these people. "It has got to be met sooner or later," he thought. "Putting it off won't make it any easier."

He turned and drove in on the church grounds. The service had not yet started; and many persons were sitting in the grass and on the stone hedge, watching the people arrive. The instant they saw Ingmar and Brita they began to nudge each other, and whisper, and point. Ingmar glanced at Brita. She sat there with clasped hands, quite unconscious of the things about her. She saw no persons, apparently, but Ingmar saw them only too well. They came running after the wagon, and did not wonder at their running or their stares. They must have thought that their eyes had deceived them. Of course, they could not believe that he had come to the house of God with her—the woman who had strangled his child. "This is too much!" he said. "I can't stand it.

"I think you'd better go inside at once, Brita," he suggested.

"Why, certainly," she answered. To attend service was her only thought; she had not come there to meet people.

Ingmar took his own time unharnessing and feeding the horse. Many eyes were fixed upon him, but nobody spoke to him. By the time he was ready to go into the church, most of the people were already in their pews, and the opening hymn was being sung. Walking down the centre isle, he glanced over at the side where the women were seated. All the pews were filled save one, and in that there was only one person. He saw at once that it was Brita and knew, of course, that no one had cared to sit with her. Ingmar went and sat down beside her. Brita looked up at him in wonderment. She had not noticed it before, but now she understood why she had the pew to herself. Then the deep feeling of devotion, which she had but just experienced, was dispelled by a sense of black despair. "How would it all end?" she wondered. She should never have come with him.

Her eyes began to fill. To keep from breaking down she took up an old prayerbook from the shelf in front of her, and opened it. She kept turning the leaves of both gospels and epistles without being able to see a word for the tears. Suddenly something bright caught her eye. It was a bookmark, with a red heart, which lay between the leaves. She took it out and slipped it toward Ingmar. She saw him close his big hand over it and steal a glance at it. Shortly afterward it lay upon the floor. "What is to become of us?" thought Brita, sobbing behind the prayerbook.

As soon as the preacher had stepped down from the pulpit they went out. Ingmar hurriedly hitched up the horse, with Brita's help. By the time the benediction was pronounced and the congregation was beginning to file out, Brita and Ingmar were already off. Both seemed to be thinking the same thought: one who has committed such a crime cannot live among people. The two fell as if they had been doing penance by appearing at church. "Neither of us will be able to stand it," they thought.

In the midst of her distress of mind, Brita caught a glimpse of the Ingmar Farm, and hardly knew it again. It looked so bright and red. She remembered having heard that the house was to be painted the year Ingmar married. Before, the wedding had been put off because he had felt that he could not afford to pay out any money just then. Now she understood that he had always meant to have everything right; but the way had been made rather hard for him.

When they arrived at the farm the folks were at dinner. "Here comes the boss," said one of the men, looking out. Mother Martha got up from the table, scarcely lifting her heavy eyelids.

"Stay where you are, all of you!" she commanded. "No one need rise from the table."

The old woman walked heavily across the room. Those who turned to look after her noticed that she had on her best dress, with her silk shawl across her shoulders, and her silk kerchief on her head, as if to emphasize her authority. When the horse stopped she was already at the door.

Ingmar jumped down at once, but Brita kept her seat. He went over to her side and unfastened the carriage apron.

"Aren't you going to get out?" he said.

"No," she replied, then covering her face with her hands, she burst into tears.

"I ought never to have come back," she sobbed.

"Oh, do get down!" he urged.

"Let me go back to the city; I'm not good enough for you."

Ingmar thought that maybe she was right about it, but said nothing. He stood with his hand on the apron, and waited.

"What does she say?" asked Mother Martha from the doorway.

"She says she isn't good enough for us," Ingmar replied, for Brita's words could scarcely be heard for her sobs.

"What is she crying about?" asked the old woman.

"Because I am such a miserable sinner," said Brita, pressing her hands to her heart which she thought would break.

"What's that?" the old woman asked once more.

"She says she is such a miserable sinner," Ingmar repeated.

When Brita heard him repeat her words in a cold and indifferent tone, the truth suddenly flashed upon her. No, he could never have stood there and repeated those words to his mother had he been fond of her, or had there been a spark of love in his heart for her.

"Why doesn't she get down?" the old woman then asked.

Suppressing her sobs, Brita spoke up: "Because I don't want to bring misfortune upon Ingmar."

"I think she is quite right," said the old mistress. "Let her go, little Ingmar! You may as well know that otherwise I'll be the one to leave: for I'll not sleep one night under the same roof with the likes of her."

"For God's sake let me go!" Brita moaned.

Ingmar ripped out an oath, turned the horse, and sprang into the cart. He was sick and tired of all this and could not stand any more of it.

Out on the highway they kept meeting church people. This annoyed Ingmar. Suddenly he turned the horse and drove in on a narrow forest road.

As he turned some one called to him. He glanced back. It was the postman with a letter for him. He took the letter, thrust it into his pocket, and drove on.

As soon as he felt sure that he could not be seen from the road, he slowed down and brought out the letter. Instantly Brita put her hand on his arm. "Don't read it!" she begged.

"Why not?" he asked.

"Never mind reading it; it's nothing."

"But how can you know?"

"It's a letter from me."

"Then tell me yourself what's in it."

"No, I can't tell you that."

He looked hard at her. She turned scarlet, her eyes growing wild with alarm. "I guess I will read that letter anyway," said Ingmar, and began to tear open the envelope.

"O Heavenly Father!" she cried, "am I then to be spared nothing? Ingmar," she implored, "read it in a day or two—when I am on my way to America."

By that time he had already opened the letter and was scanning it. She put her hand over the paper. "Listen to me, Ingmar!" she said. "It was the chaplain who got me to write that letter, and he promised not to send it till I was on board the steamer. Instead he sent it off too soon. You have no right to read it yet; wait till I'm gone, Ingmar."

Ingmar gave her an angry look and jumped out of the wagon, so that he might read the letter in peace. Brita was as much excited now as she had been in the old days, when things did not go her way.

"What I say in that letter isn't true. The chaplain talked me into writing it. I *don't* love you, Ingmar."

He looked up from the paper and gazed at her in

astonishment. Then she grew silent, and the lessons in humility which she had learned in prison profited her now. After all she suffered no greater embarrassment than she deserved.

Ingmar, meanwhile, stood puzzling over the letter. Suddenly, with an impatient snarl, he crumpled it up.

"I can't make this out!" he said, stamping his foot. "My head's all in a muddle."

He went up to Brita and gripped her by the arm.

"Does it really say in the letter that you care for me?" His tone was shockingly brutal, and the look of him was terrible.

Brita was silent.

"Does the letter say that you care for me?" he repeated savagely.

"Yes," she answered faintly.

Then his face became horribly distorted. He shook her arm and thrust it from him. "How you can lie!" he said, with a hoarse and angry laugh. "How you can lie!"

"God knows I have prayed night and day that I might see you again before I go!" she solemnly avowed.

"Where are you going?"

"I'm going to America, of course."

"The hell you are!"

Ingmar was beside himself. He staggered a few steps into the woods and cast himself upon the ground. And now it was his turn to weep!

Brita followed him and sat down beside him, she was so happy that she wanted to shout.

"Ingmar, little Ingmar!" she said, calling him by his pet name.

"But you think I'm so ugly!" he returned.

"Of course I do."

Ingmar pushed her hand away.

"Now let me tell you something," said Brita.

"Tell away."

"Do you remember what you said in court three years ago?"

"I do."

"That if I could only get to think differently of you, you would marry me?"

"Yes, I remember."

"It was after that I began to care for you. I had never imagined that any mortal could say such a thing. It seemed almost unbelievable your saying it to me, after all I had done to you. As I saw you that day, I thought you better looking than all the others, and you were wiser than any of them, and the only one with whom it would be good to share one's life. I fell so deeply in love with you that it seemed as if you belonged to me, and I to you. At first I took it for granted that you would come and fetch me, but later I hardly dared think it."

Ingmar raised his head. "Then why didn't you write?" he asked.

"But I did write."

"Asking me to forgive you, as if that were anything to write about!"

"What should I have written?"

"About the other thing."

"How would I have dared—I?"

"I came mighty near not coming at all."

"But Ingmar! do you suppose I could have written love letters to you after all I had done! My last day in prison I wrote to you because the chaplain said I must. When I gave him the letter, he promised not to send it until I was well on my way."

Ingmar took her hand and flattened it against the earth, then slapped it.

"I could beat you!" he said.

"You may do with me what you will, Ingmar."

He looked up into her face, upon which suffering had wrought a new kind of beauty. "And I came so near letting you go!" he sighed.

"You just had to come, I suppose."

"Let me tell you that I didn't care for you."

"I don't wonder at that."

"I felt relieved when I heard that you were to be sent to America."

"Yes, father wrote me that you were pleased."

"Whenever I looked at mother, I felt somehow that I couldn't ask her to accept a daughter-in-law like you."

"No, it would never do, Ingmar."

"I've had to put up with a lot on your account; no one would notice me because of my treatment of you."

"Now you are doing what you threatened to do," said Brita. "You're striking me."

"I can't begin to tell you how mad I am at you."

She kept still.

"When I think of all I've had to stand these last few weeks—" he went on.

"But Ingmar—"

"Oh, I'm not angry about that, but at the thought of how near I came to letting you go!"

"Didn't you love me, Ingmar?"

"No, indeed."

"Not during the whole journey home?"

"No, not for a second! I was just put out with you."

"When did you change?"

"When I got your letter."

"I saw that your love was over; that was why I did not want you to know that mine was but just beginning."

Ingmar chuckled.

"What amuses you, Ingmar?"

"I'm thinking of how we sneaked out of church, and of the kind of welcome we got at the Ingmar Farm."

"And you can laugh at that?"

"Why not as well laugh? I suppose we'll have to take to the road, like tramps. Wonder what father would say to that?"

"You may laugh, Ingmar, but this can't be; it can't be."

"I think it can, for now I don't care a damn about anything or anybody but you!"

Brita was ready to cry, but he just made her tell him again and again how often she had thought of him, and how much she had longed for him. Little by little he became as quiet as a child listening to a lullaby. It was all so different from what Brita had expected. She had thought of talking to him about her crime, if he came for her, and the weight of it. She would have liked to tell either him or her mother, or whoever had come for her, how unworthy she was of them. But not a word of this had she been allowed to speak.

Presently he said very gently:

"There is something you want to tell me?"

"Yes."

"And you are thinking about it all the time?"

"Day and night!"

"And it gets sort of mixed in with everything?"

"That's true."

"Now tell me about it, so there will be two instead of one to bear it."

He sat looking into her eyes; they were like the eyes of a poor, hunted fawn. But as she spoke they became calmer.

"Now you feel better," he said when she had finished.

"I feel as if a great weight had been lifted from my heart."

"That is because we are two to bear it. Now, perhaps, you won't want to go away."

"Indeed I should love to stay!" she said.

"Then let us go home," said Ingmar, rising.

"No, I'm afraid!"

"Mother is not so terrible," lie laughed, "when she sees that one has a mind of one's own."

"No, Ingmar, I could never turn her out of her home. I have no choice but to go to America."

"I'm going to tell you something," said Ingmar, with a mysterious smile. "You needn't be the least bit afraid, for there is some one who will help us."

"Who is it?"

"It's father. He'll see to it that everything comes out right."

There was some one coming along the forest road. It was Kaisa. But as she was not bearing the familiar yoke, with the baskets, they hardly knew her at first.

"Good-day to you!" greeted Ingmar and Brita, and the old woman came up and shook hands with them.

"Well, I declare, here you sit, and all the folks from the farm out looking for you! You were in such a hurry to get out of church," the old woman went on, "that I never got to meet you at all. So I went down to the farm to pay my respects to Brita. When I got there who should I see but the Dean, and he was in the house calling Mother Martha at the top of his lungs before I even had a chance to say 'how d'ye do.' And before he had so much as shaken hands with her, he was crying out: 'Now, Mother Martha, you can be proud of Ingmar! It's plain now that he belongs to the old stock; so we must begin to call him *Big Ingmar*.'

"Mother Martha, as you know, never says very much; she just stood there tying knots in her shawl. 'What's this you're telling me?' she said finally. 'He has brought Brita home,' the Dean explained, 'and, believe me, Mother Martha, he will be honoured and respected for it as long as he lives.' 'You don't tell me,' said the old lady. 'I could hardly go on with the service when I saw them sitting in church; it was a better sermon than any I could ever preach. Ingmar will be a credit to us all, as his father before him was.' 'The Dean brings us great news,' said Mother Martha. 'Isn't he home yet?" asked the Dean. 'No, he is not at home; but they may have stopped at Bergskog first.'"

"Did mother really say that?" cried Ingmar.

"Why, of course she did; and while we sat waiting for you to appear, she sent out one messenger after the other to look for you."

Kaisa kept up a steady stream of talk, but Ingmar no longer heard what she said. His thoughts were far away. "I come into the living-room, where father sits with all the old Ingmars. 'Good-day to you, Big Ingmar Ingmarsson,' says father, rising and coming toward me. 'The same to you, father,' says I, 'and thank you for your help.' 'Now you'll be well married,' says father, 'and then the other matters will all right themselves.' 'But, father, it could never have turned out so well if you hadn't stood by me.' 'That was nothing,' says father. 'All we Ingmars need do is to walk in the ways of God.'"

BOOK TWO

At The Schoolmaster's

In the early eighties there was no one in the parish where the old Ingmarsson family lived who would have thought of embracing any new kind of faith or attending any new form of sacred service. That new sects had sprung up, here and there, in other Dalecarlian parishes, and that people went out into rivers and lakes to be immersed in accordance with the new rites of the Baptists, was known; but folks only laughed at it all and said: "That sort of thing may suit those who live at Applebo and in Gagnef, but it can never touch our parish."

The people of that parish clung to their old customs and habits, one of which was a regular attendance at church on Sundays; every one that could go went, even in the severest winter weather. Then, of all times, it was almost a necessity; with the thermometer at twenty below zero outside, it would have been beyond human endurance to sit in the unheated church had it not been packed to the doors with people.

It could not be said of the parishioners that they turned out in such great numbers because they had a particularly brilliant pastor or one who had any special gift for expounding the Scriptures. In those days folks went to church to praise God and not to be entertained by fine sermons. On the way home, when fighting against the cutting wind on an open country road, one thought: "Our Lord must have noticed that you were at church this cold morning." That was the main thing. It was no fault of theirs if the preacher had said nothing more than he had been heard to say every Sunday since his appointment to the pastorate.

As a matter of fact, the majority seemed perfectly satisfied with what they got. They knew that what the pastor read to them was the Word of God, and therefore they found it altogether beautiful. Only the schoolmaster and one or two of the more intelligent farmers occasionally said among themselves: "The parson seems to have only one sermon; he talks of nothing but God's wisdom and God's government. All that is well enough so long as the Dissenters keep away. But this stronghold is poorly defended and would fall at the first attack."

Lay preachers generally passed by this parish. "What's the good of going there?" they used to say. "Those people don't want to be awakened." Not only the lay preachers, but even all the "awakened souls" in the neighbouring parishes looked upon the Ingmarssons and their fellow-parishioners as great sinners, and whenever they caught the sound of the bells from their church they would say the bells were tolling, "Sleep in your sins! Sleep in your sins!"

The whole congregation, old and young alike, were furious when they learned that people spoke in that way of their bells. They knew that their folks never forgot to repeat the Lord's Prayer whenever the church bells rang, and that every evening, at the time of the Angelus, the menfolk uncovered their heads, the women curtsied, and everybody stood still about as long as it takes to say an Our Father. All who have lived in that parish must acknowledge that God never seemed so mighty and so honoured as on summer evenings, when scythes were rested, and plows were stopped in the middle of a furrow, and the seed wagon was halted in the midst of the loading, simply at the stroke of a bell. It was as if they knew that our Lord at that moment was hovering over the parish on an evening cloud— great and powerful and good—breathing His blessing upon the whole community.

None of your college-bred men had ever taught in that parish. The schoolmaster was just a plain, old-fashioned farmer, who was self-taught. He was a capable man who could manage a hundred children single-handed. For thirty years and more he had been the only teacher there, and was looked up to by everybody. The schoolmaster seemed to feel that the spiritual welfare of the entire congregation rested with him, and was therefore quite concerned at their having called a parson who was no kind of a preacher. However, he held his peace as long as it was only a question of introducing a new form of baptism, and elsewhere at that; but on learning that there had also been some changes in the administration of the Holy Communion and that people were beginning to gather in private homes to partake of the Sacrament, he could no longer remain passive. Although a poor man himself, he managed to persuade some of the leading citizens to raise the money to build a mission house. "You know me," he said to them. "I only want to preach in order to strengthen people in the old faith. What would be the natural result if the lay preachers were to come upon us, with their new baptism and their new Sacrament, if there were no one to tell the people what was the true doctrine and what the false?"

The schoolmaster was as well liked by the clergyman as by every one else. He and the parson were frequently seen strolling together along the road between the schoolhouse and the parsonage, back and forth, back and forth, as if they had no end of things to say to each other. The parson would often drop in at the schoolmaster's of an evening to sit in the cozy kitchen by an open fire and chat with the schoolmaster's wife, Mother Stina. At times he came night after night. He had a dreary time of it at home; his wife was always ailing, and there was neither order nor comfort in his house.

One winter's evening the schoolmaster and his wife were sitting by the kitchen fire, talking in earnest whispers, while a little girl of twelve played by herself in a corner of the room. The little girl was their daughter, and her name was Gertrude. She was a fair little lass, with flaxen hair and plump, rosy cheeks, but she did not have that wise and prematurely old look which one so often sees in the children of schoolmasters.

The corner in which she sat was her playground. There she had gathered together a variety of things: bits of coloured glass, broken teacups and saucers, pebbles from the banks of the river, little square blocks of wood, and more rubbish of the same sort.

She had been let play in peace all the evening; neither her father nor her mother had disturbed her. Busy as she was she did not want to be reminded of lessons and chores. It didn't look as if there were going to be any extra sums to do for father that night, she thought.

She had a big work in hand, the little girl back there in her corner. Nothing less than making a whole parish! She was going to build up the entire district with both church and schoolhouse; the river and the bridge were also to be included. Everything had to be quite complete, of course.

She had already got a good part of it done. The whole wreath of hills that went round the parish was made up of smaller and larger stones. In all the crevices she had planted forests of little spruce twigs, and with two jagged stones she had erected Klack Mountain and Olaf's Peak on either side of the Dal River. The long valley in between the mountains had been covered with mould taken from one of her mother's flowerpots. So far everything was all right, only she had not been able to make the galley blossom. But she comforted herself by pretending it was early springtime, before grass and grain had sprouted.

The broad, beautiful Dal River that flows through the valley she had managed to lay out effectively with a long and narrow piece of glass, and the floating bridge connecting both sides of the parish, had been making on the water this long while. The more distant farms and settlements were marked off by pieces of red brick. Farthest north, amid fields and meadows, lay the Ingmar Farm. To the east was the village of Kolasen, at the foot of the mountain. At the extreme south, where the river, with rapids and falls, leaves the valley and rushes under the mountain, was Bergsana Foundry.

The entire landscape was now ready, with country roads laid out along the river, sanded and gravelled. Groves had also been set out, here and there, on the plains and near the cottages. The little girl had only to cast a glance at her structure of glass and stone and earth and twigs to see before her the whole parish. And she thought it all very beautiful.

Time after time she raised her head to call her mother and show her what she had done, then changed her mind. She had always found it wiser not to call attention to herself. But the most difficult work of all was yet to come: the building up of the

town on both sides of the river. It meant much shifting about of
stones and bits of glass. The sheriff's house wanted to crowd out
the merchant's shop; there was no room for the judge's house
next door to the doctor's. There were the church and the
parsonage, the drug-store and post-office, the peasant
homesteads, with their barns and outhouses, the inn, the hunter's
lodge, the telegraph station. To remember everything was no
small task!

Finally, the whole town of white and red houses stood
embedded in green. Now there was only one thing left: she had
worked hard to get everything else done so as to begin on the
schoolhouse. She wanted plenty of space for the school, which
was to be built on the riverside, and must have a big yard, with a
flagpole right in the middle of the lawn.

She had saved all her best blocks for the schoolhouse.
Now she wondered how she had best go about it. She wanted it
to be just like their school, with a big classroom on the ground
floor and another upstairs; then there was the kitchen and also
the big room where she and her parents lived. But all that would
take a good while. "They won't leave me in peace long enough,"
she said to herself.

Just then footsteps were heard in the entry; some one was
stamping off snow. In a twinkling she went ahead with her
building. "Here comes the parson to chat with father and
mother," she thought. Now she would have the whole evening to
herself. And with renewed courage she began to lay the
foundation of a schoolhouse as big as half the parish.

Her mother, who had also heard the steps in the hall, got
up quickly and drew an old armchair up to the fireplace. Then
turning to her husband, she said: "Shall you tell him about it to-
night?"

"Yes," answered the schoolmaster, "as soon as I can get
round to it."

Presently the pastor came in, half frozen and glad to be in
a warm room where he could sit by an open fire. He was very
talkative, as usual. It would be hard to find a more likable man
than the parson when he came in of an evening to chat about all
sorts of things, big and little. He spoke with such ease and
assurance of everything pertaining to this world, that one could

scarcely believe that he and the dull preacher were one and the same person. But if you happened to speak to him about spiritual things he grew red in the face, began fishing for words, and never said anything that was convincing, unless he chanced to mention that "God governs wisely."

When the parson had settled himself comfortably, the schoolmaster suddenly turned to him and said in a cheery tone:

"Now I must tell you the news: I'm going to build a mission house."

The clergyman became as white as a sheet and sank back in his chair.

"What are you saying, Storm?" he gasped. "Are they really thinking of building a mission house here? Then what's to become of me and the church? Are we to be dispensed with?"

"The church and the pastor will be needed just the same," returned the schoolmaster with a confident air. "It is my purpose that the mission house shall promote the welfare of the church. With so many schisms cropping up all over the country, the church is sorely in need of help."

"I thought you were my friend, Storm," said the parson, mournfully. Only a few moments before he had come in confident and happy, and now all at once his spirit was gone, and he looked as if he were entirely done for.

The schoolmaster understood quite well why the pastor was so distressed. He and every one else knew that at one time the clergyman had been a man of rare promise; but in his student days he had "gone the pace," so to speak, and, in consequence, had suffered a stroke. After that he was never the same. Sometimes he seemed to forget that he was only the ruin of a man; but when reminded of it, a sense of deep despondency came over him. Now he sat there as if paralyzed. It was a long time before any one ventured to speak.

"You mustn't take it like that, Parson," the schoolmaster said at last, trying to make his voice very soft and low.

"Hush, Storm! I know that I'm not a great preacher; still I couldn't have believed it possible that you would wish to take the living from me."

Storm made a gesture of protest, which said, in effect, that anything of the sort had never entered his mind, but he had not the courage to put it into words.

The schoolmaster was a man of sixty and, despite all the work and responsibility which had fallen to his lot, he was still master of his forces. There was a great contrast between him and the parson. Storm was one of the biggest men in Dalecarlia. His head was covered with a mass of black bushy hair, his skin was as dark as bronze, and his features were strong and clear cut. He looked singularly powerful beside the pastor, who was a little narrow-chested, bald-headed man.

The schoolmaster's wife thought that her husband, as the stronger, ought to give in, and motioned to him to drop the matter. Whatever of regret he may have felt, there was nothing in his manner to indicate that he had any idea of relinquishing his project.

Then the schoolmaster began to speak plainly and to the point. He said he was certain that before long the heretics would invade their parish; therefore, it was very necessary that they should have a meeting place where one could talk to the people in a more informal way than at a regular church service; where one might choose one's own text, expound the whole Bible, and interpret its most difficult passages to the people.

His wife again signed to him to keep still. She knew what the clergyman was thinking while her husband talked. "So I haven't taught them anything, and I haven't given them any sort of protection against unbelief? I must be a poor specimen of a pastor when the schoolmaster in my own parish thinks himself a better preacher than I."

The schoolmaster, however, did not keep still, but went on talking of all that must be done to protect the flock from the wolves.

"I haven't seen any wolves," said the pastor.

"But I know they are on their way."

"And you, Storm, are opening the door to them," declared the minister, rising. The schoolmaster's talk had irritated him. The blood mounted to his face, and he regained a little of his old dignity.

"My dear Storm, let us drop the subject," he said. Then turning to the housewife, he passed some pleasant remark about the last pretty bride she had dressed. For Mother Stina dressed all the brides in the parish.

Peasant woman though she was, she understood how it must hurt him to be so cruelly reminded of his own impotence. She wept from compassion, and could not answer him for the tears; so the pastor had to do most of the talking.

Meanwhile, he kept thinking: "Oh, if I only had some of the power and the capacity of my younger days, I would convince this peasant at once of the wrong he is doing." With that he turned again to the schoolmaster:

"Where did you get the money, Storm?" he asked.

"A company has been formed," Storm explained; then he mentioned the names of several men who had pledged their support, just to show the parson that they were the kind of people who would harm neither the church nor its pastor.

"Is Ingmar Ingmarsson in it, too?" the parson exclaimed. The effect of this was like a deathblow. "And to think that I was as sure of Ingmar Ingmarsson as I had been of you, Storm!"

He said nothing more about this just then, but instead turned to Mother Stina and talked to her. He must have seen that she was crying, but acted as if he had not noticed it. In a little while he again addressed the schoolmaster.

"Drop it, Storm!" he begged. "Drop it for my sake. You wouldn't like it if somebody put up another school next to yours."

The schoolmaster sat gazing at the floor and reflected a moment. Presently he said, almost reluctantly, "I can't, Parson."

For fully ten minutes there was a dead silence. Where upon the pastor put on his overcoat and cap, and went toward the door.

The whole evening he had been trying to find words with which to prove to Storm that he was not only doing harm to the pastor with this undertaking, but he was undermining the parish. Although thoughts and words kept crowding into his head, he could neither arrange them into an orderly sequence nor give utterance to them, because he was a broken man. Walking toward the door, he espied Gertrude sitting in her corner playing with her blocks and bits of glass. He stopped and looked at her. Evidently she had not heard a word of the conversation, for her eyes sparkled with delight and her cheeks were like fresh-blown roses.

The pastor was startled at the sight of all this innocent happiness of the child in contrast to his own heart heaviness.

"What are you making?" he asked, and went up to her.

The little girl had got through with her parish long before that; in fact, she had already pulled it down and started something new.

"If you had only come a minute sooner!" exclaimed the child. "I had made such a beautiful parish, with both church and schoolhouse—"

"But where is it now?"

"Oh, I've destroyed the parish, and now I'm building a Jerusalem, and—"

"What?" interrupted the parson. "Have you destroyed the parish in order to build a Jerusalem?"

"Yes," said Gertrude, "and it was such a fine parish! But we read about Jerusalem yesterday in school, and now I have pulled down the parish to build a Jerusalem."

The preacher stood regarding the child. He put his hand to his forehead and thought a moment, then he said: "It is surely someone greater than you that speaks through your mouth."

The child's words seemed to him so extraordinarily prophetic that he kept repeating them to himself, over and over. Gradually his thoughts drifted back into their old groove, and he began to ponder the ways of Providence and the means by which He works His will.

Presently he went back to the schoolmaster, his eyes shining with a new light, and said in his usual cheery tone:

"I'm no longer angry at you, Storm. You are only doing what you must do. All my life I have been pondering the ways of Providence, and I can't seem to get any light on them. Nor do I understand this thing, but I understand that you are doing what you needs must do."

"And They Saw Heaven Open"

The spring the mission house was built there was a great thaw, and the Dal River rose to an alarming height. And what quantities of water that spring brought! It came in showers from the skies; it came rushing down in streams from the mountainsides, and it welled out of the earth; water ran in every wheel rut and in every furrow. All this water found its way to the river, which kept rising higher and higher, and rolled onward with greater and greater force. It did not present its usual shiny and placid appearance, but had turned a dirty brown from all the muddy water that kept flowing in. The surging stream, filled with logs and cakes of ice, looked strangely weird and threatening.

At first the grown folks paid no special heed to the spring flood; only the children ran down to the banks to watch the raging river and all that it carried along.

But timber and ice floes were not the only things that went floating by! Presently the stream came driving with washing piers and bath houses, then with boats and wreckage of bridges.

"It will soon be taking our bridge, too!" the children exclaimed. They felt a bit uneasy, but were glad at the same time that something so extraordinary was likely to happen.

Suddenly a huge pine, root and branch, came sailing past, followed by a white-stemmed aspen tree, its spreading branches thick with buds which had swelled from being so long in the water. Close upon the trees came a little hay shed, bottom upward; it was still full of hay and straw, and floated on its roof like a boat on its keel.

But when things of that sort began to drift past, the grown-ups, too, bestirred themselves. They realized now that the river had overflowed its banks somewhere up north, and hurried down to the shores with poles and boat hooks, to haul up on land buildings and furniture.

At the northern end of the parish, where the houses were scattered and people were scarce, Ingmar Ingmarsson alone was standing on the bank, gazing out at the river. He was then almost sixty, and looked even older. His face was weatherbeaten and furrowed, his figure bent; he appeared to be as awkward and helpless as ever. He stood leaning on a long, heavy boat hook, his dull, sleepy-looking eyes fixed on the water. The river raged and foamed, arrogantly marching past with all that it had matched from the shores. It was as if it were deriding the peasant for his slowness. "Oh, you're not the one to wrest from me any of the things I'm carrying away!" it seemed to say.

Ingmar Ingmarsson made no attempt to rescue any of the floating bridges or boat hulls that passed quite close to the bank. "All that will be seen to down at the village," he thought. Not for a second did his gaze wander from the river. He took note of everything that drifted past. All at once he sighted something bright and yellow floating on some loosely nailed boards quite a distance up the river. "Ah, this is what I have been expecting all along!" he said aloud. At first he could not quite make out what the yellow was; but for one who knew how little children in Dalecarlia are dressed it was easy to guess. "Those must be youngsters who were out on a washing pier playing," he said, "and hadn't the sense to get back on land before the river took them."

It was not long until the peasant saw that he had guessed rightly. Now he could distinctly see three little children, in their yellow homespun frocks and round yellow hats, being carried downstream on a poorly constructed raft that was being slowly torn apart by the swift current and the moving ice floes.

The children were still a long way off. Big Ingmar knew there was a bend in the river where it touched his land. If God in His mercy would only direct the raft with the children into this current, he thought, he might be able to get them ashore.

He stood very still, watching the raft. All at once it seemed as if some one had given it a push; it swung round and headed straight for the shore. By that time the children were so close that he could see their frightened little faces and hear their cries. But they were still too far out to be reached by the boat hook, from the bank at least; so he hurried down to the water's edge, and waded into the river.

As he did so, he had a strange sort of feeling that some one was calling to him to comeback. "You are no longer a young man, Ingmar; this may prove a perilous business for you!" a voice said to him.

He reflected a moment, wondering whether he had the right to risk his life. The wife, whom he had once fetched from the prison, had died during the winter, and since her going his one longing had been that he might soon follow. But, on the other hand, there was his son who needed a father's care, for he was only a little lad and could not look after the farm.

"In any case, it must be as God wills," he said.

Now Big Ingmar was no longer either awkward or slow. As he plunged into the raging river, he planted his boat hook firmly into the bottom, so as not to be carried away by the current, and he took good care to dodge the floating ice and driftwood. When the raft with the children was quite near, he pressed his feet down in the river bed, thrust out his boat hook, and got a purchase on it.

"Hold on tight!" he shouted to the children, for just then the raft made a sudden turn and all its planks creaked. But the wretched structure held together, and Big Ingmar managed to pull it out of the strongest current. That done, he let go of it, for he knew that the raft would now drift shoreward by itself.

Touching bottom with his boat hook again, he turned to go back to the bank. This time, however, he failed to notice a huge log that was coming toward him with a rush. It caught him in the side just below the armpit. It was a terrific blow, for the log was hurled against him with a violent force that sent him staggering in the water. Yet he kept a tight grip on the boat hook until he reached the bank. When he again stood on firm ground, he hardly dared touch his body, for he felt that his chest had been crushed. Then his mouth suddenly filled with blood. "It's all up with you, Ingmar!" he thought, and sank down on the bank, for he could not go a step farther. The little children whom he had rescued gave the alarm, and soon people came running down to the bank, and Big Ingmar was carried home.

The pastor was called in, and he remained at the Ingmar Farm the whole afternoon. On his way home, he stopped at the schoolmaster's. He had experienced things in the course of the day which he felt the need of telling to some one who would understand.

Storm and Mother Stina were deeply grieved, for they had already heard that Ingmar Ingmarsson was dead. The clergyman, on the other hand, looked almost radiant as he stepped into the schoolmaster's kitchen.

Immediately Storm asked the pastor if he had been in time.

"Yes," he said, "but on this occasion I was not needed."

"Weren't you?" said Mother Stina.

"No," answered the pastor with a mysterious smile. "He would have got on just as well without me. Sometimes it is very hard to sit by a deathbed," he added.

"It is indeed," nodded the schoolmaster.

"Particularly when the one who is passing from among us happens to be the best man in your parish."

"Just so."

"But things can also be quite different from what one had imagined."

For a moment the pastor sat quietly gazing into space; his eyes looked clearer than usual behind the spectacles.

"Have you, Strong, or you, Mother Stina, ever heard of the wonderful thing that once happened to Big Ingmar when he was a young man?" he asked.

The schoolmaster said that he had heard many wonderful things about him.

"Why, of course; but this is the most wonderful of all! I never knew of it myself until to-day. Big Ingmar had a good friend who has always lived in a little cabin on his estate," the pastor continued.

"Yes, I know," said the schoolmaster. "He is also named

Ingmar; folks call him Strong Ingmar by way of distinction."

"True," said the pastor; "his father named him Ingmar in honour of the master's family. One Saturday evening, at midsummer, when the nights are almost as light as the days, Big Ingmar and his friend, Strong Ingmar, after finishing their work, put on their Sunday clothes and went down to the village in quest of amusement."

The pastor paused a moment, and pondered. "I can imagine that the night must have been a beautiful one," he went on, "clear and still—one of those nights when earth and sky seem to exchange hues, the sky turning a bright green while the earth becomes veiled in white mists, lending to everything a white or bluish tinge. When Big Ingmar and Strong Ingmar were crossing the bridge to the village, it was as if some one had told them to stop and look upward. They did so. And they saw heaven open! The whole firmament had been drawn back to right and left, like a pair of curtains, and the two stood there, hand in hand, and beheld all the glories of heaven. Have you ever heard anything like it, Mother Stina, or you, Storm?" said the pastor in awed tones. "Only think of those two standing on the bridge and seeing heaven open! But what they saw they have never divulged to a soul. Sometimes they would tell a child or a kinsman that they had once seen heaven open, but they never spoke of it to outsiders. But the vision lived in their memories as their greatest treasure, their Holy of Holies."

The pastor closed his eyes for a moment, and heaved a deep sigh. "I have never before heard tell of such things." His voice shook a little as he proceeded. "I only wish I had stood on the bridge with Big Ingmar and Strong Ingmar, and seen heaven open!

"This morning, immediately after Big Ingmar had been carried home, he requested that Strong Ingmar be sent for. At once a messenger was dispatched to the croft to fetch him, only to find that Strong Ingmar was not at home. He was in the forest somewhere, chopping firewood, and was not easy to find. Messenger after messenger went in search of him. In the meantime, Big Ingmar felt very anxious lest he should not get to see his old friend again in this life. First the doctor came, then I came, but Strong Ingmar they couldn't seem to find. Big Ingmar took very little notice of us. He was sinking fast. 'I shall soon be gone, Parson,' he said to me. 'I only wish I might see Strong Ingmar before I go.' He was lying on the broad bed in the little chamber off the living-room. His eyes were wide open and he seemed to be looking all the while at something that was far, far away, and which no one else saw. The three little children he had rescued sat huddled at the foot of his bed. Whenever his eyes wandered for an instant from that which he saw in the distance, they rested upon the children, and then his whole face was wreathed in smiles.

"At last they had succeeded in finding the crofter. Big Ingmar glanced away from the children with a sigh of relief when he heard Strong Ingmar's heavy step in the hallway. And when his friend came over to the bedside, he took his hand and patted it gently, saying: 'Do you remember the time when you and I stood on the bridge and saw heaven open?' 'As if I could ever forget that night when we two had a vision of Paradise!' Strong Ingmar responded. Then Big Ingmar turned toward him, his face beaming as if he had the most glorious news to impart. 'Now I'm going there,' he said. Then the crofter bent over him and looked straight into his eyes. 'I shall come after,' he said. Big Ingmar nodded. 'But you know I cannot come before your son returns from the pilgrimage.' 'Yes, yes, I know,' Big Ingmar whispered. Then he drew in a few deep breaths and, before we knew it, he was gone."

The schoolmaster and his wife thought, with the pastor, that it was a beautiful death. All three of them sat profoundly silent for a long while.

"But what could Strong Ingmar have meant," asked Mother Stina abruptly, "when he spoke of the pilgrimage?"

The pastor looked up, somewhat perplexed. "I don't know," he replied. "Big Ingmar died just after that was said, and I have not had time to ponder it." He fell to thinking, then he spoke kind of half to himself: "It was a strange sort of thing to say, you're right about that, Mother Stina."

"You know, of course, that it has been said of Strong Ingmar that he can see into the future?" she said reflectively.

The pastor sat stroking his forehead in an effort to collect his thoughts. "The ways of Providence cannot be reasoned out by the finite mind," he mused. "I cannot fathom them, yet seeking to know them is the most satisfying thing in all the world."

Karin, Daughter Of Ingmar

Autumn had come and school was again open. One morning, when the children were having their recess, the schoolmaster and Gertrude went into the kitchen and sat down at the table, where Mother Stina served them with coffee. Before they had finished their cups a visitor arrived.

The caller was a young peasant named Halvor Halvorsson, who had lately opened a shop in the village. He came from Tims Farm, and was familiarly known as Tims Halvor. He was a tall, good-looking chap who appeared to be somewhat dejected. Mother Stina asked him also to have some coffee; so he sat down at the table, helped himself, and began to talk to the schoolmaster.

Mother Stina sat by the window knitting; from where she was seated she could look down the road. All at once she grew red in the face and leaned forward to get a better view. Trying to appear unconcerned, she said with feigned indifference: "The grand folk seem to be out walking to-day."

Tims Halvor thought he detected a certain something in her tone that sounded a bit peculiar, and he got up and looked out. He saw a tall, stoop-shouldered woman and a half-grown boy coming toward the schoolhouse.

"Unless my eyes deceive me, that's Karin, daughter of Ingmar!" said Mother Stina.

"It's Karin all right," Tims Halvor confirmed. He said nothing more, but turned away from the window and glanced around the room, as if trying to discover some way of escape;

but in a moment he quietly went back to his seat.

The summer before, when Big Ingmar was still alive, Halvor had paid court to Karin Ingmarsson. The courtship had been a long one, with many ifs and buts on the part of her family. The old Ingmars were not quite sure that he was good enough for Karin. It had not been a question of money, for Halvor was well-to-do; his father, however, had been addicted to drink, and who could say but that this failing had been transmitted to the son. However, it was finally decided that Halvor should have Karin. The wedding day was fixed and they had asked to have the banns published. But before the day set for the first reading Karin and Halvor made a journey to Falun, to purchase the wedding ring and the prayerbook. They were away for three days, and when they got back Karin told her father that she could not marry Halvor. She had no fault to find with him save that on one occasion he had taken a drop too much, and she feared he might become like his father. Big Ingmar then said that he would not try to influence her against her better judgment, so Halvor was dismissed, and the engagement was off.

Halvor took it very much to heart. "You are heaping upon me shame that will be hard to bear," he said. "What will people think if you throw me over in this way? It isn't fair to treat a decent man like that."

But Karin was not to be moved, and ever since Halvor had been morose and unhappy. He could not forget the injustice that had been done him by the Ingmarssons. And here sat Halvor, and there came Karin! What would happen next? This much was certain: a reconciliation was out of the question. Since the previous autumn Karin had been married to one Elof Ersson. She and her husband lived at the Ingmar Farm, which they had been running since the death of Big Ingmar, in the spring. Big Ingmar had left five daughters and one son, but the son was too young to take over the property.

Meanwhile Karin had come in. She was only about two and twenty, but was one of those women who never look real young. Most people thought her exceedingly plain, for she favoured her father's family and had their heavy eyelids, their sandy hair, and hard lines about the mouth. But the schoolmaster and his wife were pleased to think that she bore such a striking resemblance to the old Ingmars. When Karin saw Halvor, her face did not change. She moved about, slowly and quietly, and greeted each of them in turn; when she offered her hand to Halvor, he put out his, and they barely touched each other with the tips of their fingers. Karin always stooped a little and, as she stood before Halvor, with head bowed, she seemed to be more bent than usual, while Halvor looked taller and straighter than ever.

"So Karin has really ventured out to-day?" said Mother Stina, drawing up the pastor's chair for her.

"Yes," she answered. "It's easy walking now that the frost has set in."

"There has been a hard frost during the night," the schoolmaster put in.

This was followed by a dead silence, which lasted several minutes. Presently Halvor got up, and the others started, as if suddenly awakened from a sound sleep.

"I must get back to the shop," said Halvor.

"What's your hurry?" asked Mother Stina.

"I hope Halvor isn't going on my account," said Karin meekly.

As soon as Halvor was gone the tension was broken, and the schoolmaster knew at once what to say. He looked at the lad Karin had brought with her, and of whom no one had taken any notice before. He was a little chap who could not have been much older than Gertrude. He had a fair, soft baby face, yet there was something about him that made him appear old for his years. It was easy to tell to what family he belonged.

"I think Karin has brought us a new pupil," said Storm.

"This is my brother," Karin replied. "He is the present Ingmar Ingmarsson."

"He's rather little for that name," Storm remarked.

"Yes, father died too soon!"

"He did indeed," said the schoolmaster and his wife, both in the same breath.

"He has been attending the school in Falun," Karin explained. "That's why he hasn't been here before."

"Aren't you going to let him go back this year, too?"

Karin dropped her eyes and a sigh escaped her. "He has

the name of being a good student," she said, evading his question.

"I'm only afraid that I can't teach him anything. He must know as much as I do."

"Well, I guess the schoolmaster knows a good deal more than a little chap like him." Then came another pause, after which Karin continued: "This is not only the question of his attending school, but I would also like to ask whether you and Mother Stina would let the boy come here to live."

The schoolmaster and his wife looked at each other in astonishment, but neither of them was prepared to answer.

"I fear our quarters are rather close," said Storm, presently.

"I thought that perhaps you might be willing to accept milk and butter and eggs as part payment."

"As to that—"

"You would be doing me a great service," said the rich peasant woman.

Mother Stina felt that Karin would never have made this singular request had there not been some good reason for it; so she promptly settled the matter.

"Karin need say no more. We will do all that we can for the Ingmarssons."

"Thank you," said Karin.

The two women talked over what had best be done for Ingmar's welfare. Meantime, Storm took the boy with him to the classroom, and gave him a seat next to Gertrude. During the whole of the first day Ingmar never said a word.

* * * * *

Tims Halvor did not go near the schoolhouse again for a week or more; it was as if he were afraid of again meeting Karin there. But one morning when it rained in torrents, and there was no likelihood of any customers coming, he decided to run over and have a chat with Mother Stina. He was hungry for a heart-to-heart talk with some kindly and sympathetic person. He had been seized by a terrible fit of the blues. "I'm no good, and no one has any respect for me," he murmured, tormenting himself, as he had been in the habit of doing ever since Karin had thrown him over.

He closed his shop, buttoned his storm coat, and went on his way to the school, through wind and rain and slush. Halvor was happy to be back once more in the friendly atmosphere of the schoolhouse, and was still there when the recess bell rang, and Storm and the two children came in for their coffee. All three went over to greet him. He arose to shake hands with the schoolmaster, but when little Ingmar put out his hand, Halvor was talking so earnestly to Mother Stina that he seemed not to have noticed the boy. Ingmar remained standing a moment, then he went up to the table and sat down. He sighed several times, just as Karin had done the day she was there.

"Halvor has come to show us his new watch," said Mother Stina.

Whereupon Halvor took from his pocket a new silver watch, which he showed to them. It was a pretty little timepiece, with a flower design engraved on the case. The schoolmaster opened it, went into the schoolroom for a magnifying glass, adjusted it to his eye, and began examining the works. He seemed quite carried away as he studied the delicate adjustment of the tiny wheels, and said he had never seen finer workmanship. Finally he gave the watch back to Halvor, who put it in his pocket, looking neither pleased nor proud, as folks generally do when you praise their purchases.

Ingmar was silent during the meal, but when he had finished his coffee, he asked Storm whether he really knew anything about watches.

"Why, of course," returned the schoolmaster. "Don't you know that I understand a little of everything?"

Ingmar then brought out a watch which he carried in his vest pocket. It was a big, round, silver *turnip* that looked ugly and clumsy as compared with Halvor's watch. The chain to which it was attached was also a clumsy contrivance. The case was quite plain and dented. It was not much of a watch: it had no crystal, and the enamel on its face was cracked.

"It has stopped," said Storm, putting the watch to his ear.

"Yes, I kn-n-ow," stammered the boy. "I was just wondering if you didn't think it could be mended."

Storm opened it and found that all the wheels were loose. "You must have been hammering nails with this watch," he said. "I can't do anything with it."

"Don't you think that Eric, the clockmaker, could fix it?"

"No, no more than I. You'd better send it to Falun and have new works put in."

"I thought so," said Ingmar, and took the watch.

"For heaven's sake, what have you been doing with it?" the schoolmaster exclaimed.

The boy swallowed hard. "It was father's watch," he explained, "and it got damaged like that when father was struck by the whirling log."

Now they all grew interested.

With an effort to control his feelings, Ingmar continued: "As you know, it happened during Holy Week, when I was at home. I was the first person to reach father when he lay on the bank. I found him with the watch in his hand. 'Now it's all over with me, Ingmar,' he said. 'I'm sorry the watch is broken, for I want you to give it, with my greetings, to some one that I have wronged.' Then he told me who was to have the watch, and bade me take it along to Falun and have it repaired before presenting it. But I never went back to Falun, and now I don't know what to do about it."

The schoolmaster was wondering whether he knew of any one who was soon going to the city, when Mother Stina turned to the boy:

"Who was to have the watch, Ingmar?" she asked.

"I don't know as I ought to tell," the boy demurred.

"Wasn't it Tims Halvor, who is sitting here?"

"Yes," he whispered.

"Then give Halvor the watch just as it is," said Mother Stina. "That will please him best."

Ingmar obediently rose, took out the watch and rubbed it in the sleeve of his coat, to shine it up a bit. Then he went over to Halvor.

"Father asked me to give you this with his compliments," he said, holding out the watch.

All this while Halvor had sat there, silent and glum. And when the boy went over to him, he put his hand up to his eyes, as if he did not want to look at him. Ingmar stood a long time holding out the watch; finally, he glanced appealingly at Mother Stina.

"Blessed are the peacemakers," she said.

Then Storm put in a word. "I don't thick you could ask for a better amend, Halvor," he said. "I've always maintained that if Ingmar Ingmarsson had lived he would have given you full justice long before this."

The next they saw was Halvor reaching out for the watch, almost as if against his will. But the moment he had got it into his hand, he put it in the inside pocket of his vest.

"There's no fear of any one taking that watch from him," said the schoolmaster with a laugh, as he saw Halvor carefully buttoning his coat.

And Halvor laughed, too. Presently he got up, straightened himself, and drew a deep breath. The colour came into his cheeks, and his eyes shone with a new-found happiness.

"Now Halvor must feel like a new man," said the schoolmaster's wife.

Then Halvor put his hand inside his overcoat and drew out his brand-new watch. Crossing over to Ingmar, who was again seated at the table, he said: "Since I have taken your father's watch from you, you must accept this one from me."

He laid the watch on the table and went out, without even saying good-bye. The rest of the day he tramped the roads and bypaths. A couple of peasants who had come from a distance to trade with him hung around outside the shop from noon till evening. But no Tims Halvor appeared.

* * * * *

Elof Ersson, the husband of Karin Ingmarsson, was the son of a cruel and avaricious peasant, who had always treated him harshly. As a child he had been half starved, and even after he was grown up his father kept him under his thumb. He had to toil and slave from morning till night, and was never allowed any pleasures. He was not even allowed to attend the country dances like other young folk, and he got no rest from his work even on Sundays. Nor did Elof become his own master when he married. He had to live at the Ingmar Farm and be under the domination of his father-in-law; and also at the Ingmar Farm hard work and frugality were the rule of the day. As long as Ingmar Ingmarsson lived Elof seemed quite content with his lot, toiling and slaving with never so much as a complaint. Folks used to say that now the Ingmarssons had got a son-in-law after their own hearts, for Elof Ersson did not know that there was anything else in life than just toil and drudgery.

But as soon as Big Ingmar was dead and buried, Elof began to drink and carouse. He made the acquaintance of all the rounders in the parish, and invited them down to the Farm, and went with them to dance halls and taverns. He quit work altogether, and drank himself full every day. In the space of two short months he became a poor drunken wretch.

The first time Karin saw him in a state of intoxication she was horrified. "This is God's judgment upon me for my treatment of Halvor," was the thought that came to her. To the husband she said very little in the way of rebuke or warning. She soon perceived that he was like a blasted tree, doomed to wither and decay, and she could not hope for either help or protection from him.

But Karin's sisters were not so wise as she was. They resented his escapades, blushed at his ribald songs and coarse jokes, by turns threatening and admonishing him. And although their brother-in-law was on the whole rather good-natured, he sometimes got into a rage and had words with them. Then Karin's only thought was how she should get her sisters away from the house, that they might escape the misery in which she herself had to live. In the course of the summer she managed to marry off the two older girls, and the two younger ones she sent to America, where they had relatives who were well-to-do.

All the sisters received their proportion of the inheritance, which amounted to twenty thousand kroner each. The farm had been left to Karin, with the understanding that young Ingmar was to take it over when he became of age.

It seemed remarkable that Karin, who was so awkward and diffident, should have been able to send so many birds from the nest, find mates for them, and homes. She arranged it all herself, for she could get no help whatever from her husband, who had now become utterly worthless.

Her greatest concern, however, was the little brother—he who was now Ingmar Ingmarsson. The boy exasperated Karin's husband even more than the sisters had done. He did it by actions rather than words. One time he poured out all the corn brandy Elof had brought home; another time the brother-in-law caught him in the act of diluting his liquor with water.

When autumn came Karin demanded that the boy be sent back to high school that year, as in former years, but her husband, who was also his guardian, would not hear of it.

"Ingmar shall be a farmer, like his father and me and my father," said Elof. "What business has he at high school? When the winter comes, he and I will go into the forest to put up charcoal kilns. That will be the best kind of schooling for him. When I was his age, I spent a whole winter working at the kiln."

As Karin could not induce him to alter his mind, she had to make the best of it and keep Ingmar at home for the time being.

Elof then tried to win the confidence of little Ingmar. Whenever he went anywhere he always wanted the boy to accompany him. The lad went, of course, but unwillingly. He did not like to go with him on his sprees. Then Elof would coax the boy, and vow that he was not going any farther than the church or the shop. But when once he got Ingmar in the cart, he would drive off with him, down to the smithies at Bergsana, or the tavern in Karmsund.

Karin was glad that her husband took the boy along; it was at least a safeguard against Elof being left in a ditch by the roadside, or driving the horse to death.

Once, when Elof came home at eight in the morning, Ingmar was sitting beside him in the cart, fast asleep.

"Come out here and look after the boy!" Elof shouted to Karin, "and carry him in. The poor brat's as full as a tick, and can't walk a step."

Karin was so shocked that she almost collapsed. She was obliged to sit down on the steps for a moment, to recover herself, before she could lift the boy. The minute she took hold of him she discovered that he was not really asleep, but stiff from the cold, and unconscious. Taking the boy in her arms, she carried him into the bedroom, locked the door after her, and tried to bring him to. After a while she stepped into the living-room, where Elof sat eating his breakfast. She walked straight up to him and put her hand on his shoulder.

"You'd better lay in a good meal while you're about it," she said, "for if you have made my brother drink himself to death, you'll soon have to put up with poorer fare than you're getting on the Ingmar Farm."

"How you talk! As if a little brandy could hurt him!"

"Mark what I say! If the boy dies, you'll get twenty years in prison, Elof."

When Karin returned to the bedroom, the boy had come out of his stupor, but was delirious and unable to move hand or foot. He suffered agonies.

"Do you think I'm going to die, Karin?" he moaned.

"No, dear, of course not," Karin assured him.

"I didn't know what they were giving me."

"Thank God for that!" said Karin fervently.

"If I die, write to my sisters and tell them I didn't know it was liquor," wailed the boy.

"Yes, dear," soothed Karin.

"Really and truly I didn't know—I swear it!"

All day Ingmar lay in a raging fever. "Please don't tell father about it!" he raved.

"Father will never know of it," she said.

"But suppose I die, then father would surely find it out, and I would be shamed before him."

"But it wasn't your fault, child."

"Maybe father will think that I shouldn't have taken what Elof offered me? Don't you suppose the whole parish must know that I have been full?" he asked. "What do the hired men say, and what does old Lisa say, and Strong Ingmar?"

"They're not saying anything," Karin replied.

"You will have to tell them how it happened. We were at the tavern in Karmsund, where Elof and some of his pals had been drinking the whole night. I was sitting in a corner on a bench, half asleep, when Elof came over and roused me. 'Wake up, Ingmar,' he said very pleasantly, 'and I'll give you something that will make you warm. Drink this,' he urged,

holding a glass to my lips. 'It's only hot water with a little sugar
in it.' I was shivering with the cold when I awoke and, as I drank
the stuff, I only noticed that it was hot and sweet. But he had
gone and mixed something strong with it! Oh, what will father
say?"

Then Karin opened the door leading to the living-room,
where Elof still lingered over his meal. She felt that it would be
well for him to hear this.

"If only father were living, Karin, if only father were
living!"

"What then, Ingmar?"

"Don't you think he'd kill him?"

Elof broke into a loud laugh, and when the boy heard
him, he turned so pale with fright that Karin promptly closed the
door again.

It had this good effect upon Elof, at all events: he put up
no objection when Karin decided to take the boy to Storm's
school.

* * * * *

Soon after Halvor had received the watch, his shop was
always full of people. Every farmer in the parish, when in town,
would stop at Halvor's shop in order to hear the story of Big
Ingmar's watch. The peasants in their long white fur coats stood
hanging over the counter by the hour, their solemn, furrowed
faces turned toward Halvor as he talked to them. Sometimes he
would take out the watch, and show them the dented case and
the cracked face.

"So it was there the blow caught him," the peasants
would say. And they seemed to see before them what had
happened when Big Ingmar was hurt. "It is a great thing for you,
Halvor, to have that watch!"

When Halvor was showing the watch he would never let
it out of his hands, but would always keep a tight grip on the
chain.

One day Halvor stood talking to a group of peasants,
telling them the usual story, and at the climax the watch was of
course brought out. As it was being passed from one to the other

(he holding the chain) there fell upon all a solemn hush. In the meantime Elof had come into the shop, but as every one's attention was riveted upon the watch, no one had remarked his presence. Elof had also heard the story of his father-in-law's watch, and knew at once what was going on. He did not begrudge Halvor his souvenir; he was simply amused at the sight of him and the others standing there looking so solemn over nothing but an old and battered silver watch.

Elof stole quietly up behind the men, reached over, and snatched the watch from Halvor. It was only meant in fun. He had no thought of taking the watch only from Halvor; he just wanted to tease him a bit.

When Halvor tried to snatch it again, Elof stepped back and held it up, as if he were holding out a lump of sugar to a dog. Then Halvor vaulted the counter; and he looked so angry that Elof got frightened and, instead of standing still and handing him back the watch, he ran for the door.

Outside were some badly worn wooden steps; Elof's foot caught in a hole, and down he went. Halvor fell upon him, seized the watch, then gave him several hard kicks.

"You'd better quit kicking me, and find out what's wrong with my back," said Elof.

Halvor stopped at once, but Elof made no move to raise himself.

"Help me up," he said.

"You can help yourself when you've slept off your jag."

"I'm not full," Elof protested. "The fact is, as I started to run down the stairs I thought I saw Big Ingmar coming toward me, to take the watch. That's how I got such an ugly fall."

Then Halvor bent down and gave the poor wretch a lift, for his back was broken. He had to be put into a wagon and driven home. He would never again have the use of his legs. From that time forth Elof was confined to his bed, a helpless cripple. But he could talk, and all day long he kept begging for brandy. The doctor had left strict orders with Karin not to give him any spirits, lest he drink himself to death. Then Elof tried to get what he wanted by shrieking and making the most hideous noises, especially at night. He behaved like a madman, and disturbed every one's rest.

That was Karin's most trying year. Her husband sometimes tormented her until it seemed as though she could not stand it any longer. The very air became polluted by his vile talk and profanity, so that the home was like a hell. Karin begged the Storms to keep little Ingmar with them also during the holidays; she did not want her brother to be at home with her for a day, not even at Christmas.

All the servants at the Ingmar Farm were distantly related to the family, and had always lived on the place. But for the feeling that they belonged to the Ingmarssons, they could not have gone on serving under such conditions. There were precious few nights that they were allowed to sleep in peace. Elof was constantly hitting upon new ways of tormenting both the servants and Karin, to make them give in to his demands.

In this misery Karin passed a winter and a summer and another winter.

But Karin had a retreat to which she would flee at times in order to be alone with her thoughts. Behind the hop garden there was a narrow seat upon which she often sat, with her elbows on her knees and her chin resting in her hands, staring straight ahead, yet seeing nothing. Fronting her were great stretches of cornfields, beyond which was the forest, and in the distance the range of hills and Mount Klack.

One evening in April she sat on her bench, feeling tired and listless, as one often does in the springtime when the snow turns to slush and the ground is still unwashed by spring rains. The hops lay sleeping under a cover of fir brush. Over against the hills hung a thick mist, such as always accompanies a thaw. The birch tops were beginning to turn brown, but all along the skirt of the forest there was still a deep border of snow. Spring would soon be there in earnest, and the thought of it made her feel even more tired. She felt that she could never live through another summer like the last one. She thought of all the work ahead of her—sowing and haymaking; spring baking and spring cleaning; weaving and sewing—and wondered how she would ever get through with it all.

"I might better be dead," she sighed. "I seem to be here for no other purpose than to prevent Elof killing himself with drink."

Suddenly she looked up, as if she had heard some one calling her. Leaning against the hedge, looking straight at her, stood Halvor Halvorsson. She did not know just when he had come, but apparently he had been standing there a good while.

"I thought I should find you over here," Halvor said.

"Oh, did you?"

"I remembered how in days gone by you used to step away, and come here to sit and brood."

"I didn't have much to brood over at that time."

"Then your troubles were mostly imaginary."

Karin mused as she looked at Halvor: "He must be thinking what a fool I was not to have married him, who is such a handsome and dignified man. Now he's got me where he can crow over me, and he has come only to laugh at me."

"I've been inside talking with Elof," Halvor enlightened. "It was really him I wanted to see."

Karin made no reply, but sat there, frigid and unresponsive, her eyes fixed on the ground and her hands crossed, prepared to meet all the scorn she fancied Halvor would now heap upon her.

"I said to him," Halvor continued, "that I considered myself largely to blame for his misfortune, since it was at my place that he got hurt." He paused a moment, as if waiting for some expression from her, either of approval or disapproval. But Karin was silent. "So I have asked him to come and live with me for a while. It would at least be a change, and he could see more people than he meets here."

Then Karin raised her eyes, but otherwise remained as motionless as before.

"We have arranged to have him sent to my place to-morrow morning. I know he'll come, because he thinks he can get his liquor. But, of course, you must know, Karin, that that's out of the question. No, indeed! It's no more to be had with me than with you. I shall expect him to-morrow. He is to occupy the little room off the shop, and I've promised him that I'll let his door stand open, so that he may see all persons who come and go."

At Halvor's first words Karin wondered whether this was not something he had made up, but gradually it dawned on her that he was in earnest.

As a matter of fact, Karin had always imagined that Halvor had courted her only because of her money and good connections. It had never occurred to her that he might have loved her for herself alone. She probably knew she was not the kind of girl that men care for. Nor had she herself been in love, either with Halvor or Elof. But now that Halvor had come to her in her trouble, and wanted to help her, she was completely overwhelmed by the bigness of the man. She marvelled that he could be so kind. She felt that surely he must like her a little, since he had come like that, to help her.

Karin's heart began to beat violently and anxiously. She awoke to something she had never before experienced, and wondered what it meant. Then all at once she realized that Halvor's kindness had thawed her frozen heart, and that love was beginning to flame up in her. Halvor went on unfolding his plan, fearing all the while that she might oppose him. "It's hard for Elof, too," he pleaded. "He needs a change of scene, and he won't make as much trouble for me as he has made for you. It will be quite different when he's got a man to reckon with."

Karin hardly knew what she should do. She felt that she could not make a movement or say a word without letting Halvor see that she was in love with him; yet she knew she would have to give him some kind of an answer.

Presently Halvor stopped talking and simply looked at her.

Then Karin rose, involuntarily went up to him, and patted him on the hand. "God bless you, Halvor!" she said in broken tones. "God bless you!"

Despite all her precautions, Halvor must have divined something, for he quickly grasped her hands and drew her to him.

"No! No!" she cried in alarm, freeing herself; then she hurried away.

* * * * *

Elof had gone to live with Halvor. All summer he lay in the little bedroom off the shop. Halvor was not troubled with the care of him for a great while, for in the autumn he died.

Shortly after his death Mother Stina said to Halvor: "Now you must promise me one thing: promise me that you will exercise patience as regards Karin."

"Of course I'll have patience," Halvor returned, wonderingly.

"She's somebody worth winning, even if one has to wait seven long years."

But it was not so easy for Halvor to have patience, for he soon learned that this one and that one was paying court to Karin. This began within a fortnight of Elof's funeral.

One Sunday afternoon Halvor sat on the steps in front of his shop, watching the people coming and going. Presently it occurred to him that an unusual number of fine rigs were moving in the direction of the Ingmar Farm. In the first carriage sat an inspector from Bergsana Foundry, in the second was the son of the proprietor of the Karmsund Inn, and last came the Magistrate Berger Sven Persson, who was the richest man in western Dalecarlia, and a sensible and highly esteemed man, too. He was not young, to be sure; he had been twice married, and was now a widower for the second time.

When Halvor saw Berger Sven Persson driving by, he could not contain himself any longer. He jumped to his feet and started down the road; in almost no time he was over the bridge and on the side of the river where the Ingmar Farm lay.

"I'd like to know where all those carriages have gone to," he said to himself. He followed the wheel ruts, half running, but all the while becoming more and more determined. "I know this is stupid of me," he thought, remembering Mother Stina's warning. "But I'm only going as far as the gate, to see what they're up to down there."

In the best room at the Ingmars sat Berger Sven Persson and two other men, drinking coffee. Ingmar Ingmarsson, who still lived at the schoolhouse, was at home over Sunday. He sat at table with them and acted as host, for Karin had excused herself, saying she had some work to do in the kitchen, as the maids had gone down to the mission house to hear the schoolmaster preach.

It was deadly dull in the parlour. All the men sat drinking

their coffee without exchanging a word. The suitors were practically strangers to one another, and all three of them were watching for an opportunity to slip into the kitchen for a private word with Karin.

Presently the door opened and in stepped another caller, who was received by Ingmar, and conducted to the table.

"This is Tims Halvor Halvorsson," said Ingmar, introducing the newcomer to Berger Sven Persson.

Sven Persson did not rise, but greeted Halvor with a sweep of the hand, saying, somewhat facetiously:

"It is a pleasure to meet so distinguished a personage."

Ingmar noisily drew up a chair for Halvor, so that he was spared the embarrassment of replying.

From the moment Halvor entered the room, all the suitors became chatty and began to talk big. Each in turn praised and championed the others. It was as if they had all agreed among themselves to stand together until Halvor was well out of the game.

"The magistrate is driving a fine horse to-day," the inspector began.

Berger Sven Persson took up the fun by complimenting the inspector on having shot a bear the winter before. Then the two turned to the innkeeper's son, and said something in praise of a house his father was building.

Finally all three of them bragged about the wealth of Bergen Sven Persson. They waxed eloquent, and with every word they gave Halvor to understand that he was too lowly a man to think of pitting himself against them. And Halvor certainly did feel very insignificant, and bitterly regretted having come.

Just then Karin came along with fresh coffee. At sight of Halvor she brightened for an instant; then it occurred to her that his calling on her so soon after her husband's death looked rather bad. "If he is in such a hurry, people will surely say that he hadn't given Elof proper care, and that he wanted him out of the way so he could marry me." She would rather he had waited two or three years before coming; that would have been long enough to make folks see that he had not been impatient for Elof's departure. "Why need he be in such haste?" she wondered.

"Surely he must know that I don't want anyone but him."

Every one had stopped talking the moment Karin appeared, wondering how she and Halvor would greet each other. They barely touched hands. .At which the magistrate expressed his delight by a short whistle, while the inspector broke into a loud guffaw. Haldor quietly turned to him. "What are you laughing at?" he said.

The inspector was at a loss for an answer. With Karin there he did not wish to say anything that might give offence.

"He is thinking of a hound that raises a hare and allows some one else to catch it," remarked the innkeeper's son, insinuatingly.

Karin turned blood red, but refilled the coffee cups. "Berger Sven Persson and the rest of you will have to be satisfied with plain coffee," she said. "We no longer serve spirits to any one on this farm."

"Nor do I at my home," said the magistrate approvingly.

The inspector and the innkeeper's son kept quiet; they understood that Sven Persson had scored heavily.

The magistrate straightway began to discourse on temperance and its salutary effects. Karin listened to him with interest, and agreed with all that he said. Seeing that this was the kind of talk that would appeal to her, the magistrate began to spread himself, and delivered long-winded harangue on the curse of liquor and drunkenness. Karin recognized all her own thoughts on the subject, and was glad to find that they were shared by so intelligent a man as the magistrate.

In the middle of his monologue Berger Sven Persson glanced over at Halvor, who sat at the table, looking glum and sulky, his coffee cup untouched.

"It's pretty rough on him," thought Berger Sven Persson, "particularly if there's any truth in what people say about his having given Elof a little lift on his way into the next world. Anyway, he did Karin a good service by relieving her of that dreadful sot." And since the magistrate seemed to think that he had as good as won the game, he felt rather friendly toward Halvor. Raising his cup, he said: "Here's to you, Halvor! You certainly did Karin a good turn when you took her drunken sot of a husband off her hands."

Halvor did not respond to the toast. He sat looking the man straight in the eyes, and wondered how he should take this.

The inspector again burst out laughing. "Yes, yes, a good turn," he haw-hawed, "a real good turn."

"Yes, yes, a real good turn," echoed the innkeeper's son, with a chuckle.

Before they were done laughing, Karin had vanished like a shadow through the kitchen door; but she could hear from the kitchen all that was said inside. She was both sorry and distressed over Halvor's untimely visit. It would probably result in her never being able to marry Halvor. It was plain that the gossips were already spreading evil reports. "I can't bear the thought of losing him," she sighed.

For a time no sound came from the sitting-room, but presently she heard a noise as if a chair were being pushed back. Some one had evidently risen.

"Are you going already, Halvor?" young Ingmar was heard to say.

"Yes," Halvor replied. "I can't stop any longer. Please say good-bye to Karin for me."

"Why don't you go into the kitchen and say it for yourself?"

"No," Halvor was heard to answer, "we two have nothing more to say to each other."

Karin's heart began to pump hard, and thoughts came rushing into her head, as if on wings. Now Halvor was angry at her—and no wonder! She had hardly dared even to shake hands with him, and when the others had scoffed at him, she never opened her mouth in his defence, but quietly sneaked away. Now he must think she did not care for him, and was therefore going, never to return. She could not understand why she should have treated him so shabbily—she who was so fond of him. Then, all at once her father's old saying came to her: "The Ingmarssons need have no fear of men; they have only to walk in the ways of God."

Karin hastily opened the door, and stood facing Halvor before he could manage to leave the room. "Are you leaving so soon, Halvor?" she asked. "I thought you were going to stay to supper."

Halvor stood staring at Karin. She seemed to be completely changed; her cheeks were aglow, and there was something tender and appealing about her which he had never seen before.

"I'm going, and I'm not coming back," said Halvor. He had not caught her meaning, apparently.

"Do stay and finish your coffee," she urged. Then she took him by the hand and led him back to the table. She turned both white and red, and several times she all but lost her courage. Just the same she braved it out, although there was nothing she feared so much as scorn and contempt. "Now he will at least see that I'm willing to stand by him," she thought. Turning toward her guests, she said: "Berger Sven Persson and all of you! Halvor and I have not spoken of this matter—as I have so recently become a widow—but now it seems best that you should all know that I would rather marry Halvor than any one else in the world." She paused to get control of her voice, then concluded: "Folks may say what they like about this, but Halvor and I have done nothing wrong."

When Karin had finished speaking, she drew nearer to Halvor, as if seeking protection against all the cruel slander that would come now.

The men were speechless, mostly from astonishment at Karin Ingmarsson, who looked younger and more girlish than ever before in her life.

Then Halvor said in a voice vibrant with feeling: "Karin, when I received your father's watch, I felt that nothing greater could have happened to me; but this thing which you have just done transcends everything."

Whereupon Berger Sven Persson, who was in many ways an excellent man, arose.

"Let us all congratulate Karin and Halvor," he said, graciously, "for every one must know that he whom Karin, daughter of Ingmar, has chosen is a man of sterling worth."

In Zion

That an old country schoolmaster should sometimes be a little too self-confident is not surprising: for well nigh a lifetime he has imparted knowledge and given advice to his fellowmen. He sees that all the peasants are living by what he has taught, and that not one among them knows more than what he, their schoolmaster, has told them. How can he help but regard all the people in the parish as mere school children, however old they may have grown? It is only natural that he should consider himself wiser than every one else. It seems almost an impossibility for one of these regular old school persons to treat any one as a grown-up, for he looks upon each and every one as a child with dimpled cheeks and wide innocent baby eyes.

One Sunday, in the winter, just after service, the pastor and the schoolmaster stood talking together in the vestry; the conversation had turned upon the Salvation Army.

"It's a singular idea to have hit upon," the pastor remarked. "I never imagined that I should live to see anything of that sort!"

The schoolmaster glanced sharply at the pastor; he thought his remark entirely irrelevant. Surely the pastor could never think that such an absurd innovation would find its way into their parish.

"I don't believe you are likely to see it, either," he said emphatically.

The pastor, knowing that he himself was a weak and broken-down man, let the schoolmaster have things pretty much his own way, but all the same, he could not refrain from chaffing him a little, occasionally.

"How can you feel so cocksure that we shall escape the Salvation Army, Storm?" he said. "You see, when pastor and schoolmaster stand together, there's no fear of any nuisance of that sort crowding in. Yet I'm not altogether certain, Storm, that you do stand by me. You preach to suit yourself in your Zion."

To this the schoolmaster did not reply at once. Presently he said, quite meekly: "The pastor has never heard me preach."

The mission house was a veritable rock of offence. The clergyman had never set foot in the place. And now that this mooted question had come up, both men were sorry they had said anything to hurt each other's feelings. "Perhaps I'm unjust to Storm," thought the pastor. "During the four years that he has been holding his afternoon Bible Talks, on Sundays, there has been a larger attendance at the morning church services than ever before, and I haven't seen the least sign of division in the church. Storm has not destroyed the parish, as I feared he would. He is a faithful friend and servant, and I mean to show him how much I appreciate him."

The little misunderstanding of the forenoon resulted in the pastor's attending the schoolmaster's meeting in the afternoon.

"I'll give Storm a pleasant surprise," he thought. "I will go to hear him preach in his Zion."

On the way to the mission house the pastor's thoughts went back to the time it was built. How full the air had been of prophecies, and how firmly he had believed that God had intended it to be something great! But nothing much had happened. "Our Lord must have changed His mind," he thought, amused at his entertaining such queer ideas regarding our Lord.

The schoolmaster's Zion was a large hall with light-coloured walls. On either side hung wood engravings of Luther and Melanchton, in fur-trimmed cloaks; along the borders, close to the ceiling, ran highly illuminated Bible texts, embellished with flowers and heavenly trumpets and bassoons. At the front of the room, above the speaker's platform, hung an oleograph representing the Good Shepherd.

The large bare room was full of people, which was all

that seemed necessary to create an atmosphere of impressive
solemnity. Most of the people were dressed in the picturesque
peasant costume of the parish, and the starched and flaring white
headgear of the women made the room look as if it were filled
with large white-winged birds.

Storm had already commenced his address, when he saw
the pastor come down the aisle, and take a seat in the front row.

"You're a wonderful man, Storm!" thought the schoolmaster. "Everything comes your way. Here's the pastor himself
to do you honour."

During the time that the schoolmaster had been holding
meetings, he had explained the Bible from cover to cover. That
afternoon he spoke of the Heavenly Jerusalem and everlasting
bliss, as given in the Book of the Revelation. He was so pleased
at the parson having come, that he kept thinking to himself: "For
my part I shouldn't ask for anything better than to stand on a
platform through all eternity, teaching good and obedient
children; and if, on occasion, our Lord Himself should drop in to
hear me, as the pastor has done to-day, no one in heaven would
be more delighted than I."

The pastor became interested when the schoolmaster
began to talk about Jerusalem, and the strange misgivings which
he had had long ago flashed through his mind again. In the
middle of the service the door opened, and a number of people
came in. There were about twenty, and they stopped at the door
so as not to disturb the meeting. "Ah!" thought the parson. "I
knew something was going to happen."

Storm had no sooner said "Amen" than a voice, coming
from some one in the group down by the door, piped up: "I
should very much like to say a few words."

"That must be Hök Matts Ericsson," thought the pastor,
and others with him. For no one else in the parish had such a
sweet and childlike treble.

The next moment a little meek-faced man made his way
up to the platform, followed by a score of men and women who
seemed to be there for the purpose of supporting and
encouraging him.

The pastor, the schoolmaster, and the entire congregation
sat in suspense. "Hök Matts has come to tell us of some awful

calamity," they thought. "Either the king is dead, or war has been declared, or perhaps some poor creature has fallen into the river and been drowned." Still Hök Matts did not look as if he had any bad news to impart. He seemed to be in earnest and somewhat stirred, but at the same time he looked so pleased that he could hardly keep from smiling.

"I want to say to the schoolmaster and to the congregation," he began, "that Sunday before last, while I was sitting at home with my family, the Spirit descended upon me, and I began to preach. We couldn't get down here to listen to Storm, on account of the ice and sleet, and we sat longing to hear the Word of God. Then all at once I had the feeling that I could speak myself. I've been preaching now for two Sundays, and all my folks at home and our neighbours, too, have told me that I ought to come down here and let all the people hear me."

Hök Matts also said he was astonished that the gift of speech should have fallen upon so humble a man. "But the schoolmaster himself is only a peasant," he added, with a little more confidence.

After this preamble, Hök Matts folded his hands and was ready to begin preaching at once. But by that time the schoolmaster had recovered from his first shock of surprise.

"Do you think of speaking here now, Hök Matts— immediately?"

"Yes, that's my intention," the man replied. He grew as frightened as a child when Storm glowered at him. "It was my purpose, of course, to first ask leave of the schoolmaster and the rest," he stammered.

"We're all through for the day," said Storm, conclusively.

Then the meek little man began to beg with tears in his voice: "Won't you please let me say a few words? I only want to tell of the things that have come to me when walking behind the plow and when working by myself at the kiln; and now they want to come out."

But the schoolmaster, though he had had such a day of triumph himself, felt no pity for the poor little man. "Matts Ericsson comes here with his own peculiar notions, and claims that they are messages from God," he declared rebukingly.

Hök Matts dared not venture a protest, and the schoolmaster opened the hymnbook.

"Let us all join in singing hymn one hundred and eighty-seven," he said. Whereupon he read out the hymn in stentorian tones, then he began to sing at the top of his voice, "Are your windows open toward Jerusalem."

Meanwhile, he thought: "It was well after all that the pastor happened in to-day; now he can see that I know how to maintain order in my Zion."

But no sooner was the hymn finished than a man jumped to his feet. It was proud and dignified Ljung Björn Olafsson, who was married to one of the Ingmar girls, and was the owner of a large farmstead in the heart of the parish.

"We down at this end think that the schoolmaster might have consulted our wishes before turning Matts Ericsson down," he mildly protested.

"Oh, you think so, do you, Sonny?" The schoolmaster spoke in just the kind of tone he would have used in reproving some young whippersnapper. "Then let me tell you that no one but myself has any say here, in this hall."

Ljung Björn turned blood red. He had not meant to provoke a quarrel with Storm, but had simply wished to soften the blow for Hök Matts, who was an inoffensive man. Just the same, he could not help feeling chagrined over the reply he had got; but before he could think of a retort, one of the men who had come in with Hök Matts spoke up:

"Twice I have heard Hök Matts preach, and must say that he is wonderful. I believe that every one present would be helped by hearing him."

The schoolmaster answered pleasantly enough, but in the old admonishing tone of the classroom: "Surely you understand, Krister Larsson, that I can't allow this. Were I to let Hök Matts preach to-day, then you, Krister, would want to preach next Sunday, and Ljung Björn the Sunday after!"

At this several persons laughed; but Ljung Björn was ready with a sharp rejoinder: "I see no reason why Krister and I shouldn't be as well qualified to preach as the schoolmaster," he said.

Thereupon Tims Halvor arose and tried to quiet them and

to prevent possible strife. "Those of us who have furnished the money to build and run this mission should be consulted before any new preacher is allowed to speak."

By that time Krister Larsson had become aroused and was on his feet again. "I recall to mind that when we built this hall we were all agreed that it should be a free-for-all meetinghouse and not a church where only one man is allowed to preach the Word."

When Krister had spoken every one seemed to breathe freer. Only one short hour before it had not occurred to them that they could ever wish to hear any speaker but the schoolmaster. Now they thought it would be a treat to hear something different. "We'd like to hear something new and to see a fresh face behind the rostrum," somebody muttered.

In all likelihood there would have been no further disturbance if only Bullet Gunner had remained away that day. He, too, was a brother-in-law of Tims Halvor and a tall, gaunt-looking fellow, with a swarthy skin and piercing eyes. Gunner, as well as every one else, liked the schoolmaster, but what he liked even more was a good scrap.

"There was a lot of talk about freedom while we were building this house," said Gunner "but I haven't heard a liberal word since the place was first opened."

The schoolmaster grew purple. Gunner's remark was the first evidence of any actual hostility or revolt. "Let me remind you, Bullet Gunner, that here you have heard the true freedom preached, as Luther taught it; but here there has been no license to preach the kind of new-fangled ideas that spring up one day and fall to the ground the next."

"The schoolmaster would have us think that everything new is worthless as soon as it touches upon doctrine," Gunner replied soothingly and half regretfully. "He approves of our using new methods of caring for our cattle, and wants us to adopt the latest agricultural machinery; but we are not allowed to know anything about the new implements with which God's acres are now being tilled."

Storm began to think that Bullet Gunner's bark was worse than his bite. "Is it your meaning," he said, adopting a facetious tone, "that we should preach a different doctrine here from the Lutheran?"

"It is not a question of a new doctrine," roared Gunner, "but as to who shall preach; and, as far as I know, Matts Ericsson is as good a Lutheran as either the schoolmaster or the parson."

For the moment the schoolmaster had forgotten about the parson; but now he glanced down at him. The clergyman sat quietly musing, his chin resting upon the knob of his cane. There was a curious gleam in his eyes, which were fixed upon Storm, never leaving him for a second.

"After all, perhaps it would have been just as well if the parson hadn't come to-day," thought the schoolmaster. What was then taking place reminded Storm of something he had experienced before. It could be just like this in school sometimes, on a bright spring morning, when a little bird perched itself outside the schoolroom window and warbled lustily. Then all at once the children would tease and beg to be excused from school; they abandoned their studies and made so much fuss and noise that it was almost impossible to bring them to order. Something of the same sort had come over the congregation after Hök Matts's arrival. However, the schoolmaster meant to show the pastor and all of them that he was man enough to quell the mutiny. "First, I will leave them alone and let the ringleaders talk themselves hoarse," he thought, and went and sat down on a chair behind the table on which the water bottle stood.

Instantly there arose against him a perfect storm of protests; for by that time every one had become inflated with the idea that they were all of them just as good as the schoolmaster. "Why should he alone be allowed to tell us what to believe and what not to believe!" they shouted.

These ideas seemed to be new to most of them, yet from the talk it became evident that they had been germinating in their minds ever since the schoolmaster had built the mission house, and shown them that a plain, ordinary man can preach the Word of God.

After a bit Storm remarked to himself: "The tempest of the children must have spent itself by this. Now is the time to show them who is master here." Whereupon he rose up, pounded the table with his fist, and thundered: "Stop! What's the meaning of all this racketing? I'm going now, and you must go, too, so that I may put out the lights and lock up."

Some of them actually did get up, for they had all gone to Storm's school, and knew that when their teacher rapped on the table it meant that everybody had to mind. Yet the majority stoically kept their seats.

"The schoolmaster forgets that now we are grown men," said one; "but he still seems to think we should run just because he happens to rap on the table!" said another.

They went right on talking about their wanting to hear some new speakers, and which ones they should call in. They were already quarrelling among themselves as to whether it should be the Waldenstromites or colporteurs from the National Evangelical Union.

The schoolmaster stood staring at the assemblage as if he were looking at some weird monstrosity. For up to that time he had seen only the child in each individual face. But now all the round baby cheeks, the soft baby curls, and the mild baby eyes had vanished, and he saw only a gathering of adults, with hard, set faces; he felt that over such as these he had no control. He did not even know what to say to them.

The tumult continued, growing louder and louder. The schoolmaster kept still and let them rage. Bullet Gunner, Ljung Björn, and Krister Larsson led the attack. Hök Matts, who was the innocent cause of all the trouble, rose to his feet time and again and begged them to be quiet, but no one listened to him.

Once again the schoolmaster glanced down at the parson, who was still quietly musing, the same gleam in his eyes, which were fixed on the schoolmaster.

"He's probably thinking of that evening four years ago when I told him I would build a mission," thought Storm. "He was right, too. Everything has turned out just as he said it would: heresy, revolt, and division. Perhaps we might have escaped all this if I hadn't been so bent upon building my Zion."

The instant this became clear to the schoolmaster, his head went up and his backbone straightened. He drew from his pocket a small key of polished steel. It was the key to Zion! He held it toward the light so that it could be seen from all parts of the hall.

"Now I'm going to lay this key upon the table," he said, "and I shall never touch it again, for I see now that it has unlocked the door to everything which I had hoped to shut out."

Whereupon the schoolmaster put the key down, took up his hat, and walked straight over to the pastor.

"I want to thank you, Parson, for coming to hear me to-day," he said; "for if you hadn't come to-day you never could have heard me."

The Wild Hunt

There were many who thought that Elof Ersson should have found no peace in his grave for the shameful way in which he had dealt with Karin and young Ingmar. He had deliberately made way with all of his and Karin's money, so she would suffer hardship after his death. And he left the farm so heavily mortgaged, that Karin would have been forced to turn it over to the creditors, had not Halvor been rich enough to buy in the property and pay off the debts. Ingmar Ingmarsson's twenty thousand kroner, of which Elof had been sole trustee, had entirely disappeared. Some people thought that Elof had buried the money, others that he had given it away; in any case, it was not to be found.

When Ingmar learned that he was penniless, he consulted Karin as to what he should do. Ingmar told his sister that of all things he would prefer to be a teacher, and begged her to let him remain with the Storms until he was old enough to enter college. Down at the village he would always be able to borrow books from the schoolmaster or the pastor, he said, and, moreover, he could help Storm at the school, by reading with the children; that would be excellent practice.

Karin turned this over in her mind before answering. "I suppose you wouldn't care to remain at home, since you can't become master here?" she said.

When Storm's daughter heard that Ingmar was coming back, she pulled a long face. It seemed to her that if they must have a boy living with them, they might better have the judge's good-looking son, Bertil, or there was jolly Gabriel, the son of Hök Matts Ericsson.

Gertrude liked both Gabriel and Bertil, but as for Ingmar, she couldn't exactly tell what her feelings were toward him. She liked him because he helped her with her lessons and minded her like a slave; but she could also become thoroughly put out with him sometimes, because he was clumsy and tiresome and did not know how to play. She had to admire his diligence and his aptitude for learning, yet at times she fairly despised him for not being able to show off what he could do.

Gertrude's head was always full of droll fancies and dreams, which she confided to Ingmar. If the lad happened to be away for a few days, she grew restless, and felt that she had no one to talk to; but as soon as he got back she hardly knew what she had been longing for.

The girl had never thought of Ingmar as a boy of means and good family connections, but treated him rather as though he were a little beneath her. Yet when she heard that Ingmar had become poor, she wept for him, and when he told her that he would not try to get back his property, but meant to earn his own living as a teacher, she was so indignant she could hardly control herself.

The Lord only knows all she had dreamed that he would be some day!

The children at Storm's school were given very rigid training. They were held strictly to their tasks, and only on rare occasions were they allowed any amusements. However, all this was changed the spring Storm gave up his preaching. Then Mother Stina said to him: "Now, Storm, we must let the young folks be young. Remember that you and I were young once. Why, when we were seventeen, we danced many a night from sundown to sunup."

So, one Saturday night, when young Gabriel and Gunhild, the councilman's daughter, paid a visit to the Storms, they actually had a dance at the schoolhouse.

Gertrude was wild with delight at being allowed to dance, but Ingmar would not join in. Instead, he took up a book, and went and sat down on the sofa by the window. Time and again Gertrude tried to make him lay down his book, but Ingmar, sulky and shy, refused to budge. Mother Stina looked at him and shook her head. "It's plain he comes of an old, old stock," she thought. "That kind can never be really young."

The three who did dance had such a good time! They talked of going to a regular dance the next Saturday evening, and asked the schoolmaster and Mother Stina what they thought about it.

"If you will do your dancing at Strong Ingmar's, I give my consent," said Mother Stina; "for there you will meet only respectable folk."

Then Storm also made it conditional. "I can't allow Gertrude to go to a dance unless Ingmar goes along to look after her," he said.

Whereupon all three rushed up to Ingmar and begged him to accompany them.

"No!" he growled, without even glancing up from his book.

"It's no good asking him!" said Gertrude in a tone that made Ingmar raise his eyes. Gertrude looked radiantly beautiful after the dance. She smiled scornfully, and her eyes flashed as she turned away. It was plainly to be seen how much she despised him for sitting there so ugly and sulky, like some crotchety old man. Ingmar had to alter his mind and say "yes"— there was no way out of it.

A few evenings later while Gertrude and Mother Stina sat spinning in the kitchen, the girl suddenly noticed that her mother was getting uneasy. Every little while she would stop her spinning-wheel and listen. "I can't imagine what that noise is," she said. "Do you hear anything, Gertrude?"

"Yes, I do," replied the girl. "There must be some one upstairs in the classroom."

"Who could be there at this hour?" Mother Stina flouted. "Only listen to the rustling and the pattering from one end of the room to the other!"

And there certainly was a rustling and a pattering and a bumping about over their heads, that made both Gertrude and her mother feel creepy.

"There must surely be some one up there," insisted Gertrude.

"There can't be," Mother Stina declared. "Let me tell you that this thing has been going on every night since you danced here."

Gertrude perceived that her mother imagined the house had been haunted since the night of the dance. If that idea were allowed to become fixed in Mother Stina's mind, there would be no more dancing for Gertrude.

"I'm going up there to see what it is," said the girl, rising; but her mother caught hold of her skirt.

"I don't know whether I dare let you go," she said.

"Nonsense, mother! It's best to find out what this is."

"Then I'd better go with you," the mother decided.

They crept softly up the stairs. When they got to the door they were afraid to open it. Mother Stina bent down and peeped through the keyhole. Presently she gave a little chuckle.

"What pleases you, mother" asked Gertrude.

"See for yourself, only be very quiet!"

Then Gertrude put her eye to the keyhole. Inside, benches and desks had been pushed against the wall, and in the centre of the schoolroom, amid a cloud of dust, Ingmar Ingmarsson was whirling round, with a chair in his arms.

"Has Ingmar gone mad!" exclaimed Gertrude.

"Ssh!" warned the mother, drawing her away from the door and down the stairs. "He must be trying to teach himself to dance. I suppose he wants to learn how, so he'll be able to dance at the party," she added, with smirk. Then Mother Stina began to shake with laughter. "He came near frightening the life out of me," she confessed. "Thank God he can be young for once!" When she had got over her fit of laughing, she said: "You're not to say a word about this to anybody, do you hear!"

* * * * *

Saturday evening the four young people stood on the steps of the schoolhouse, ready to start. Mother Stina looked them over approvingly. The boys had on yellow buckskin breeches and green homespun waistcoats, with bright red sleeves. Gunhild and Gertrude wore stripe skirts bordered with red cloth, and white blouses, with big puffed sleeves; flowered

kerchiefs were crossed over their bodices, and they had on
aprons that were as flowered as their kerchiefs.

As the four of them walked along in the twilight of a
perfect spring evening, nothing was said for quite a long time.
Now and then Gertrude would cast a side glance at Ingmar
thinking of how he had worked to learn to dance. Whatever the
reason—whether it was the memory of Ingmar's weird dancing,
or the anticipation of attending a regular dance—her thoughts
became light and airy. She managed to keep just a little behind
the others, that she might muse undisturbed. She had made up
quite little story about how the trees had come by their new
leaves.

It happened in this way, she thought: the trees, after
sleeping peacefully and quietly the whole winter, suddenly
began to dream. They dreamt that summer had come. They
seemed to see the fields dressed in green grass and waving corn;
the hawthorn shimmered with new-blown roses; brooks and
ponds were spread with the leaves of the water-lily; the stones
were hidden under the creeping tendrils of the twin flower, and
the forest carpet was thick with star flowers. And amid all this
that was clothed and decked out, the trees saw themselves
standing gaunt and naked. They began to feel ashamed of their
nakedness, as often happens in dreams.

In their confusion and embarrassment, the trees fancied
that all the rest were making fun of them. The bumblebees came
buzzingly up to mock at them, the magpies laughed them to
scorn, while the other birds sang taunting ditties.

"Where shall we find something to put on?" asked the
trees in despair; but they had not a leaf to their names on either
twig or branch, and their distress was so terrible that it awakened
them.

And glancing about, drowsy like, their first thought was:
"Thank God it was only a dream! There is certainly no summer
hereabout. It's lucky for us that we haven't overslept."

But as they looked around more carefully, they noticed
that the streams were clear of ice, grass blades and crocuses
beeped out from their beds of soil, and under their own ark the
sap was running. "Spring is here at all events," said the trees, "so
it was well we awoke. We have slept long enough for this year;

now it's high time we were getting dressed."

So the birches hurriedly put on some sticky pale green leaves, and the maples a few green flowers. The leaves of the alder came forth in such a crinkly and unfinished state that they looked quite malformed, but the slender leave: of the willow slipped out of their buds smooth and shapely from the start.

Gertrude smiled to herself as she walked along and thought this up. She only wished she had been alone with Ingmar so she could have told it all to him.

They had a long way to go to get to the Ingmar Farm—more than an hour's tramp. They followed the riverside; all the while Gertrude kept walking a little behind the others. Her fancy had begun to play around the red glow of the sunset, which flamed now above the river, now above the strand. Gray alder and green birch were enveloped by the shimmer, flashing red one instant, the next taking on their natural hues.

Suddenly Ingmar stopped, and broke off in the middle of something he was telling.

"What's the matter, Ingmar?" asked Gunhild.

Ingmar, pale as a ghost, stood gazing at something in front of him. The others saw only a wide plain covered with grain fields and encircled by a range of hills, and in the centre of the plain a big farmstead. At that moment the glow of sunset rested upon the farm; all the window pans glittered, and the old roofs and walls had a bright red glimmer about them.

Gertrude promptly stepped up to the others, and after a quick glance at Ingmar, she drew Gunhild and Gabriel aside.

"We mustn't question him about anything around here," she said under her breath. "That place over yonder is the Ingmar Farm. The sight of it has probably made him sad. He hasn't been at home in two years—not since he lost all his money."

The road which they had taken was the one leading past the farm and down to Strong Ingmar's cabin, at the edge of the forest.

Soon Ingmar came running after, calling, "Hadn't we better go this way instead?" Then he led them in on a bypath that wound around the edge of the forest, and by which they could reach the cabin without having to cross the farm proper.

"You know Strong Ingmar, I suppose?" said Gabriel.

"Oh, yes," young Ingmar replied. "We used to be good friends in the old days."

"Is it true that he understands magic?" asked Gunhild.

"Well—no!" Ingmar answered rather hesitatingly, as if half-believing it himself.

"You may as well tell us what you know," persisted Gunhild.

"The schoolmaster says we mustn't believe in such things."

"The schoolmaster can't prevent a person seeing what he sees and believing what he knows," Gabriel declared.

Ingmar wanted to tell them all about his home; memories of his childhood came back to him at sight of the old place. "I can tell you about something that I saw once," he said. "It happened one winter when father and Strong Ingmar were up in the forest working at the kiln. When Christmas came around, Strong Ingmar offered to tend the kiln by himself, so that father could come home for the holidays. The day before Christmas, mother sent me up to the forest with a basket of good fare for Strong Ingmar. I started early, so as to be there before the midday dinner hour. When I came up, father and Strong Ingmar had just finished drawing a kiln, and all the charcoal had been spread on the ground to cool. It was still smoking and, where the coals lay thickest, it was ready to take fire, which is something that must not happen. To prevent that is the most important part of the entire process of charcoal making. Therefore, father said as soon as he saw me: 'I'm afraid you'll have to go home alone, little Ingmar. I can't leave Strong Ingmar with all this work.' Strong Ingmar walked along the side of the heap where the smoke rose thickest. 'You can go, Big Ingmar,' he said. 'I've managed worse things than this.' In a little while the smoke grew less. 'Now let's see what kind of a Christmas treat Brita has sent me,' said Strong Ingmar, taking the basket from me. 'Come, let me show you what a fine house we've got here.' Then he took me into the hut where he and father lived. At the back was a rude stone, and the other walls were made up of branches of spruce and blackthorn. 'Well, my lad, you never guessed that your father had a royal castle like this in the forest, eh?' said Strong Ingmar. 'Here are walls that keep out both storm and frost,' he laughed, thrusting his arm clean through the spruce branches.

"Soon father came in laughing. He and the old man were black with soot and reeking with the odour of sour charcoal smoke. But never had I seen father so happy and full of fun. Neither of them could stand upright in the hut, and the only furniture in the place were two bunks made of spruce twigs and a couple of flat stones on which they had built a fire; yet they were perfectly contented. They sat down, side by side, on one of the bunks, and opened the basket. 'I don't know whether you can have any of this,' said Strong Ingmar to father, 'for it's my Christmas dinner, you know.' 'Seeing it's Christmas Eve you must be a good to me,' said father. 'At a time like this I suppose it would never do to let a poor old charcoal burner starve,' Strong Ingmar then said.

"They carried on like that all the time they were eating. Mother had sent a little brandy along with the food. I marvelled that people could be so happy over food and drink. 'You'll have to tell your mother that Big Ingmar has eaten up everything,' said the old man, 'and that she will have to send more to-morrow.' 'So I see,' said I.

"Just then I was startled by a crackling noise in the fireplace. It sounded as if some one had cast a handful of pebbles on the stones. Father did not notice it, but at once Strong Ingmar said: 'What, so soon?' Yet he went on eating. Then there was more crackling; this time it was much louder. Now it sounded as if a shovelful of stones had been thrown on the fire. 'Well, well, is it so urgent!' Strong Ingmar exclaimed. Then he went out. 'The charcoal must be afire!' he shouted back. 'Just you sit still, Big Ingmar. I'll attend to this myself.' Father and I sat very quiet.

"In a little while Strong Ingmar returned, and the fun began anew. 'I haven't had such a merry Christmas in years,' he laughed. He had no sooner got the words out of his mouth than the crackling started afresh. 'What, again? Well, I never!' and out he flew in a jiffy. The charcoal was afire again. When the old man came back for the second time, father said to him: 'I see now that you have such good help up here that you can get along by yourself.' 'Yes, you can safely go home and keep your

Christmas, Big Ingmar, for here there are those who will help me.' Then father and I went home, and everything was all right. And never, either before or afterward, was any kiln tended by Strong Ingmar known to get afire."

Gunhild thanked Ingmar for his story, but Gertrude walked on in silence, as if she had become frightened. It was beginning to get dark; everything that had looked so rosy a while ago was now either blue or gray. Here and there in the forest could be seen a shiny leaf that gleamed in the twilight like the red eye of a troll.

Gertrude was astonished at Ingmar having talked so much and so long. He seemed like another person since coming in on home ground; he carried his head higher than usual, and stepped with firmer tread. Gertrude did not quite like this change in him; it made her feel uneasy. All the same she spunked up, and began to tease Ingmar about his going home to dance.

Then at last they came to a little gray hut. Candles were burning inside, the windows being too small to let in much light. They caught the sound of violin music and the clatter of dancing feet. Still the girls paused, wonderingly. "Is it here?" they questioned. "Can any one dance here? The place looks too small to hold even one couple."

"Go along inside," said Gabriel; "the hut isn't as tiny as looks."

Outside the door, which was open, stood a group of boys and girls who had danced themselves into a warm glow; the girls were fanning themselves with their headshawls, and the boys had pulled off their short black jackets in order to dance in their bright green red-sleeved waistcoats.

The newcomers edged their way through the crowd by the door into the hut. The first person they saw was Strong Ingmar—a little fat man, with a big head and a long beard.

"He must be related to the elves and the trolls," thought Gertrude. The old man was standing upon the hearth, playing his fiddle, so as not to be in the way of the dancers.

The hut was larger than it had appeared from the outside, but it looked poor and dilapidated. The bare pine walls were worm-eaten, and the beams were blackened by smoke. There were no curtains at the windows, and no cover on the table. It was evident that Strong Ingmar lived by himself. His children had all left him and gone to America, and the only pleasure the old man had in his loneliness was to gather the young folks around him on a Saturday evening, and let them dance to his fiddle.

It was dim in the hut, and suffocatingly close. Couple after couple were whirling around in there. Gertrude could scarcely breathe, and wanted to hurry out again, but it was an impossibility to get past the tight wedge of humanity that blocked the doorway.

Strong Ingmar played with a sure stroke and in perfect time, but the instant that young Ingmarsson came into the room he drew his bow across the strings, making a rasping noise that brought all the dancers to a stop. "It's nothing," he shouted. "Go on with the dance!"

Ingmar placed his arm around Gertrude's waist to dance out the figure. Gertrude seemed very much surprised at his wanting to dance. But they could get nowhere, for the dancers followed each other so closely that no one who had not been there at the start could squeeze in between them.

The old man stopped short, rapped on the fender with his bow, and said in a commanding voice: "Room must be made for Big Ingmar's son when there's any dancing in my shack!"

With that every one turned to have a look at Ingmar, who became so embarrassed that he could not stir. Gertrude had to take hold of him and fairly drag him across the floor.

As soon as the dance was finished, the fiddler came down to greet Ingmar. When he felt Ingmar's hand in his, the old man pretended to be very much concerned, and instantly let go of it. "My goodness!" he exclaimed, "be careful of those delicate schoolmaster hands! A clumsy old fellow like me could easily crush them."

He took young Ingmar and his friends up to the table, driving away several old women who were sitting there, looking on. Presently he went over to the cupboard and brought out some bread and butter and root beer.

"I don't, as a rule, offer refreshments at these affairs," he said. "The others have to be content with just music and dancing, but Ingmar Ingmarsson must have a bite to eat under my roof."

Drawing up a little three-legged stool, the old man sat down in front of Ingmar, and looked sharply at him.

"So you're going to be a school-teacher, eh?" he queried.

Ingmar closed his eyes for a moment, and there was the shadow of a smile on his lips, but all the same he answered rather mournfully: "They have no use for me at home."

"No use for *you*?" cried the old man. "You don't know how soon you may be needed on the farm. Elof lived only two years, and who knows how long Halvor will hold out?"

"Halvor is a strong, hearty fellow," Ingmar reminded.

"You must know, of course, that Halvor will turn the farm over to you as soon as you're able to buy it back."

"He'd be a fool to give up the Ingmar Farm now that it has fallen into his hands."

During this colloquy Ingmar sat gripping the edge of the plain deal table. Suddenly a noise was heard as of something cracking. Ingmar had broken off a corner of the table. "If you become a school-teacher, he'll never let you have the farm," the old man went on.

"You think not?"

"Think—think? Well it's plain how you have been brought up. Have you ever driven a plow?"

"No."

"Or tended a kiln, or felled a huge pine?"

Ingmar sat there looking quite placid, but the table kept crumbling under his fingers. Finally the old man began to take notice.

"See here, young man!" he said when he saw what was happening, "I shall have to take you in hand once more." Then he picked up some of the splinters of the table and tried to fit them into place. "You rogue! You ought to be going around to fairs, showing your tricks for money!" he laughed, and dealing Ingmar a hard whack on the shoulder, he remarked: "Oh, you'd make a fine school-teacher, you would!"

In a twinkling he was back at the fireplace, fiddling away. Now there was a snap and a go to his performance. He beat time with his foot and set the dancers whirling. "This is young Ingmar's polka," he called out. "Hoop-la! Now the whole house must dance for young Ingmar!"

Two such pretty girls as Gertrude and Gunhild had to be in every dance, of course. Ingmar did not do much dancing. He stood talking most of the time with some of the older men at the farther end of the room. Between dances the people crowded around him as if it did them good just to look at him.

Gertrude thought Ingmar had entirely forgotten her, which made her quite miserable. "Now he feels that he is the son of Big Ingmar, and that I am only the school-master's Gertrude," she pouted. It seemed strange to her that she should take this so to heart. Between the dances some of the young folks went out for a breath of air. The night had grown piercingly cold. It was quite dark, and as no one wanted to go home, they all said: "We'd better wait a little while; the moon will soon be out. Now it's too dark to start for home."

Once, when Ingmar and Gertrude happened to be standing outside the door, the old man came and drew the boy away. "Come, let me show you something," he said, and taking Ingmar by the hand, he led him through a thicket a short distance away from the house. "Stand still now and look down!" he said presently. Then Ingmar found himself looking down a cleft, at the bottom of which something white shimmered. "This must be Langfors Rapids," said young Ingmar.

"Right you are," nodded the old man. "Now what do you suppose a waterfall like that can be used for, eh?"

"It might be used to run a mill," said Ingmar thoughtfully.

The old man laughed to himself. He patted Ingmar on the back, then gave him a dig in the ribs that almost sent him into the rapids. "But who's going to put up a mill here? Who's going to get rich, and who's going to buy the Ingmar Farm, eh?" he chuckled.

"I'd just like to know," said Ingmar.

Then the old man began unfolding a big plan he had in mind: Ingmar was to persuade Tims Halvor to put up a sawmill below the rapids, and afterward lease it to him. For many years the old man's dream had been to find a way by which Big Ingmar's son might come into his own again. Ingmar stood quietly looking down at the foaming rapids.

"Come, let's go back to the house and the dancing!" said

the old man, but as Ingmar did not stir he waited patiently. "If he's the right sort, he won't reply to this today, nor yet to-morrow," he remarked to himself. "An Ingmarsson has to have time to consider."

And as they stood there, all at once they heard a sharp and angry bark that seemed to come from some dog running loose in the forest.

"Do you hear that, Ingmar?" asked the old man.

"Yes; that must be a dog on the rampage."

Then they heard the bark more distinctly; it seemed to be coming nearer, as if the beast were heading straight for the hut. The old man seized Ingmar by the wrist. "Come, boy!" he said. "Get into the house as quick as you can!"

"What's the matter?" asked Ingmar, astonished.

"Get in, I tell you!"

As they made for the hut, the angry barking sounded as if it were quite close to them.

"What kind of dog is it?" Ingmar asked, again and again.

"Get inside, only get inside!" cried the old man, fairly pushing Ingmar into the narrow passageway. Before closing the outer door he shouted: "If there are any of you outside, come in at once!" As he stood holding the door open, people came running from all directions. "In with you, in with you!" he shrieked at them, and stamped impatiently.

Meanwhile the people in the hut were becoming alarmed. They all wanted to know what was amiss. When the old man had made sure that everybody was inside, he closed and bolted the door.

"Are you mad, to be running about when you hear the mountain dog!" At that moment the barking was heard just outside the hut; it was as if the mountain dog were chasing round and round the house, emitting hideous yowls.

"Isn't it a real dog?" asked a young rustic.

"You can go out and call to it if you like, Nils Jansson."

Then all were silent, listening to the howling thing which continued to go round and round without a stop. It sounded weird and dreadful. They began to shudder and shake, and some turned as white as death. No, indeed, this was no ordinary dog; anybody could tell that! It was doubtless some demon let loose from hell, they thought.

The little old man was the only one who moved about. First he closed the flue, then he went around and snuffed out the candles.

"No, no!" cried the womenfolk, "don't put out the lights!"

"You must let me do what is best for all of us," said the old man.

One of the girls caught hold of his coat. "Is the mountain dog dangerous?" she asked.

"No, not he, but what comes after."

"And what comes after?"

Again the old man listened. Presently he said: "Now we must all be very still."

Instantly there was breathless silence. Once again the terrible howling seemed to circle the hut, but it grew less distinct as it went across the marsh and up the mountains on the other side of the valley. Then came an ominous stillness. Presently some man, who couldn't hold in any longer, said that the *dog* was gone.

Without a word Strong Ingmar raised his hand and dealt the man a blow across the mouth.

From far away at the top of Mount Flack came a piercing sound; it was like a howling wind, but it could also have been a blast from a horn. Now and again prolonged blare could be heard, then roaring and tramping and snorting.

All at once the thing came dashing down from the mountain with an awful roar. They could tell when it had reached the foot of the slope; they could tell when it swept the skirt of the forest; and when it was directly above them. It was like the rolling of thunder across the face of the earth; it was as if the whole mountain had come tumbling into the valley. When it seemed to be almost upon them, every head went down. "It will crush us," they all thought. "It will surely crush us."

But what they felt was not so much the fear of death, as terror lest it might be the prince of darkness himself coming, with all his demons. What frightened them most were the shrieks and moans that could be heard above the other noises. There were wails and groans, laughter and bellowings, whines and hisses. When that which they had supposed was a big thunderstorm was right upon them, it seemed to be a mingling of groans and curses, of sobs and angry cries, of the blast of horns, of crackling fire, of the plaints of doomed spirits, of the mocking laughter of demons, of the flapping of huge wings.

They thought all the furies of the infernal regions had been let loose that night, and would overwhelm them. The ground trembled, and the hut swayed as if it were going to topple over. It was as if wild horses were prancing on the roof; as if howling ghosts rushed past the door, and as if owls and bats were beating their wings against the chimney.

While this was happening, some one put an arm around Gertrude's waist and drew her to her knees. Then she heard Ingmar whisper: "We must kneel down, Gertrude, and ask God to help us."

Only the moment before Gertrude had imagined she was dying, so terrible was the fear that held her. "I don't mind having to die," she thought; "the awful part of it is that the powers of evil are hovering over us."

But Gertrude had no sooner felt Ingmar's protecting arm around her than her heart began to beat once more, and the feeling of numbness in her limbs was gone. She snuggled close to him. She was not frightened now. How wonderful! Ingmar must have felt afraid also, yet he was able to impart to her a sense of security and protection.

Finally the terrible noises died away; they heard only the faintest echoes of them in the distance. They seemed to have followed in the trail of the dog, down through the marsh and up into the mountain passes beyond Olaf's Peak.

And yet the silence in Strong Ingmar's but was unbroken. No one moved, no one spoke; at times it was as if fear had extinguished all life there. Now and then through the stillness a deep sigh was heard. No one moved for a long, long time. Some of the people were standing up against the walls, others had sunk down on the benches, but most of them were kneeling upon the floor in anxious prayer. All were motionless, stunned by fear.

Thus hour after hour passed, and during that time there was many a one in that room who ransacked his soul and resolved to live a new life—nearer to God and farther away from His enemies, for each of those present thought: "It is something that *I* have done which has brought this upon us. This has happened because of *my* sins. I could hear how the fiends kept calling to me and threatening me, and shrieking my name, as they rushed by."

As for Gertrude, her only thought was: "I know now that I can never live without Ingmar; I must always be near him because of that feeling of confidence he gives one."

Then gradually the day began to break, the faint light of dawn came stealing into the hut, revealing the many blanched faces. The twitter of a bird was heard, then of another, and another. Strong Ingmar's cow began to low for her breakfast, and his cat, who never slept in the house on nights when there was dancing, came to the door and mewed. But no one inside moved until the sun rolled up from behind the eastern hills. Then, one by one, they stole out without a word or even a good-bye.

Outside the house the departing guests beheld the signs of the night's devastation. A huge pine, which had stood close to the gate, had been torn up by the roots and thrown down; branches and fence posts were littered over the ground; bats and owls had been crushed against the side walls of the hut.

Along the broad roadway leading to the top of Mount Klack all the trees had been blown down. No one could bear to look at this long, so they all hurried on toward the village.

It was Sunday, and most people were still in their beds, but a few persons were already out tending to their cattle. An old man had just emerged from his house with his Sunday coat, to brush and air it. From another house came father, mother, and children—all dressed up for a holiday outing. It was a great relief to see people quietly going about their business, unconscious of the awful things that had happened in the forest during the night.

At last they came to the riverside, where the houses were less scattered, and then to the village. They were glad to see the old church and everything else. It was comforting to see that everything down here looked natural: the sign-board in front of the shop creaked on its hinges as usual; the post-office horn was in its regular place; and the inn-keeper's dog lay sleeping, as always, outside his kennel. It was also a gladsome surprise to them to see a little bird-berry bush that had blossomed overnight, and the green seats in the pastor's garden, which must have been put out late in the evening. All this was decidedly reassuring. But just the same no one ventured to speak until they had reached their several homes.

When Gertrude stood on the steps of the schoolhouse, she said to Ingmar: "I have danced my last dance, Ingmar."

"And I, too," Ingmar solemnly declared.

"And you'll become a clergyman, won't you, Ingmar? And if you can't become a preacher, you must at least be a teacher. There is so much evil in the world one has to fight against."

Ingmar looked straight at Gertrude. "What did those voices say to you?" he asked.

"They said that I had been caught in the toils of sin, and that the devil would come and take me, because I was so fond of dancing."

"Now I must tell you what I heard," said Ingmar. "It seemed to me that all the old Ingmarssons were threatening and cursing me because I wanted to be something more than a peasant, and to do something besides just tilling the soil and working in the forest."

Hellgum

The night of the dance at Strong Ingmar's, Tims Halvor was away from home, and his wife, Karin, slept alone in the little chamber off the living-room. In the night Karin had a frightful dream. She dreamt that Elof was alive and was holding a big revel. She could hear him in the next room clinking glasses, laughing loudly, and singing ribald songs. She thought, in the dream, that Elof and his boon companions were getting noisier and noisier, and at last it sounded as though they were trying to break up both tables and chairs. Then Karin became so frightened that she awoke. But even after she had awakened the noise continued. The earth shook, the windows rattled, the tiles on the roof were loosened, and the old pear trees at the gables lashed the house with their stout branches. It was as if Judgment Day had come.

Just when the noise was at its height a window pane was sprung, and the shattered glass fell jingling against the floor. A violent gust of wind rushed through the room, and then Karin thought she heard a laugh quite close to her ear—the same kind of laugh that she had heard in the dream. She fancied she was about to die. Never had she felt such a sense of terror; her heart stopped, and her whole body became numb and cold as ice.

All at once the noise died down, and Karin, as it were, came back to life. The raw night wind came sweeping into the room; so after a little Karin decided to get up and stuff something into the broken window pane. As she stepped out of the bed, her legs gave way, and she found that she could not walk. She did not cry for help, but quietly laid down again. "I'll surely be able to walk when I feel more composed," she thought. In a few moments she made another attempt. This time, too, her legs failed her, and she fell prone on the floor beside the bed.

In the morning, when people were astir in the house, the doctor was called in. He was at a loss to understand what had come over Karin. She did not appear to be ill, nor was she paralyzed. He was of the opinion that her trouble had been brought on by fright.

"You'll soon be all right again," he assured her. Karin listened to the doctor, but said nothing. She felt certain that Elof had been in the room during the night, and that he was the cause of her trouble. She also had the feeling that she would never recover from this shock.

All that morning she sat up in bed, and brooded. She tried to reason out why God had let this trial come upon her. She examined her conscience thoroughly, but could not discover that she had committed any special sin that merited such a terrible punishment. "God is unjust to me," she thought.

In the afternoon she was taken to Storm's mission house, where at that time a lay preacher named Dagson led the meetings. She hoped that he could tell her why she had been punished in this way.

Dagson was a popular speaker, and never had he had so many hearers as on that afternoon. My, but what a gathering of people down at the mission house! And no one talked of anything but what had happened in the night at Strong Ingmar's hut. The whole community was in a state of terror, and had turned out in full force, in order to hear the Word of God preached with a force that would annihilate their fears. Hardly a quarter of the people could get inside; but windows and doors were wide open, and Dagson had such a powerful voice that he could be heard even by those on the outside. Of course he knew what had occurred, and what the people wanted to hear. He opened his address with a terror-striking word picture of hell and the prince of darkness. He reminded them of the evil one who skulks about in the dark to capture souls, who lays the snares of sin and sets the traps of vice. The people shuddered. They seemed to see a world full of devils, tempting and enticing them to destruction. Everything was a sin and a danger. They were wandering among pitfalls, hunted and tormented like the wild beasts of the forest. When Dagson talked in this strain, his voice pierced the room like a blasting wind, and his words were like tongues of fire.

All who heard Dagson's sermon likened it to a roaring torrent of flame. With all this talk about demons and fire and smoke, they had the same feeling as when trapped in a burning forest—when the fire creeps along the moss upon which you are treading, and smoke clouds fill the air you breathe, and the heat singes your hair, while the roar of the fire fills your ears, and flying sparks set fire to your clothing.

Thus did Dagson drive the people through flame and smoke and desolation. They had fire in front of them, fire behind them, and fire to left and right of them, and saw only destruction ahead of them. Yet, after taking them through all these horrors, he finally led them to a green spot in the forest, where it was peaceful and cool and safe. In the centre of a flowery meadow sat Jesus, with His arms outstretched toward the fleeing and hunted men and women who cast themselves at His feet. Now all danger was past, and they suffered no further distress nor persecution.

Dagson spoke as he himself felt. If he could only lay himself down at Jesus' feet, a sense of great peace and serenity would come to him, and he had no more fear of the snares of the world.

After the service there was great emotional excitement. Many persons rushed up to the speaker and thanked him, with tears streaming down their faces. They told him that his words had awakened them to a true faith in God. But all this time Karin sat unmoved. When Dagson had finished speaking, she raised her heavy eyelids and looked up at him, as if reproaching him for not having given her anything. Just then some one outside cried in a voice loud enough to be heard by the entire congregation:

"Woe, woe, woe to those who give stones for bread! Woe, woe, woe to those who give stones for bread!"

Whereupon everybody rushed out, curious to see who it was that had spoken those words, and Karin was left sitting there in her helplessness. Presently members of her own household came back, and told her that the person who had cried out like that was a tall, dark stranger. He and a pretty, fair-haired woman had been seen coming down the road, in a cart, during the service. They had stopped to listen, and just as they were about to drive on, the man had risen up and spoken. Some folks thought they knew the woman. They said she was one of Strong Ingmar's daughters—one of those who had gone to America and married there. The man was evidently her husband. Of course it is not so easy to recognize a person whom one has known as a young girl in the ordinary peasant costume, when she comes back a grown woman dressed up in city clothes.

Karin and the stranger were evidently of the same mind regarding Dagson. Karin never went to the mission house again. But later in the summer, when a Baptist layman came to the parish, baptizing and exhorting, she went to hear him, and when the Salvation Army began to hold meetings in the village, she also attended one of these.

The parish was in the throes of a great religious upheaval. At all the meetings there were awakenings and conversions. The people seemed to find what they had been seeking. Yet among all those whom Karin had heard preach, not one could give her any consolation.

* * * * *

A blacksmith named Birger Larsson had a smithy close by the highroad. His shop was small and dark, with a low door, and an aperture in place of a window. Birger Larsson made common knives, mended locks, put tires on wheels and on sled runners. When there was nothing else to be done, he forged nails.

One evening, in the summer, there was a rush of work at the smithy. At one anvil stood Birger Larsson flattening the heads of nails; his eldest son was at another anvil forging iron rods and cutting off pins. A second son was blowing the bellows, a third carried coal to the forge, turned the iron, and, when at white heat, brought it to the smiths. The fourth son, who was not more than seven years old, gathered up the finished nails and threw them into a trough filled with water, afterward bunching and tying them.

While they were all hard at work a stranger came up and stationed himself in the doorway. He was a tall, swarthy-looking man, and he had to bend almost double to look in. Birger Larsson glanced up from his work to see what the man wanted.

"I hope you don't mind my looking in, although I have no special errand here," said the stranger. "I was a blacksmith myself in my younger days, and can never pass by a smithy without first stopping to glance in at the work."

Birger Larsson noticed that the man had large, sinewy hands—regular blacksmith's hands. He at once began to question him as to who he was and whence he came. The man answered pleasantly, but without disclosing his identity. Birger thought him clever and likable, and after showing him around the shop, he went outside with him and began to brag about his sons. He had seen hard times, he said, before the boys were big enough to help with the work; but now that all of them were able to lend a hand, everything went well. "In a few years I expect to be a rich man," he declared.

The stranger smiled a little at that and said he was pleased to hear that Birger's sons were so helpful to him. Placing his heavy hand on Birger's shoulder, and looking him square in the eyes, he said: "Since you have had such good aid from your sons in a material way, I suppose you also let them help you in the things that pertain to the spirit?" Birger stared stupidly. "I see that this is a new thought to you," the stranger added. "Ponder it till we meet again." Then he went on his way smiling, and Birger Larsson, scratching his head, returned to his work. But the stranger's query haunted his mind for several days. "I wonder what made him say that?" he mused. "There must be something back of it all that I don't understand."

* * * * *

The day after the stranger had talked with Birger Larsson an extraordinary thing took place at Tims Halvor's old shop, which since his marriage to Karin had been turned over to his brother-in-law, Bullet Gunner. Gunner was away at the time, and, in his absence, Brita Ingmarsson tended the shop. Brita was named after her mother, Big Ingmar's handsome wife, whose good looks she had inherited. Moreover, she had the distinction of being the prettiest girl ever born and reared on the Ingmar Farm. Although she bore no outward resemblance to the old Ingmars, she was, nevertheless, quite as conscientious and upright as any of them.

When Gunner was absent Brita always ran the business in her own way. Whenever old Corporal Felt would come stumbling in, tipsy and shaky, and ask for a bottle of beer, Brita would give him a blunt "No," and when poor Kolbjörn's Lena came and wanted to buy a fine brooch, Brita sent her home with several pounds of rye meal. The peasant woman who dropped in to buy some light flimsy fabric was told to go home and weave suitable and durable cloth on her own loom. And no children dared come into the shop to spend their poor coppers for candy and raisins when Brita was in charge there.

That day Brita had not many customers. So for hours and hours she sat quite alone, staring into vacancy, despair burning in her eyes. By and by she got up and took out a rope; then she moved a little stepladder from the shop into the back room. After that she made a loop in one end of the rope, and fastened the other end to a hook in the ceiling. Just as she was about to slip her head into the noose, she happened to look down.

At that moment the door opened and in walked a tall, dark man. He had evidently entered the shop without her having heard him, and on finding no one in attendance, had stepped behind the counter and opened the door to the next room.

Brita quietly came down from the ladder. The man did not speak, but withdrew into the shop, Brita slowly following him. She had never seen the man before. She noticed that he had black curly hair, throat whiskers, keen eyes, and big, sinewy hands. He was well dressed, but his bearing was that of a labourer. After seating himself on a rickety chair near the door, he began to stare hard at Brita.

By that time Brita was again standing behind the counter. She did not ask him what he wanted; she only wished he would go away. The man just stared and stared, never once taking his eyes off her. Brita felt that she was being held by his gaze, and could not move. Presently she grew impatient, and said, in her mind: "What's the use of your sitting there watching me? Can't you understand that I'm going to do what I want to do, anyhow, as soon as I'm left alone? If this were only something that could be helped," Brita argued mentally, "I wouldn't mind your hindering me, but it can't be remedied now."

All the while the man sat gazing intently at her.

"Let me say to you that we Ingmars are not fitted to be shopkeepers," Brita continued in her thoughts. "You don't know how happy we were, Gunner and I, till he took up with this business. Folks certainly warned me against marrying him; they didn't like him, on account of his black hair, his piercing eyes, and his sharp tongue. But we two were fond of each other, you see, and there was never a cross word between us till Gunner took over the shop. But since then all has not been well. I want him to conduct the business in my way. I can't abide his selling wine and beer to drunkards, and it seems to me that he ought to encourage people in buying only such things as are useful and necessary; but Gunner thinks this a ridiculous notion. Neither of us will give in to the other, so we are forever wrangling, and now he doesn't care for me any more."

She gave the man a savage look, amazed at his not yielding to her mute entreaties.

"Surely you must understand that I cannot go on living under the shame of knowing that he lets the bailiff serve executions upon poor people and take from them their only cow or a couple of sheep! Can't you see that this thing will never come right? Why don't you go, and let me put an end to it all!"

Brita, under the man's gaze, gradually became quieter in her mind, and in a little while she began to cry softly. She was touched by his sitting there and protecting her against herself.

As soon as the man saw that Brita was weeping, he rose and went toward the door. When he was on the doorstep, he turned and again looked straight into her eyes, and said in a deep voice: "Do thyself no harm, for the time is nearing when thou shalt live in righteousness."

Then he went his way. She could hear his heavy footsteps as he walked, down the road. Brita ran into the little room, took down the rope, and carried the stepladder back into

the shop. Then she dropped down on a box, where she sat
quietly musing for two full hours. She felt, somehow, that for a
long time she had wandered in a darkness so thick that she could
not see her hand before her. She had lost her way and knew not
whither she had strayed, and with every step she had been afraid
of sinking into a quagmire or stumbling headlong into an abyss.
Now some one had called to her not to go any farther, but to sit
down and wait for the break of day. She was glad that she would
not have to continue her perilous wanderings; now she sat
quietly waiting for the dawn.

* * * * *

Strong Ingmar had a daughter who was called Anna Lisa.
She had lived in Chicago for a number of years, and had married
there a Swede named John Hellgum, who was the leader of a
little band of religionists with a faith and doctrine of their own.
The day after the memorable dance night at Strong Ingmar's,
Anna Lisa and her husband had come home to pay a visit to her
old father.

Hellgum passed his time taking long walks about the
parish. He struck up an acquaintance with all whom he met on
the way. He talked with them at first of commonplace things; but
just before parting with a person, he would always place his
large hand upon his or her shoulder, and speak a few words of
comfort or warning.

Strong Ingmar saw very little of his son-in-law, for that
summer the old man and young Ingmar, who had now gone back
to the Ingmar Farm to live, were hard at work daytimes putting
up a sawmill below the rapids. It was a proud day for Strong
Ingmar when the sawmill was ready and the first log had been
turned into white planks by the buzzing saws.

One evening on his way home from work, the old man
met Anna Lisa on the road. She looked frightened, and wanted to
run away. Strong Ingmar, seeing this, quickened his pace,
thinking all was not well at home. When he reached his but he
stopped short, frowning. As far back as he could remember, a
certain rosebush had been growing outside the door. It had been
the apple of his eye. He had never allowed any one to pluck a

rose or a leaf from that bush. Strong Ingmar had always guarded
the bush very tenderly, because he believed it sheltered elves and
fairies. But now it had been cut down. Of course it was his son-
in-law, the preacher, who had done this, as the sight of the bush
had always been an eyesore to him.

Strong Ingmar had his axe with him, and his grip on the
handle tightened as he entered the hut. Inside sat Hellgum with
an open Bible before him. He raised his eyes and gave the old
man a piercing look, then went on with his reading; this time
aloud:

"Even as ye think, we will be as the heathen, as the
families of the countries, to serve wood and stone, it shall not be
at all as ye think. As I live, saith the Lord God, surely with a
mighty hand, and with stretched-out arm, and with fury poured
out, will I rule over you—"

Without a word Strong Ingmar turned and walked out of
the house. That night he slept in the barn. The following day he
and Ingmar Ingmarsson set out for the forest to burn charcoal
and fell timber. They were to be gone the whole winter.

On two or three occasions Hellgum had spoken at prayer
meetings and outlined his teaching, which he maintained was the
only true Christianity. But Hellgum, who was not as eloquent a
speaker as Dagson, had made no converts. Those who had met
him outside and had only heard him say a few telling words,
expected great things from him; but when he tried to deliver a
lengthy address he became heavy, prosy, and tiresome.

* * * * *

Toward the close of summer Karin became utterly
despondent over her condition. She rarely spoke. All day long
she sat motionless in her chair. She went to hear no more
preachers, but stayed at home, brooding over her misfortune.
Once in a while she would repeat to Halvor her father's old
saying about the Ingmars not having anything to fear so long as
they walked in the ways of God. Now she had come to the
conclusion that there was no truth even in that.

Halvor, not knowing what to do, on one occasion
suggested that she talk with the newest preacher, but Karin

declared that she would never again look to a parson for help.

One Sunday, toward the end of August, Karin sat at the window in the living-room. A Sabbath stillness rested over the farm, and she could hardly keep awake. Her head kept sinking nearer and nearer her breast, and presently she dropped into a doze.

She was suddenly awakened by the sound of a voice just outside her window. She could not see who the speaker was, but the voice was strong and deep. A more beautiful voice she had never heard.

"I know, Halvor, that it doesn't seem reasonable to you that a poor, uneducated blacksmith should have found the truth, when so many learned men have failed," said the voice.

"I don't see how you can be so sure of that," Halvor questioned.

"It's Hellgum talking to Halvor," thought Karin, trying to close the window, which she was unable to reach.

"It has been said, as you know," Hellgum went on, "that if somebody strikes us on one cheek we must turn the other cheek also, and that we should not resist evil, and other things of the same sort; all of which none of us can live up to. Why, people would rob you of your house and home, they'd steal your potatoes and carry off your grain, if you failed to protect what was yours. I guess they'd take the whole Ingmar Farm from you."

"Maybe you're right," Halvor admitted.

"Well, then, I suppose Christ didn't mean anything when He said all that; He was just talking into the air, eh?"

"I don't know what you're driving at!" said Halvor.

"Now here's something to set you thinking," Hellgum continued. "We are supposed to be very far advanced in our Christianity. There's no one nowadays who steals, no one who commits murder or wrongs the widow and the fatherless, and of course no one hates or persecutes his neighbour any more, and it wouldn't occur to any of us, who have such a good religion, to do any wrong!"

"There are many things that aren't just as they ought to be," drawled Halvor. He sounded sleepy, and anything but interested.

"Now if you had a threshing machine that wouldn't work, you'd find out what was wrong with it. You wouldn't give yourself any rest till you had discovered wherein it was faulty. But when you see that it is simply impossible to get people to lead a Christian life, shouldn't you try to find out whether there is anything the matter with Christianity itself?"

"I can't believe there are any flaws in the teachings of Jesus," said Halvor.

"No, they were unquestionably sound from the start; but it may be that they have become a little rusty, as it were, from neglect. In any perfect mechanism, if a cog happens to slip— only one tiny little cog—instantly the whole machinery stops!"

He paused a moment as if searching for words and proofs.

"Now let me tell you what happened to me a few years ago," he resumed. "I then tried for the first time in my life to really live by the teachings. Do you know what the result was? I was at that time working in a factory. When my fellow-workmen found out what manner of man I was, they let me do a good share of their work in addition to my own. In thanks they took the job away from me by conniving to throw the blame on me for a theft committed by one of them. I was arrested, of course, and sent to the penitentiary."

"One doesn't ordinarily run across such bad people," returned Halvor indifferently.

"Then said I to myself: It wouldn't be very hard to be a Christian if one were only alone on this earth, and there were no fellow humans to be reckoned with. I must confess that I really enjoyed being in prison, for there I was allowed to lead a righteous life, undisturbed and unmolested. But after a time I began to think that this trying to be good in solitude was about as effective as the automatic turning of a mill when there's no corn in the grinder. Inasmuch as God had seen fit to place so many people in the world," I reasoned, "it must have been done with the idea that they should be a help and a comfort to one another, and not a menace. It occurred tome, finally, that Satan must have taken something away from the Bible, so that Christianity should go to smash."

"But surely he never had the power to do that," said

Halvor.

"Yes; he has taken out this precept: *Ye who would lead a Christian life must seek help among your fellowmen.*"

Halvor did not venture a reply, but Karin nodded approvingly. She had listened very carefully, and had not missed a word.

"As soon as I was released from prison," Hellgum continued, "I went to see an old friend, and asked him to help me lead a righteous life. And, mind, when we were two about it, at once it became easier. Soon a third party joined with us, then a fourth, and it became easier and easier. Now there are thirty of us who live together in a house in Chicago. All our interests are common interests; we share and share alike. We watch over each other's lives, and the way of righteousness lies before us, smooth and even. We are able to deal with one another in a Christly manner, for one brother does not abuse the kindness of another, nor trample him down in his humility."

As Halvor remained silent, Hellgum spoke on convincingly: "You know, of course, that he who wishes to do something big always allies himself with others who help him. Now you couldn't run this farm by yourself. If you wanted to start a factory, you'd have to organize a company to coöperate with you, and if you wanted to build a railway, just think how many helpers you'd have to take on!

"But the most difficult work in the world is to live a Christian life; yet that you would accomplish single-handed and without the support of others. Or maybe you don't even try to do so, since you know beforehand that it can't be done. But we—I and those who have joined me back there in Chicago—have found a way. Our little community is in truth the New Jerusalem come down from Heaven. You may know it by these signs: the gifts of the Spirit which descended upon the early Christians, have also fallen upon us. There are some among us who hear the Voice of God, others who prophesy, and others, again, who heal the sick—"

"Can you heal the sick?" Halvor broke in eagerly.

"Yes," answered Hellgum. "I can heal those who have faith in me."

"It's rather hard to believe something different from what

one was taught as a child," said Halvor thoughtfully.

"Nevertheless, I feel certain, Halvor, that very soon you will give your full support to the upbuilding of the New Jerusalem," Hellgum declared.

Then came a moment of silence, after which Karin heard Hellgum say good-bye.

Presently Halvor went into the house. On seeing Karin seated by the open window, he remarked: "You must have heard all that Hellgum said."

"Yes," she replied.

"Did you hear him say that he could heal any one who had faith in him?"

Karin reddened a little. She had liked what Hellgum said better than anything she had heard that summer. There was something sound and practical about his teaching which appealed to her common sense. Here were works and service and no mere emotionalism, which meant nothing to her. However, she would not admit this, for she had made up her mind to have no further dealings with preachers. So she said to Halvor: "My father's faith is good enough for me."

* * * * *

A fortnight later Karin was again seated in the living-room. Autumn had just set in; the wind howled round the house and a fire crackled on the hearth. There was nobody in the room but herself and her baby daughter, who was almost a year old and had just learned to walk. The child was sitting on the floor at her mother's feet, playing.

As Karin sat watching the child, the door opened, and in came a tall, dark man, with keen eyes and large sinewy hands. Before Karin had heard him say a word, she guessed that it was Hellgum.

After passing the time of day, the man asked after Halvor. He learned that Karin's husband had gone to a town meeting, and was expected home shortly. Hellgum sat down. Now and then he glanced over at Karin, and after a little he said:

"I've been told that you are ill."

"I have not been able to walk for the past six months,"

Karin replied.

"I have been thinking of coming here to pray for you," volunteered the preacher.

Karin closed her eyes and retired within herself.

"You have perhaps heard that by the Grace of God I am able to heal the sick?"

The woman opened her eyes and sent him a look of distrust. "I'm much obliged to you for thinking of me," she said, "but it isn't likely that you can help me, as I'm not the kind that changes faith easily."

"Possibly God will help you, anyhow, since you have always tried to live an upright life."

"I'm afraid I don't stand well enough in the sight of God to expect help from Him in this matter."

In a little while Hellgum asked her if she had looked within to get at the cause of this affliction. "Has Mother Karin ever asked herself why this affliction has been visited upon her?"

Karin made no reply; again she seemed to retire within herself.

"Something tells me that God has done this that His Name might be glorified," said Hellgum.

At that Karin grew angry and two bright red spots appeared in her cheeks. She thought it very presumptuous in Hellgum to think this illness had come upon her simply to give him an opportunity to perform a miracle.

Presently the preacher got up and went over to Karin. Placing his heavy hand on her head, he asked: "Do you want me to pray for you?"

Karin immediately felt a current of life and health shoot through her body, but she was so offended at the man for his obtrusiveness that she pushed away his hand and raised her own as if to strike him. Her indignation was beyond words.

Hellgum withdrew toward the door. "One should not reject the help which God sends, but accept it thankfully."

"That's true," Karin returned. "Whatever God sends one is obliged to accept."

"Mark well what I say to you! This day shall salvation come unto this house," the man proclaimed.

Karin did not answer.

"Think of me when you receive the help!" he said. The next instant he was gone.

Karin sat bolt upright in her chair, the red spots still burning in her cheeks. "Am I to have no peace even in my own house?" she muttered. "It's singular how many there are nowadays who think themselves sent of God."

Suddenly Karin's little girl got up and toddled toward the fireplace. The bright blaze had attracted the child, who, shrieking with delight, was making for it as fast as her tiny feet could carry her.

Karin called to her to come back, but the child paid no heed to her; at that moment she was trying to clamber up into the fireplace. After tumbling down a couple of times, she finally managed to get upon the hearth, where the fire blazed.

"God help me! God help me!" cried Karin. Then she began to shout for help, although she knew there was no one near.

The little girl bent laughingly over the fire. Suddenly a burning ember rolled out and fell on her little yellow frock. Instantly Karin sprang to her feet, rushed over to the fireplace, and snatched the child in her arms. Not until she had brushed away all the sparks from the child's dress, and had made sure that her baby was unharmed, did she realize what had happened to herself. She was actually on her feet; she had been walking again, and would always be able to walk!

Karin experienced the greatest mental shake-up she had ever felt in her life, and at the same time the greatest sense of happiness. She had the feeling that she was under God's special care and protection, and that God Himself had sent a holy man to her house to strengthen her and to heal her.

* * * * *

That autumn Hellgum often stood on the little porch of Strong Ingmar's cottage, looking out across the landscape. The country round about was growing more beautiful every day: the ground was now a golden brown, and all the leafy trees had turned either a bright red or a bright yellow. Here and there loomed stretches of woodland that shimmered in the breeze like a billowy sea of gold. Against the shadowy background of the fir-clad hills could be seen splashes of yellow; they were the leaf trees that had strayed in among the pines and spruces and taken root there.

As an humble gray hut, when ablaze, gives out light and brilliancy, thus did this humble Swedish landscape flame into a marvel of splendour. Everything was so wondrously golden, exactly as one might imagine that a landscape on the surface of the sun would look.

Hellgum was thinking, as he viewed this scene, that a time was coming when God would let the land reflect the brightness of His Glory, and when the seeds of Truth which had been sawn during the summer would yield golden harvests of righteousness.

Then, to and behold, one evening Tims Halvor came over to the croft and invited Hellgum and his wife to come with him to the Ingmar Farm!

On arriving they found everything in holiday order; around the house all the old dry birch leaves had been cleared away; farm implements and carts, which at other times were scattered about the yard, had now been put out of sight.

"They must be having a number of visitors here," thought Anna Lisa. Just then Halvor opened the front door, and they stepped inside.

The living-room was full of people who were seated upon benches all along the walls, solemnly expectant. Hellgum noticed that they were the leading people of the parish. The first persons he recognized were Ljung Björn Olofsson and his wife, Martha Ingmarsson; also Bullet Gunner and his wife. Then he saw Krister Larsson and Israel Tomasson with their wives, all of whom were members of the Ingmar family. Presently he saw Hök Matts Ericsson and his son Gabriel, the councillor's daughter Gunhild, and several persons besides. Altogether there were about twenty people present.

When Hellgum and Anna Lisa had gone round and shaken hands with every one, Tims Halvor said:

"We who are assembled here have been thinking over the things Hellgum has said to us during the summer. Most of us belong to an old family whose wish it has ever been to walk in the ways of God. If Hellgum can help us do this, we are ready to follow him."

The next day the news spread like wildfire throughout the parish that a new religious sect had sprung up on the Ingmar Farm, which was supposed to embody the only correct and true principles of Christianity.

The New Way

In the spring, soon after the snow had disappeared, young Ingmar and Strong Ingmar returned to the village to start the sawmill. They had been up in the forest the whole winter cutting timber and making charcoal. And when Ingmar got back to the lowlands he fell like a bear that had just crawled out from its lair. He could hardly accustom himself to the glaring sunlight of an open sky, and blinked as if the light hurt him. The roaring of the rapids and the sound of human voices seemed almost intolerable to him, and all the noises on the farm were a veritable torture to his ears. At the same time he was glad; heaven knows he did not show it, either in speech or manner, but that spring he felt as young as the fresh shoots on the birches.

Oh, but it seemed good to him to sleep once more in a comfortable bed, and to eat properly cooked food! And then to be at home with Karin, who looked after his comfort as tenderly as a mother! She had ordered new clothes for him; and she had a way of coming in from the kitchen and handing him some dainty or other, as if he were still a little boy. And what wonderful things had happened at home while he was up in the forest! Ingmar had heard only a few vague rumours about Hellgum's teachings; but now Karin and Halvor told him of the great happiness that had come to them, and of how they and their friends were trying to help one another to walk in the ways of God.

"We are sure you will want to join us," said Karin.

Ingmar replied that maybe he would, but that he must

think it over first.

"All winter I longed for you to come home and share our bliss," the sister went on, "for now we no longer live upon earth, but in 'The New Jerusalem which is come down from Heaven!'"

Ingmar said he was glad to hear that Hellgum was still in the neighbourhood. The summer before the preacher had often dropped in at the mill to chat with Ingmar, and the two had become good friends. Ingmar thought him the finest chap he had ever met. Never had he come across any one who was so much of a man, so firm in his convictions, and so sure of himself. Sometimes, when there had been a great rush of work at the mill, Hellgum had pulled off his coat and given them a lift. Ingmar had been amazed at the man's cleverness; he had never seen any one who was so quick at his work. Just then Hellgum happened to be away for a few days, but was Expected back shortly.

"Once you've talked with Hellgum, I think that you will join us," Karin said. Ingmar thought so, too, although he felt a little reluctant about accepting anything which had not been approved by his father.

"But wasn't it father himself who taught us that we must always walk in the ways of God?" argued Karin.

Everything seemed to be so bright and so promising! Ingmar had never dreamed that it would be so delightful to get back among people once more. There was only one thing wanting: no one ever spoke of the schoolmaster and his wife, or of Gertrude, which was most disquieting to him. He had not seen Gertrude for a whole year. In the summer he had never been without news of her; for then hardly a day went by that some one did not speak of the Storms. He thought that perhaps this silence regarding his old friends was accidental. When one feels timid about asking questions, and when no one voluntarily speaks of that which one longs above everything to hear about, it is mighty provoking, to say the least.

But if young Ingmar seemed to be happy and content, the same could not be said of Strong Ingmar. The old man had of late become sullen and taciturn and difficult to get on with.

"I believe you are homesick for the forest," Ingmar said to him one afternoon as they sat on separate logs eating their sandwiches.

"God knows I am!" the old man burst forth. "I only wish I had never come back at all!"

"Why, what's gone wrong at home?"

"How can you ask! You must know as well as I that Hellgum has been raising the deuce around here."

Ingmar answered that, on the contrary, he had heard that Hellgum had become a big man.

"Yes, he has grown so big and strong that he's been able to upset the whole parish," Strong Ingmar sneered.

It seemed strange to Ingmar that the old man never evinced a particle of affection for any of his own kin. He cared for nobody and for nothing save the Ingmarssons and the Ingmar Farm. Therefore Ingmar felt that he must stand up for the son-in-law.

"I think his doctrine a good one," he said.

"Oh, you do, do you?" snapped the old man; and he gave him a withering look. "Do you think Big Ingmar would have thought so?"

Ingmar replied that his father would have upheld any one who worked for righteousness.

"It's your belief, then, that Big Ingmar would have approved of calling all persons who do not belong to Hellgum's band devils and anti-Christs, and that he would have refused to associate with his old friends because they held to their old faith?"

"I hardly think that such people as Hellgum and Halvor and Karin would behave in that way," said Ingmar.

"Just you try to oppose them once, and you'll soon hear what they think of you!"

Ingmar cut off a big corner of his sandwich and stuffed his mouth full, so he would not have to talk. It irritated him to see Strong Ingmar in such bad humour.

"Heigho, hum! It's a queer world," sighed the old man. "Here you sit, the son of Big Ingmar, with nothing to say, while my Anna Lisa and her husband are living on the fat of your land. The best people in the parish bow and scrape to them, and every day they're being fêted, here, there, and everywhere."

Ingmar kept on munching and swallowing. There was nothing he could say. Strong Ingmar, however, went at him again.

"Yes, it's a fine doctrine that Hellgum is spreading! That's why half the parish has gone over to him. No one has ever had such absolute influence over the people, not even Strong Ingmar himself. He separates children from their parents by preaching that those who are of his fold must not live among sinners. Hellgum need only beckon, and brother leaves brother, friend leaves friend, and the lover deserts his betrothed. He has used his power to create strife and dissension in every household. Of course, Big Ingmar would have been pleased to death with that sort of thing! Doubtless he would have backed Hellgum up in all this! I can just picture him doing it!"

Ingmar looked up and down; he wanted to get away. He knew, to be sure, that the old man had been drawing heavily on his imagination, but all the same this talk depressed him.

"I don't deny that Hellgum has done wonders," he modified. "The way in which he manages to hold his people together, and the way he can get those who formerly would have nothing to do with each other to live on friendly terms, is certainly remarkable. And look how he takes from the rich to give to the poor, and how he makes each person protect the other's welfare. I'm only sorry for those on the outside, who are called children of the devil and are not allowed in the game. But, of course, you don't feel that way."

Ingmar was thoroughly put out with the old man for speaking so disparagingly of Hellgum.

"There used to be such peace and harmony in this parish!" the old man rattled on. "But that's all past and gone. In Big Ingmar's time we lived in such unity that we had the name of being the friendliest people in all Dalecarlia. Now there are angels bucking against devils, and sheep against goats."

"If we could only get the saws going," thought Ingmar, "I wouldn't have to hear any more of this talk!"

"It won't be long either till it's all over between you and me," Strong Ingmar continued. "For if you join Hellgum's *angels* it isn't likely that they will let you associate with me."

With an oath Ingmar jumped to his feet. "If you go on talking in this strain it may turn out just as you say," he warned. "You may as well understand, once for all, that it is of no use your trying to turn me against my own people, or against Hellgum, who is the grandest man I know."

That silenced the old man. In a little while he left his work, saying that he was going down to the village to see his friend Corporal Felt. He had not talked with a sensible person for a long time, he declared.

Ingmar was glad to have him go. Naturally, when a person has been away from home for a long time he does not care to be told unpleasant things, but wants every one around him to be bright and cheerful.

At five the next morning Ingmar got down to the mill, but Strong Ingmar was there ahead of him.

"To-day you can see Hellgum," the old man began. "He and Anna Lisa got back late last night. I think they must have hurried home from their round of feasts in order to convert you."

"So you're at it again!" scowled Ingmar. The old man's words had been ringing in his ears all night, and he could not help wondering who was in the right. But now he did not want to listen to any more talk against his relatives. The old man held his peace for a time; presently he began to chuckle.

"What are you laughing at?" Ingmar demanded, his hand on the sluice gate ready to set the sawmill going.

"I was just thinking of the schoolmaster's Gertrude."

"What about her?"

"They said down at the village yesterday that she was the only person who had any influence over Hellgum—"

"What's Gertrude got to do with Hellgum?"

Ingmar, meanwhile, had not opened the sluice gate, for with the saws going he could not have heard a word. The old man eyed him questioningly. Ingmar smiled a little. "You always manage somehow to have your own way," he said.

"It was that silly goose, Gunhild, Councillor Clementsson's daughter, who—"

"She's no silly goose!" Ingmar broke in.

"Oh, call it anything you like, but she happened to be at the Ingmar Farm when this new sect was founded. As soon as she got home, she informed her parents that she had accepted the only true faith, and that she would there fore have to leave them and make her home at the Ingmar Farm. Her parents asked her, of course, why she wanted to leave home. So she'd be able to lead a righteous life, she up and told them. But they seemed to think that could be done just as effectively at home with them. Oh, no, that wouldn't be possible, she declared, unless one could live with those who were of the same faith. Her father then asked her if all of them were going to live on the Ingmar Farm. No, only herself; the others had true Christians in their own homes. Now Clementsson is a pretty good sort, as you know, and both he and his wife tried to reason with Gunhild in all kindness, but she stood firm. At last her father became so exasperated that he just took her and locked her up in her room, telling her she'd have to stay there till this crazy fit had passed."

"I thought you were going to tell me about Gertrude," Ingmar reminded him.

"I'll get round to her by and by, if you'll only have patience. I may as well tell you at once that early the next morning, while Gertrude and Mother Stina were sitting in the kitchen spinning, Mrs. Clementsson called to see them. When they saw her they became alarmed. She, who was usually so happy and light of heart, now looked as if she'd been crying her eyes out. 'What's the matter? What has happened? And why do you look so forlorn?' they asked. Then Mother Clementsson answered that when one has lost one's dearest treasure, one can't very well look cheerful. I'd like to give them a good beating!" said the old man.

"Who?" asked Ingmar.

"Why, Hellgum and Anna Lisa. They marched themselves down to Clementsson's in the night and kidnapped Gunhild."

A cry of amazement escaped Ingmar.

"I'm beginning to think my Anna Lisa is married to a brigand!" said the old man. "In the middle of the night they came and tapped on Gunhild's window, and asked her why she wasn't at the Ingmar Farm. She told them about her parents having locked her in. ''Twas Satan who made 'em do it,' said Hellgum. All this her father and mother overheard."

"Did they really?"

"Yes, they slept in the next room, and the door between was partly open; so they heard all that Hellgum said to entice their daughter."

"But they could have sent him away."

"They felt that Gunhild should decide for herself. How could they think she would want to leave them, after all they had done for her? They lay there expecting her to say that she would never desert her old parents."

"Did she go?"

"Yes, Hellgum wouldn't budge till the girl went along with them. When Clementsson and his wife realized that she couldn't resist Hellgum, they let her go. Some folks are like that, you see. In the morning the mother regretted it, and begged the father to drive down to the Ingmar Farm and get their daughter. 'No indeed!' he said, 'I'll do nothing of the sort, and what's more, I never want to set eyes on her again unless she comes home of her own accord.' Then Mrs. Clementsson hurried down to the school to see if Gertrude wouldn't go and talk to Gunhild."

"Did Gertrude go?"

"Yes; she tried to reason with Gunhild, but Gunhild wouldn't listen."

"I have not seen Gunhild at our house," said Ingmar thoughtfully.

"No, for now she is back with her parents. It seems that when Gertrude left Gunhild she met Hellgum. 'There stands the one who is to blame for all this,' she thought, and then she went straight up to him, and gave him a tongue lashing. She wouldn't have minded striking him."

"Oh, Gertrude can talk all right," said Ingmar approvingly.

"She told Hellgum that he had behaved like a heathen warrior and not as a Christian preacher, in skulking about like that in the night and abducting a young girl."

"What did Hellgum say to that?"

"He stood quietly listening for a while; then he said as meek as you please that she was right, he had acted in haste. And in the afternoon he took Gunhild back to her parents and made everything right again."

Ingmar glanced up at the old man with a smile. "Gertrude is splendid," he said, "and Hellgum is a fine fellow, even if he is a little eccentric."

"So that's the way you take it, eh? I thought you would wonder why Hellgum had given in like that to Gertrude."

Ingmar did not reply to this.

After a moment's reflection the old man began again. "There are many in the village who want to know on which side you stand."

"I don't see as it matters which party I belong to."

"Let me remind you of one thing," said the old man: "In this parish we are accustomed to having somebody that we can look up to as a leader. But now that Big Ingmar is gone, and the schoolmaster has lost his power over the people, while the pastor, as you know, was never any good at ruling, they run after Hellgum, and they're going to follow him just as long as you choose to remain in the background."

Ingmar's hands dropped; he looked quite worn out. "But I don't know who is in the right," he protested.

"The people are looking to you for deliverance from Hellgum. You may be sure that we were spared a lot of unpleasantness by being away from home all winter. It must have been something dreadful in the beginning, before people had got used to this converting craze and to being called devils and hellhounds. But the worst of all was when the converted children started in to preach!"

"You don't mean to tell me that even the children preached," said Ingmar doubtingly.

"Oh, yes!" the old man returned. "Hellgum told them that they should serve the Lord instead of playing, so they started in to convert their elders. They lay in ambush along the roadside, and pounced upon innocent passers-by with such ravings as these: 'Aren't you going to begin the fight against the devil? Shall you continue to live in sin?'"

Young Ingmar did not want to believe what Strong Ingmar was recounting. "Old man Felt must have put all that into your head," he concluded.

"By the way, this was what I wanted to tell you," said Strong Ingmar: "Felt is done for, too! When I think that all this mischief has been hatched on the Ingmar Farm, I feel ashamed to look people in the face."

"Have they wronged Felt in any way?" asked Ingmar.

"It was the work of those youngsters, drat them! One evening, when they had nothing else to do, they took it into their heads to go and convert Felt, for of course they had heard that he was a great sinner."

"But in the old days all the children were as afraid of Felt as they were of witches and trolls," Ingmar reminded.

"Oh, these youngsters were scared, too, but they must have had their hearts set upon doing something very heroic. So one evening, as Felt sat stirring his evening porridge, they stormed his cabin. When they opened the door and saw the old Corporal, with his bristling moustaches, his broken nose, and his game eye, sitting before the fire, they were terribly frightened, and two of the littlest ones ran away. The dozen or so that went in knelt in a circle around the old man, and began to sing and pray."

"And didn't he drive them out?" asked Ingmar.

"If only he had!" sighed the old man. "I don't know what had come over the Corporal. The poor wretch must have been sitting there brooding over the loneliness and desolation of his old age. And then I suppose it was because those who had come to him were children. The fact that children had always been afraid of him must have been a source of grief to the old man; and when he saw all those baby faces, with their upturned eyes filled with shining tears, he was powerless. The children were only waiting for him to rush at them and strike them. Although they kept right on singing and praying, they were ready to cut and run the instant he made a move. Presently a pair of them noticed that Felt's face was beginning to twitch. 'Now he'll go for us,' they thought, getting up to flee. But the old man blinked his one good eye, and a tear rolled down his cheek. 'Hallelujah!' the youngsters shouted, and now, as I've already told you, it's all up with Felt. Now he does nothing but run about to meetings, and fasts and prays, and fancies he hears the voice of God."

"I don't see anything hurtful in all that," said Ingmar. "Felt was killing himself with drink when the Hellgumists took him into camp."

"Well, you've got so many friends to lose that a little thing like this wouldn't matter to you. No doubt you would have liked it if the children had succeeded in converting the schoolmaster."

"I can't imagine those poor little kids trying to tackle Storm!" Ingmar was dumfounded. What Strong Ingmar had said about the parish being turned upside down must be true after all, he thought.

"But they did, though," Strong Ingmar replied. "One evening, as Storm was sitting in the classroom writing, a score of them came in and began preaching to him."

"And what did Storm do?" asked Ingmar, unable to keep from laughing.

"He was so astounded at first that he couldn't say or do a thing. But, as luck would have it, Hellgum had arrived a few moments before and was in the kitchen talking with Gertrude."

"Was Hellgum with Gertrude?"

"Yes; Hellgum and Gertrude have been friends ever since the day that he acted upon her advice in the little matter with Gunhild. When Gertrude heard the racket in the schoolroom, she said: 'You're just in time to see something new, Hellgum. It would seem that henceforth the children are to instruct the schoolmaster.' Then Hellgum laughed, for he comprehended that this sort of thing was ludicrous. He promptly drove the children out, and abolished the nuisance."

Ingmar noticed that the old man was eying him in a peculiar way; it was as if a hunter were looking at a wounded bear and wondering whether he should give it another shot.

"I don't know what you expect of me," said Ingmar.

"What could I expect of you, who are only a boy! Why, you haven't a penny to your name. All you've got in the world are your two empty hands."

"I verily believe you want me to throttle Hellgum!"

"They said down at the village that this would soon blow over if you could only induce Hellgum to leave these parts."

"Whenever a new religious sect springs up there's always strife and dissension," said Ingmar. "So this is nothing out of the common."

"All the same, this will be a good way for you to show people what sort of stuff you're made of," the old man persisted.

Ingmar turned away and set the saws going. He would

have liked above everything to ask how Gertrude was getting along, and whether she had already joined the Hellgumists; but he was too proud to betray his fears.

At eight o'clock he went home to his breakfast. As usual, the table was heaped with tempting dishes, and both Halvor and Karin were especially nice to him. Seeing them so kind and gentle, he could not believe a word of Strong Ingmar's chatter. He felt light of heart once more, and positive that the old man had exaggerated. In a little while his anxiety about Gertrude returned, with a force so overwhelming that it took away his appetite, and he could not touch his food. Suddenly he turned to Karin and said abruptly:

"Have you seen anything of the Storms lately?"

"No!" replied Karin stiffly. "I don't care to associate with such ungodly people."

Here was an answer that set Ingmar thinking. He wondered whether he had better speak or be silent. If he were to speak it might end in a break with his family; at the same time he did not want them to think that he up held them in matters that were altogether wrong. "I have never seen any signs of ungodliness about the schoolmaster's folks," he retorted. "And yet I have lived with them for four years."

The very thought that had occurred to Ingmar the moment before, now came to Karin. She, too, wondered whether she should or should not speak. But she felt that she would have to hold to the truth, even if it hurt Ingmar; therefore she said that if people would not hearken to the voice of God, one could not help but think them ungodly.

Then Halvor joined in. "The question of the children is a vital one," he said. "They should be given the right kind of training."

"Storm has trained the entire parish, and you, too, Halvor," Ingmar reminded him.

"But he has not taught us how to live rightly," said Karin.

"It seems to me that you have always tried to do that, Karin."

"Let me tell you how it was to live by the old teaching. It was like trying to walk upon a round beam: one minute you were up, the next you were down. But when I let my fellow-Christians take me by the hand and support me, I can tread the straight and narrow path of Righteousness without stumbling."

"I dare say," Ingmar smiled; "but that's too easy."

"Even so, it's quite difficult enough, but no longer impossible."

"But what about the Storms?"

"Those who belong with us took their children out of the school. You see we didn't want the children to absorb any of the old teaching."

"What did the schoolmaster say to that?"

"He said it was against the law to take children away from school, and promptly sent a constable over to Israel Tomasson's and Krister Larsson's to fetch their children."

"And now you are not on friendly terms with the Storms?"

"We simply keep to ourselves."

"You seem to be at odds with every one."

"We only keep away from those who would tempt us to sin."

As the three went on talking, they lowered their voices. They were all very fearful of every word they let drop, for they felt that the conversation had taken a painful turn.

"But I can give you greetings from Gertrude," said Karin, trying to assume a more cheerful tone. "Hellgum had many talks with her last winter; he says that she expects to join us this evening."

Ingmar's lips began to quiver. It was as if he had been going about blindfolded all day, expecting to be shot, and now the shot had come; the bullet had pierced his heart.

"So she wants to become one of you!" he murmured faintly. "Many things can happen here while one is up in the dark forest." Ingmar seemed to think that all this time Hellgum had been ingratiating himself with Gertrude, and had laid snares to catch her. "But what's to become of me?" he asked suddenly. And there was a strange, helpless appeal in his voice.

"You must embrace our faith," said Halvor decisively. "Hellgum is back now, and if he talks to you once, you'll soon become converted."

"But maybe I don't care to be converted!"

Halvor and Karin stared at Ingmar in speechless amazement.

"Maybe I don't want any faith but my father's."

"Don't say anything until you have had a talk with Hellgum," begged Karin.

"But if I don't join you I suppose you won't want me to remain under your roof?" said Ingmar, rising. As they did not reply, it seemed to him that all at once he had been cut off from everything. Then he pulled himself together and looked more determined. "Now I want to know what you're going to do about the sawmill!" he demanded, thinking it was best to have this matter settled once for all.

Halvor and Karin exchanged glances; both were afraid of committing themselves.

"You know, Ingmar, that there is no one in the world who is more dear to us than you," said Halvor.

"Yes, yes; but what about the sawmill?" Ingmar insisted.

"The principal thing is to get all your timber sawed."

At Halvor's evasive reply, Ingmar drew his own conclusions. "Maybe Hellgum wants to run the sawmill, too?"

Karin and Halvor were perplexed at Ingmar's show of temper; since telling him that about Gertrude, they could not seem to get anywhere near him.

"Let Hellgum talk to you," pleaded Karin.

"Oh, I'll let him talk to me," said Ingmar, "but first I'd like to know just where I stand."

"Surely, Ingmar, you must know that we wish you well!"

"But Hellgum is to run the sawmill?"

"We must find some suitable employment for Hellgum so that he may remain in his own country. We have been thinking that possibly you and he might become business partners, provided you accept the only true faith. Hellgum is a good worker." This from Halvor.

"Since when have you been afraid to speak plainly, Halvor?" said Ingmar. "All I want to know is whether Hellgum is to have the sawmill."

"He is to have it if you resist God," Halvor declared.

"I'm obliged to you for telling me what a good stroke of business it would be for me to adopt your faith."

"You know well enough it wasn't meant in that way," said Karin reprovingly.

"I understand quite well what you mean," returned Ingmar. "I'm to lose Gertrude and the sawmill and the old home unless I go over to the Hellgumists." Then Ingmar turned suddenly and walked out of the house.

Once outside, the thought came to him that he might as well end this suspense, and find out at once where he stood with Gertrude. So he went straight down to the school-house. When Ingmar opened the gate a mild spring rain was falling. In the schoolmaster's beautiful garden all things had started sprouting and budding. The ground was turning green so rapidly that one could almost see the grass growing. Gertrude was standing on the steps watching the rain, and two large bird-cherry bushes, thick with newly sprung leaves, spread their branches over her. Ingmar paused a moment, astonished at finding everything down here so lovely and peaceful. He was already beginning to feel less disquieted. Gertrude had not yet seen him. He closed the gate very gently, then went toward her. When he was quite close he stopped and gazed at her in rapt wonder. When he had last seen her she was hardly more than a child, but in one short year she had developed into a dignified and beautiful young lady. She was now tall and slender and quite grown up, her head was finely poised on a graceful neck; her skin was soft and fair, shading into a fresh pink about the cheeks; her eyes were deep and thoughtful, and her mouth, around which mischief and merriment had once played, now expressed seriousness and wistful longing.

On seeing Gertrude so changed, a sense of supreme happiness came to Ingmar. A peaceful stillness pervaded his whole being; it was as though he were in the presence of something great and holy. It was all so beautiful that he wanted to go down on his knees and thank God.

But when Gertrude saw Ingmar she suddenly stiffened, her eyebrows contracted, and between her eyes there appeared the shadow of a wrinkle. He saw at once that she did not like his being there, and it cut him to the quick. "They want to take her from me," he thought; "they have already taken her from me." The feeling of Sabbath peace vanished, and the old fear and anxiety returned. Waving all ceremony, he asked Gertrude if it was true that she intended to join Hellgum and his followers. She answered that it was. Then Ingmar asked her if she had considered that the Hellgumists would not allow her to associate with persons who did not think as they did. Gertrude quietly answered that she had carefully considered this matter.

"Have you the consent of your father and mother?" asked Ingmar.

"No," she replied; "they know nothing as yet."

"But, Gertrude—"

"Hush, Ingmar! I must do this to find peace. God compels me."

"No," he cried, "not God, but—"

Gertrude suddenly turned toward him.

Then Ingmar told her that he would never join the Hellgumists. "If you go over to them, that will part us for ever."

Gertrude looked at him as much as to say that she did not see how this could affect her.

"Don't do it, Gertrude!" he implored.

"You mustn't think that I'm acting heedlessly, for I have given this matter very serious thought."

"Then think it over once more before you act."

Gertrude turned from him impatiently.

"You should also think it over for Hellgum's sake," said Ingmar with rising anger, seizing her by the arm.

She shook off his hand. "Are you out of your senses, Ingmar?" she gasped.

"Yes," he answered; "these doings of Hellgum are driving me mad. They must be stopped!"

"What must be stopped?"

"You'll find out before long."

Gertrude shrugged her shoulders.

"Good-bye, Gertrude!" he said in a choking voice. "And remember what I tell you. You will never join the Hellgumists!"

"What do you intend to do, Ingmar?" asked the girl, for she was beginning to feel uneasy.

"Good-bye, Gertrude, and think of what I have said!" Ingmar shouted back, for by that time he was halfway down the gravel walk.

Then he went on his way. "If I were only as wise as my father!" he mused. "But what can I do? I'm about to lose all that is dearest to me, and I see no way of preventing it." There was one thing, however, of which Ingmar was certain: if all this misery was to be forced upon him, Hellgum should not escape with his skin.

He went down to Strong Ingmar's but in the hope of meeting the preacher. When he got to the door, he caught the sound of loud and angry voices. There seemed to be a number of visitors inside, so he turned back at once. As he walked away he heard a man say in angry tones: "We are three brothers who have come a long way to call you to account, John Hellgum, for what has befallen our younger brother. Two years ago he went over to America, where he joined your community. The other day we received a letter telling us that he had gone out of his mind, brooding over your teaching."

Then Ingmar hurried away. Apparently there were others besides himself who had cause for complaint against Hellgum, and they were all of them equally helpless.

He went down to the sawmill, which had already been set going by Strong Ingmar. Above the buzzing noise of the saws and the roar of the rapids he heard a shriek; but he paid no special heed to it. He had no thought for anything save his strong hatred of Hellgum. He was going over in his mind all that this man had robbed him of: Gertrude and Karin, his home and his business.

Again he seemed to hear a cry. It occurred to him that possibly a quarrel had arisen between Hellgum and the strangers. "There would be no harm done if they were to beat the life out of him," he thought.

Then he heard a loud shout for help. Ingmar dropped his work and went rushing up the hill. The nearer he approached the hut the plainer he heard Hellgum's cries of distress, and when he finally reached the cabin it seemed as if the very earth around it shook from the scuffling and struggling inside.

He cautiously opened the door and tiptoed in. Over against the wall stood Hellgum defending himself with an axe. The three strangers—all of them big, powerful men—were attacking him with clubs. They carried no guns, so it was evident that they had come simply to give Hellgum a sound thrashing. But because he had put up a good fight, they were so enraged that they went at him with intent to kill. They hardly noticed Ingmar; they regarded him as nothing but a lank gawk of a boy who had just happened in.

For a moment Ingmar stood quietly looking on. To him it was like a dream, wherein the thing one desires most suddenly appears without one's knowing whence or how it came about. Now and again Hellgum cried for help.

"Surely you can't think I'm such a fool as to help you!" Ingmar said in his mind.

Suddenly one of the men dealt Hellgum a terrific blow on the head that made him let go his hold on the axe and fall to the floor. Then the others threw down their clubs, drew their knives, and cast themselves upon him. Instantly a thought flashed across Ingmar's mind. There was an old saying about the folk of his family, to the effect that every one of them was destined at some time or other during his lifetime to commit a dastardly and wrong deed. Was it his turn now, he wondered?

All at once one of the assailants felt himself in the grip of a pair of strong arms that lifted him off his feet and threw him bodily out of the house; the second one had hardly time to think of rising before the same thing happened to him; and the third, who had managed to scramble to his feet, got a blow that sent him headlong after the others.

After Ingmar had thrown them all out, he went and stood in the doorway. "Don't you want to come back?" he challenged laughingly. He would not have minded their attacking him; testing his strength was good sport.

The three brothers seemed quite ready to renew the fight, when one of them shouted that they had better take to their heels he had seen a figure coming along the path behind the elms. They were furiously disappointed at not having finished Hellgum, and, as they turned to go, one of them ran back, pounced upon Ingmar, and stabbed him in the neck.

"That's for meddling with our affair!" he shouted.

Ingmar sank down, and the man ran off, with a taunting laugh.

A few minutes later Karin came along and found Ingmar

sitting on the doorstep with a wound in his neck, and inside she discovered Hellgum, who by that time had got to his feet again and was now leaning against the wall, axe in hand and his face covered with blood. Karin had not seen the fleeing men; she supposed that Ingmar was the one who had attacked Hellgum and wounded him. She was so horrified that her knees shook. "No, no!" she thought, "it can't be possible that any one in our family is a murderer." Then she recalled the story of her mother. "That accounts for it," she muttered, and hurried past Ingmar over to Hellgum.

"Ingmar first!" cried Hellgum.

"The murderer should not be helped before his victim," said Karin.

"Ingmar first! Ingmar first!" Hellgum kept shouting. He was so excited that he raised his axe against her. "He has fought the would-be murderers and saved my life!" he said.

When Karin finally understood, and turned to help Ingmar, he was gone. She saw him stagger across the yard, and ran after him, calling, "Ingmar! Ingmar!"

Ingmar went on without even turning his head. But she soon caught up with him. Placing her hand on his arm, she said:

"Stop, Ingmar, and let me bind up your wound!"

He shook off her hand and went ahead like a blind man, following neither road nor bypath. The blood from his open wound trickled down underneath his clothes into one of his shoes. With every step that he made, blood was pressed out of the shoe, leaving a red track on the ground.

Karin followed him, wringing her hands. "Stop, Ingmar, stop!" she implored. "Where are you going? Stop, I say!"

Ingmar wandered on, straight into the wood, where there was no one to succor him. Karin kept her eyes fixed on his shoe, which was oozing blood. Every second the footprints were becoming redder and redder.

"He's going into the forest to lie down and bleed to death!" thought Karin. "God bless you, Ingmar, for helping Hellgum!" she said gently. "It took a man's courage to do that, and a man's strength, too!"

Ingmar tramped straight ahead, paying no heed whatever to his sister. Then Karin ran past him and planted herself in his way. He stepped aside without so much as glancing at her. "Go and help Hellgum!" he muttered.

"Let me explain, Ingmar! Halvor and I were very sorry for what we said to you this morning, and I was just on' my way to Hellgum to let him know that, whichever way it turned out, you were to keep the sawmill."

"Now you can give it to Hellgum," was Ingmar's answer. He walked on, stumbling over stones and tree stumps.

Karin kept close behind, trying her best to conciliate him. "Can't you forgive me for my mistake of a moment in thinking you had fought with Hellgum? I could hardly have thought differently."

"You were very ready to believe your own brother a murderer," Ingmar retorted, without giving her a look. He still walked on. When the grass blades he had trampled down came up again, blood dripped from them. It was only after Karin had noticed the peculiar way in which Ingmar had spoken Hellgum's name, that she began to realize how he hated the preacher. At the same time she saw what a big thing he had done.

"Every one will be singing your praises for what you did to-day, Ingmar; it will be known far and wide," she said. "You don't want to die and miss all the honours, do you?"

Ingmar laughed scornfully. Then he turned toward her a face that was pale and haggard. "Why don't you go home, Karin?" he said. "I know well enough whom you would prefer to help." His steps became more and more uncertain, and now, where he had walked, there was a continuous streak of blood on the ground.

Karin was about beside herself at the sight of all this blood. The great love which she had always felt or Ingmar kindled with new ardour. Now she was proud of her brother, and thought him a stout branch of the good old family tree.

"Oh, Ingmar!" she cried, "you'll have to answer before God and your fellowmen if you go on spilling your life's blood in this way. You know, if there is anything I can do to make you want to live, you have only to speak."

Ingmar halted, and put his arm around the stem of a tree to hold himself up. Then, with a cynical laugh, he said: "Perhaps you'll send Hellgum back to America?"

Karin stood looking down at the pool of blood that was forming around Ingmar's left foot, pondering over the thing her brother wanted her to do. Could it be that he expected her to leave the beautiful Garden of Paradise where she had lived all winter, and go back to the wretched world of sin she had come out of?

Ingmar turned round squarely; his face was waxen, the skin across his temples was tightly drawn, and his nose was like that of a dead person; but his under lip protruded with a determination that he had never before shown, and the set look about the mouth was sharply defined. It was not likely that he would modify his demand.

"I don't think that Hellgum and I can live in the same parish," he said, "but it's plain enough that I must make way for him."

"No," cried Karin quickly, "if you will only let me care for you, so that your life may be spared to us, I promise you that I will see that Hellgum goes away. God will surely find us another shepherd," thought Karin, "but for the time being it seems best to let Ingmar have his way."

After she had staunched the wound, she helped Ingmar home and put him to bed. He was not badly wounded. All he needed was to rest quietly for a few days. He lay abed in a room upstairs, and Karin tended him and watched over him like a baby.

The first day Ingmar was delirious, and lived over all that had happened to him in the morning. Karin soon discovered that Hellgum and the sawmill were not the only things that had caused him anxiety. By evening his mind was clear and tranquil; then Karin said to him: "There is some one who wishes to speak to you."

Ingmar replied that he felt too tired to talk to any one.

"But I think this will do you good."

Directly afterward Gertrude came into the room. She looked quite solemn and troubled. Ingmar had been fond of Gertrude even in the old days, when she was full of fun, and provoking. But at that time something within him had always fought against his love. But now Gertrude had passed through a trying year of longing and unrest, which had wrought such a wonderful change in her that Ingmar felt an uncontrollable longing to win her. When Gertrude came over to the bed, Ingmar put his hand up to his eyes.

"Don't you want to see me?" she asked.

Ingmar shook his head. He was like a wilful child.

"I only want to say a few words to you," said Gertrude.

"I suppose you've come to tell me that you have joined the Hellgumists?"

Then Gertrude knelt down beside the bed and lifted his hand from his eyes. "There is something which you don't know, Ingmar," she whispered.

He looked inquiringly at her, but did not speak. Gertrude blushed and hesitated. Finally she said:

"Last year, just as you were leaving us, I had begun to care for you in the right way."

Ingmar coloured to the roots of his hair, and a look of joy came into his eyes; but immediately he became grave and distrustful again.

"I have missed you so, Ingmar!" she murmured.

He smiled doubtingly, but patted her hand a little as thanks for her wanting to be kind to him.

"And you never once came back to see me," she said reproachfully. "It was as if I no longer existed for you."

"I didn't want to see you again until I was a well-to-do man and could propose to you," said Ingmar, as if this were a self-evident matter.

"But I thought you had forgotten me!" Gertrude's eyes filled up. "You don't know what a terrible year it has been. Hellgum has been very kind, and has tried to comfort me. He said my heart would be at rest if I would give it wholly to God."

Ingmar now looked at her with a newborn hope in his gaze.

"I was so frightened when you came this morning," she confessed, "I felt that I couldn't resist you, and that the old struggle would begin anew."

Ingmar's face was beaming.

"But this evening, when I heard about your having helped the one man whom you hated, I couldn't hold out any longer." Gertrude grew scarlet. "I felt somehow that I had not the strength to do a thing that would part me from you." Then she bowed her head over Ingmar's hand, and kissed it.

And it seemed to Ingmar as if great bells were ringing in a holy day. Within reigned Sabbath peace and stillness, while love, honey sweet, rested upon his lips, filling his whole being with a blissful solace.

BOOK THREE

Loss Of "L'Univers"

One misty night in the summer of 1880—about two years before the schoolmaster's mission house was built and Hellgum's return from America—the great French liner *L'Univers* was steaming across the Atlantic, from New York and bound for Havre.

It was about four o'clock in the morning and all the passengers, as well as most of the crew, were asleep in their berths. The big decks were entirely empty of people.

Just then, at the break of day, an old French sailor lay twisting and turning in his hammock, unable to rest. There was quite a sea on, and the ship's timbers creaked incessantly; but it was certainly not this that kept him from falling asleep. He and his mates occupied a large but exceedingly low compartment between decks. It was lighted by a couple of lanterns, so that he could see the gray hammocks, which hung in close rows, slowly swinging to and fro with their slumbering occupants. Now and again a strong gust of wind swept in through one of the hatches, which was so searchingly cold and damp that it brought to his mind's eye a vivid picture of the vast sea around him, rolling its grayish green waves beneath its veil of mists.

"There's nothing like the sea!" thought the old sailor.

As he lay there musing, all at once everything became strangely still around him, he heard neither the churning of the propeller, nor the rattling of the rudder chains, nor the lapping of the waves, nor the whistling of the wind, nor any other sound. It seemed to him that the ship had suddenly gone to the bottom,

and that he and his mates would never be shrouded or laid in
their coffins, but must remain hanging in their gray hammocks in
the depths of the sea till the Day of Judgment.

Before, he had always dreaded the thought that his end
might be a watery grave, but now the idea of it was pleasing to
him. He was glad it was the moving and transparent water that
covered him, and not the heavy, black, suffocating mould of the
churchyard. "There's nothing like the sea," he thought again.

Then he fell to thinking of something that made him
uneasy. He wondered whether his lying at the bottom of the
ocean without having received Extreme Unction would not be
bad for his soul; he began to fear that now his soul would never
be able to find its way up to Heaven.

At that moment his eye caught a faint glimmer of light
coming from the forecastle. He raised himself, and leaned over
the side of the hammock to see what it was. Presently he saw
two persons coming, each of whom was carrying a lighted
candle. He bent still farther forward so as to see who they were.
The hammocks were hung so close together and so near to the
floor that any one wanting to pass through the room, without
pushing or knocking against those who were sleeping there,
would have to crawl on hands and knees. The old seaman
wondered who the persons could be that were able to pass in this
crowded place. He soon discovered that they were two
diminutive acolytes, in surplice and cassock, each bearing a
lighted candle.

The sailor was not at all surprised. It seemed only natural
that such little folk should be able to walk with burning candles
under hammocks. "I wonder if there is a priest with them?" he
said. Immediately he heard the tinkling sound of a little bell, and
saw some one following them. However, it was no priest, but an
old woman who was not much bigger than the boys.

The old woman looked familiar to him. "It must be
mother," he thought. "I've never seen any one as tiny as mother,
and surely no one but mother could be coming along so softly
and quietly without waking people."

He noticed that his mother wore over her black dress a
long white linen surplice, edged with a wide border of lace, such
as is worn by priests. In her hand she held the large missal with

the gold cross which he had seen hundreds of times lying on the altar in the church at home.

The little acolytes now placed their candles at the side of his hammock and knelt down, each swinging a censer. The old sailor caught the sweet odour of burning incense, saw blue clouds ascend, and heard the rhythmical click, click of the censer chains. In the meantime, his mother had opened the big book and was reading the prayers for the dead. Now it seemed good to him to be lying at the bottom of the sea—much better than being in the churchyard. He stretched himself in the hammock, and for a long time he could hear his mother's voice mumbling Latin words. The smoke of the incense curled round him as he listened to the even click, click of the moving censers.

Then it all ceased. The acolytes took up their candles and walked away, followed by his mother, who suddenly closed the book with a bang. He saw all three disappear beneath the gray hammocks.

The instant they had gone the silence was at an end. He heard the breathing of his comrades, the timbers creaked, the wind whistled, and the waves swish-swashed against the ship. Then he knew that he was still among the living, and on top of the sea.

"Jesu Maria! What can be the meaning of the things I have seen this night?" he asked himself.

Ten minutes later L'Univers was struck amidships. It was as if the steamer had been cut in two.

"This was what I expected," thought the old seaman.

During the terrible confusion that ensued while the other sailors, only half awake, rolled out of their hammocks, he carefully dressed himself in his best clothes. He had had a foretaste of death which was sweet and mild, and it seemed to him that the sea had already claimed him as its own.

* * * * *

A little cabin boy lay sleeping in the deckhouse near the dining salon when the collision occurred. Startled by the shock, he sat up in his bunk, half dazed, and wondering what had happened. Just over his head there was a small porthole, through which he peered. All he could see was fog and some shadowy gray object which had, as it were, sprung from the fog. He seemed to see monstrous gray wings. A mammoth bird must have swooped down on the ship, he thought. The steamer rolled and heeled as the huge monster went at it with claws and beak and flapping wings.

The little cabin boy thought he would die from fright. In a second he was wide awake. Then he discovered that a large sailing vessel had collided with the steamer. He saw great sails and a strange deck, where men in oilskin coats were rushing about in mad terror. The wind freshened, and the sails became as taut as drums. The masts bulged, while the yards snapped with a succession of reports that sounded like pistol shots. A great three-master, which in the dense fog had sailed straight into *L'Univers*, had somehow got her bowsprit wedged into the side of the liner, and could not free herself. The passenger steamer listed considerably, but its propellers went right on working, so that now both ships moved along together.

"Lord God!" exclaimed the cabin boy as he rushed out on deck, "that poor boat has run into us, and now it will surely sink!"

It never occurred to him that the steamer could be imperilled, big and fine as she was. The officers came hurrying up; but when they saw it was only a sailing vessel that had collided with their ship, they felt quite safe, and with the utmost confidence took the necessary steps for getting the boats clear of each other.

The little cabin boy stood on the deck barelegged, his shirt fluttering in the wind, and beckoned to the unhappy men on the sailing vessel to come over to the steamer and save themselves. At first no one seemed to take any notice of him, but presently a big man with a red beard began motioning to him.

"Come over here, boy!" the man shouted, running to the side of the vessel. "The steamer is sinking!"

The little boy had not the faintest notion of going over to the sailing vessel. He shouted as loud as he could that the people on the doomed boat should come over to *L'Univers*, and save their lives.

While the other men on the three-master were working

with poles and boat hooks to free their vessel from the steamer, the man with the red beard could think of nothing but the little cabin boy, for whom he had evidently conceived an extraordinary pity. He put his hands to his mouth, trumpet-like, and called: "Come over here, come over here!"

The little lad looked forlorn and cold, standing on the deck in his thin shirt. He stamped his foot and shook his fist at the men on the other boat, because they would not mind him and board the steamer. A huge greyhound like *L'Univers*, with six hundred passengers and a crew of two hundred men, couldn't possibly go down, he reasoned. And, of course, he could see that both the captain and the sailors were just as calm as he was.

Of a sudden the man with the red beard seized a boat hook, thrust it out toward the boy, got him by the shirt, and tried to pull him on to the other ship. The boy was dragged as far as the ship's railing, but there he managed to free himself of the hook. He was not going to let himself be dragged over to a strange vessel that was doomed.

Immediately afterward another crash was heard. The bowsprit of the three-master had snapped, and the two ships were now clear of each other. As the liner steamed ahead, the boy saw the big broken bowsprit dangling in the bow of the other vessel, and he also saw great clouds of sails drop down upon the crew.

The liner proceeded on her course at full speed, and the sailing vessel was soon lost to sight in the fog. The last thing the boy saw was the men trying to get out from under the mass of sails. Thereupon the vessel disappeared as completely as if it had slipped in behind a great wall. "It has already gone down," thought the lad. And now he stood listening for distress calls.

Then a rough and powerful voice was heard to shout across to the steamer: "Save your passengers! Put out your boats!"

Again there was silence, and again the boy listened for distress calls. Then the voice was heard as if from far away: "Pray to God, for you are lost!"

At that moment an old sailor stepped up to the captain. "We have a big hole amidships; we are going down," he said, quietly and impressively.

* * * * *

Soon after the nature of the accident had become known on the steamer, a little lady appeared on deck. She had come from one of the first-class cabins with certain and determined step. She was dressed from top to toe, and her bonnet strings were tied in a natty bowknot. She was a little old lady, with crimped hair, round, owlish-looking eyes, and a florid complexion.

During the short time the voyage had lasted she had managed to become acquainted with every one on board. Everybody knew that her name was Miss Hoggs, and she had told them all—the crew as well as passengers—time and again, that she was never afraid. She didn't see why she need have any fear, she would have to die at one time or another, she had said, and whether it happened soon or late was immaterial to her. Nor was she afraid now; she had gone up on deck simply to see if anything interesting or exciting was going on there.

The first thing she saw was two sailors darting past with wild, terrified faces. Stewards, half dressed, came running out from their quarters to go down and waken the passengers and get them on deck. An old sailor came up with an armful of life belts, which he tossed on the deck. A little cabin boy in his shirt was crouching in a corner, sobbing and shrieking that he was going to die. The captain was on his bridge, and Miss Hoggs heard him give orders to stop the engines and to man the lifeboats.

Engineers and stokers came rushing up the grimy ladder leading from the engine room, shouting that the water had already reached the fires. Miss Hoggs had hardly been on deck a moment before it was thronged with steerage passengers, who had come up in a body, shrieking that they would have to hurry and make for the boats, otherwise none but the first and second class passengers would be saved.

As the excitement and confusion increased, Miss Hoggs began to realize that they were in actual danger; so she quietly slipped away to the upper deck, where several life-boats hung in their davits, just outside the railing. Up here there was not a soul, and Miss Hoggs, without being seen, climbed over the railing and scrambled into one of the boats suspended above the watery abyss. As soon as she was well inside, she congratulated herself upon her wisdom and foresight. That was the advantage of having a clear and cool head, she thought. She knew that when once the boat was lowered there would be a wild scramble for it; the crush in the gangway and on the companion ladder would be something awful. Again and again she congratulated herself on having thought of getting into the boat beforehand.

Miss Hoggs's boat was hung far aft, but by leaning over the edge of it she could see the companion ladder. Then she saw that a boat had been manned, and that people were getting into it. Suddenly a terrible cry went up. Some one in the excitement had fallen overboard. This must have frightened the others, for cries arose from all sides of the ship, and the passengers heedlessly crowded the gangway, pushing and fighting their way toward the ladder. In the struggle many of them went overboard. A few persons, who saw that it would be impossible to get to the ladder, jumped into the sea, thinking they would swim to the boat. Just then the lifeboat, already loaded to its full capacity, rowed away. The people that were in it drew their knives and threatened to cut of the fingers of any one who attempted to get inside.

Miss Hoggs saw one boat after another launched. She also saw one boat after another capsize under the weight of those who hurled themselves down into them.

The lifeboats near to hers were .lowered, but for some unaccountable reason no one had touched the one in which she was seated. "Thank God they are leaving my boat alone till the worst is over," she thought.

And Miss Hoggs heard and saw dreadful things. It seemed to her that she was suspended over a hell. She could not see the deck itself, but from the sounds that reached her, she gathered that a frightful struggle was taking place there. She heard pistol shots and saw blue smoke clouds rise in the air.

At last there came a moment when everything was hushed. "This would be the right time to lower my boat," thought Miss Hoggs. She was not at all afraid, but sat back with perfect composure until the steamer began to settle. Then, for the first time, it dawned on Miss Hoggs that *L'Univers* was sinking, and that her boat had been forgotten.

* * * * *

On board the steamer was a young American matron, a
Mrs. Gordon, who was on her way to Europe to visit her parents,
who for some years had been living in Paris. She had her two
little boys with her, and all three were asleep in their cabin when
the accident occurred. The mother was immediately awakened,
and soon managed to get the children partly dressed; then
throwing a cloak over her night robe, she went out into the
narrow passageway between the cabins.

The passage was full of people who had rushed out from
their staterooms to hurry on deck. Here it was not difficult to
pass; but in the companionway there was a terrible crush. She
saw people pushing and crowding, with no thought of any one
but themselves, as more than a hundred persons, all at one time,
tried to rush up. The young American woman stood holding her
two children by the hand. She looked longingly up the stairway,
wondering how she could manage to press through the throng
with her little ones. The people fought and struggled, thinking
only of themselves. No one even noticed her.

Mrs. Gordon glanced anxiously about in the hope of
finding some one who would take one of the boys and carry him
to the deck, while she herself took the other. But she saw no one
she dared approach. The men came dashing past, dressed every
which way. Some were wrapped in blankets, others had on
ulsters over their nightshirts, and many of them carried canes.
When she saw the desperate look in the eyes of these men, she
felt that it would not be safe to speak to them.

Of the women, on the other hand, she had no fear; but
there was not one, even among them, to whom she would dare
entrust her child. They were all out of their senses, and could not
have comprehended what she wanted of them. She stood
regarding them, wondering whether there might not be one,
perhaps, who had a bit of reason left. But seeing them rush
wildly past—some hugging the flowers they had received on
their departure from New York, others shrieking and wringing
their hands—she knew it was useless to appeal to such frenzied

people. Finally, she attempted to stop a young man who had
been her neighbour at table, and had shown her marked
attention.

"Oh, Mr. Martens—"

The man glowered at her with the same fixed savage
stare that she had seen in the eyes of the other men. He raised his
cane threateningly, and had she tried to detain him, he would
have struck her. The next moment she heard a howl, which was
hardly a howl, but rather an angry murmur, as when a strong and
sweeping wind becomes bottled up in a narrow passage. It came
from the people on the companionway, whose progress had been
suddenly impeded.

A cripple had been borne part way up the stairs—a man
who was so entirely helpless that he had to be carried to and
from the table. He was a large, heavy man, and his valet had
with the greatest difficulty managed to bear him on his back
halfway up the stairs, where he had paused to take breath. In the
meantime, the pressure from behind had become so tremendous
that it had forced him to his knees; and he and his master were
taking up the whole width of the stairway, thus creating an
impassable obstruction.

Presently Mrs. Gordon saw a big, rough-looking man
bend down, lift up the cripple, and throw him over the banister.
She also marked that, horrible as was this spectacle, no one
seemed to be either shocked or moved by it. For nobody thought
of anything save to rush ahead. It was as if a stone lying in the
road had been picked up and tossed into the ditch—nothing
more.

The young American mother saw that among these
people there was no hope of being saved; she and her children
were doomed.

* * * * *

There were a young bride and groom on board who were
on their honeymoon. Their cabin was far down in the body of the
ship, and they had slept so soundly that they had not even heard
the collision. Nor was there much commotion in their part of the
boat afterward. And as no one had thought of calling them, they

were still asleep when every one else was on deck fighting for
the lifeboats. But they woke when the propeller, which the
whole night had been revolving directly under their heads,
suddenly stopped. The husband hurriedly drew on a garment or
two, and ran out to see what was up. In a few minutes he
returned. He carefully closed the cabin door after him before
uttering a word. Then he said:

"The ship is sinking."

At the same time he sat down, and when his wife would
have rushed out, he begged her to remain with him.

"The boats have all gone," he said. "Most of the
passengers have been drowned, and those who are still on the
ship are now up on deck, fighting desperately for rafts and life
belts." He told her that in the gangway he was obliged to step
over a woman who had been trampled to death, and that he had
heard the cries of the doomed on all sides. "There's no chance of
our being saved, so don't go out! Let us die together!"

The young bride felt that he was right, and resignedly sat
down beside him.

"You wouldn't like to see all those people struggling and
fighting," he said. "Since we've got to die anyway, let us at least
have a peaceful death."

She knew that it was no more than right that she should
stay there with him the few short moments of life still left to
them. Had she not promised to give him a whole life time of
devotion?

"I had hoped," he went on, "that after we had been
married many, many years, you would be sitting by me when I
lay on my deathbed, and I would thank you for a long and happy
life partnership."

At that moment she saw a thin streak of water trickling in
through the crack under the door. This was too much for her.
She threw up her arms in despair. "I can't!" she cried. "Let me
go! I can't stay shut in here waiting for death. I love you, but I
can't do it!"

She rushed out just as the ship heeled over before going
down.

* * * * *

Young Mrs. Gordon was lying in the water, the steamer had sunk, her children were lost, and she herself had been deep under the sea. She had then come to the surface for the third time and knew that in another moment she would be sinking again, and that that would mean death.

Then her mind no longer dwelt upon her husband or children, or upon anything else of this earth. She thought only of lifting up her soul to God. And her soul rose like a liberated prisoner. Her spirit, rejoicing in the thought of casting off the heavy shackles of human existence, jubilantly prepared to ascend to its real home. "Is death so easy?" she mused.

As that thought came to her the medley of confusing noises around her—the surging of the waves, the murmur of the wind, the shrieks of the drowning, and the noises made by the colliding of the various objects that were drifting around on the water—all seemed to resolve themselves into words in the same way as shapeless clouds sometimes form themselves into pictures. And this was what she heard:

"It is a fact that death is easy, but to live, that is the difficult thing!"

"Ah, so it is!" she thought, and wondered what was needed to make living as easy as dying.

Round about her the shipwrecked people fought and struggled for the floating wreckage and the overturned boats. But amid the mad cries and curses, again the noises resolved themselves into clear and powerful words:

"That which is needed to make life as easy as death is UNITY, UNITY, UNITY."

It seemed to her that the Lord of all the earth had converted these noises into a speaking tube, through which He himself had answered her.

While the words that had been spoken were still ringing in her ears, she was rescued. She had been drawn up into a small boat in which there were only three persons besides herself—a brawny old sailor dressed in his best, an elderly woman with round, owlish eyes, and a poor little heartbroken boy, who had on nothing but a torn shirt.

* * * * *

Late in the afternoon of the following day a Norwegian
ship sailed along the great banks of Newfoundland in the
direction of the fishing grounds. The sky was clear, and the sea
was like a mirror. The vessel could make but little headway. All
the sails were set so as to catch the last breaths of the dying
breeze.

The sea looked very beautiful. It was a clear blue and
smooth as glass, but where the faintest breeze passed over it, it
was a silvery white.

When the afternoon stillness had continued for a while,
the ship's crew sighted a dark object floating on the water.
Gradually it came nearer, and soon they discovered that it was a
human body. As it was being carried by the current past the ship,
they could tell by the clothing that it was the body of a sailor. It
was lying on its back, with eyes wide open, and with a look of
peace on its face. Evidently the body had not been long enough
in the water to become disfigured. It was as if the sailor were
complacently letting himself be rocked by the tiny rippling
wavelets.

When the sailors turned their gaze in the opposite
direction, they let out a cry. Before they could turn their faces,
another body appeared on the surface close to the bow of the
boat. They came near passing over it, but at the last moment it
was washed away by the swell. Now they all rushed to the side
of the ship and looked down. This time they saw the body of a
child, a daintily dressed little girl. "Dear, dear!" said the sailors,
drying their eyes. "The poor little kiddie!"

As the body of the little girl drifted past it seemed as if
the child were looking up at them. And there was such a serious
expression in its wistful eyes-as if it were out upon some very
urgent errand. Immediately after, one of the sailors shouted that
he saw another body, and the same thing was said by one who
was looking in an opposite direction. All at once they saw five
bodies, they saw ten, and then there were so many they could not
count them.

The ship moved slowly on among all these dead people,
who surrounded the vessel as if they wanted something. Some

came floating in large groups; they looked like driftwood that had been carried away from land; but they were just a mass of dead bodies.

The sailors stood aghast, afraid to move. They could hardly believe that what they saw was real. All at once they seemed to see an island rising up out of the sea. From a distance it looked like land, but, on coming nearer, they saw hundreds of bodies floating close together, and surrounding the vessel on all sides. They moved with the ship, as if wanting to make the voyage across the water in its company. Then the skipper turned the rudder, so as to coax a little wind into the sails; but it did not help much. The sails hung limp, and the dead bodies continued to follow.

The sailors turned ashen, and silence fell upon them. The ship had so little headway that she could not seem to get clear of the dead. They were fearful lest it should go on like this the whole night. Then a Swedish seaman stood up in the bow and repeated the Lord's Prayer. Thereupon, he began to sing a hymn. When he had got half through the hymn the sun went down, and the evening breeze came along and carried the ship away from the region of the dead.

Hellgum's Letter

An old woman came out from her little log cabin in the woods. Although it was only a week day, she was dressed in her best, as if for church. After locking her door she put the key in its usual place, under the stoop.

When the old woman had gone a few paces, she turned round to look at her cabin, which appeared very small and very gray under the shadow of the towering snow-clad fir trees. She glanced at her humble home with an affectionate gaze. "Many a happy day have I spent in that little old hut!" she mused solemnly. "Ah me! The Lord giveth, and the Lord taketh away."

Then she went on her way, down the forest road. She was very old and exceeding fragile, but she was one of those who hold themselves erect and firm, however much old age may try to bend them. She had a sweet face and soft white hair. She looked so mild and gentle that it was surprising to hear her speak with a voice that was as strident and solemn as that of some old evangelist.

She had a long tramp ahead of her, for she was going down to the Ingmar Farm to a meeting of the Hellgumists. Old Eva Gunnersdotter was one of the most zealous converts to Hellgum's teachings. "Ah, those were glorious times," she mumbled to herself as she trudged on, "in the beginning when half the parish had gone over to Hellgum! Who would have thought that so many were going to backslide, and that after five years there would be hardly more than a score of us left—not counting the children, of course!"

Her thoughts went back to the time when she, who for many years had lived in solitude in the heart of the forest, forgotten by every one, all at once had found a lot of brothers and sisters who came to her in her loneliness, who never forgot to clear a path to her cabin after a big snowfall, and who always kept her little shed well filled with dry firewood—and all without her having to ask for it. She recalled to mind the time when Karin, daughter of Ingmar, and her sisters, and many more of the best people in the parish, used to come and hold love feasts in her little gray cabin.

"Alas, that so many should have abandoned the only true way of salvation!" she sighed. "Now retribution will come upon us. Next summer we must all perish because so few among us have heard the call, and because those who have heard it have not continued steadfast."

The old woman then fell to pondering over Hellgum's letters, those letters which the Hellgumists regarded as Apostolic writings and read aloud at all their meetings, as the Bible is read in the churches. "There was a time when Hellgum was as milk and honey to us," she reflected. "Then he commanded us to be kind and tolerant toward the unconverted, and to show gentle forbearance toward those who had fallen away; he taught the rich that in their works of charity they must treat the just and the unjust alike. But lately he has been as wormwood and gall. He writes about nothing but trials and punishments."

The old woman had now reached the edge of the forest, from where she could look down over the village. It was a lovely day in February. The snow had spread its white purity over the whole district; all the trees were deep in their winter sleep, and not a breath of wind stirred. But she was thinking that all this beautiful country, wrapped in peaceful slumber, would soon be awakened only to be consumed by a rain of fire and brimstone. Everything that was now lying under a cover of snow, she seemed to see enveloped in flame.

"He hasn't put it into plain words," thought the old woman, "but he keeps writing all the while about a *sore trial*. Mercy me! Who could wonder at it if this parish were to be punished as was Sodom, and overthrown like Babylon!"

As Eva Gunnersdotter wandered through the village, she

could not look up at a single house without picturing to herself how the coming earthquake would shake it and crumble it into dust and ashes. And when she met people along the way, she thought of how the monsters of hell would soon hunt and devour them.

"Ah, here comes the schoolmaster's Gertrude!" she remarked to herself as she saw a pretty young girl coming down the road. "Her eyes sparkle like sunbeams on the snow. She feels happy now because she expects to be married in the fall to young Ingmar Ingmarsson. I see she has a bundle of thread tucked under her arm. She is going to weave table covers and bed hangings for her new home. But before that weaving is done, destruction will be upon us."

The old woman cast dark glances about her. She could see that the village had grown and developed into an astonishing thing of beauty, but she thought that all these pretty white-and-yellow houses, with their fancy gables and their big bowed windows, would collapse the same as her humble gray cabin, where moss grew in the cracks between the logs, and the windows were only holes in the wall. When she reached the heart of the town, she stopped short and struck her cane hard against the pavement. A sudden feeling of indignation had seized her. "Woe, woe!" she cried, in so loud a voice that people in the street paused and looked round. "Yea, in all these houses live such as have rejected the Gospel of Christ and cling to the enemy's teaching. Why didn't they listen to the call and turn away from their sins? On their account we must all perish. God's hand strikes heavily. It strikes both the just and the unjust."

When she had crossed the river she was overtaken by some of the other Hellgumists. They were Corporal Felt and Bullet Gunner and his wife, Brita. Shortly afterward, they were joined by Hök Matts Ericsson, his son Gabriel, and Gunhild, the daughter of Councilman Clementsson.

All these people in their gayly coloured national costumes made a pretty picture walking along the snow-covered road. But to the mind of Eva Gunnersdotter, they were only doomed prisoners being led to the place of execution, like cattle driven to slaughter.

The Hellgumists looked quite dejected. They walked

along, their eyes on the ground, as if weighed down by a terrible
load of discouragement. They had all expected that the Celestial
Kingdom would suddenly spread over the whole earth, and that
they would live to see the day when the New Jerusalem should
come down from the clouds of heaven. But now that they had
become so few in number, and could not help seeing that theirs
was a forlorn hope, it was as if something within them had
snapped. They moved slowly and with dragging steps. Now and
then a sigh would escape them, but they seemed to have nothing
to say to each other. For this had been a matter of supreme
earnest with them. They had staked their all upon it, and had
lost.

"Why do they look so down-in-the-mouth?" wondered
the old woman. "They don't seem to believe the worst, and don't
want to understand what Hellgum writes. I've tried to explain his
words to them, but they won't even listen to me. Alas! those
who live on the lowlands, under an open sky, can never
understand what it is to be afraid. They don't think the same
thoughts as do those of us who live in the solitude of the dark
forest."

She could see that the Hellgumists were uneasy because
Halvor had called them together on a week day. They feared that
he was going to tell them of more desertions from their ranks.
They glanced anxiously at one another, with a look of distrust in
their eyes that seemed to say: "How long will you hold out? And
you—and you?"

"We might as well stop right now," they thought, "and
break up the Society at once. After all, sudden death would be
easier than slowly wasting away."

Alas! that this little community with its gospel of peace,
this blissful life of unity and brotherly love which had meant so
much to all of them, that this should now be doomed.

As these disheartened people walked along toward the
farm the sparkling winter sun rolled merrily on across the blue
sky. From the glistening snow rose a refreshing coolness, which
should have put life and courage into them; while from the fir-
clad hills encircling the parish, there fell a soothing peace and
stillness.

At last they were at the Ingmar Farm.

In the living-room of the farmhouse, close to the ceiling, hung an old picture which had been painted by some local artist a hundred years before their time. It represented a city surrounded by a high wall, above which could be seen the roofs and gables of many buildings, some of which were red farmhouses with turf roofs. Others were white manor houses with slate roofs. Others, again, showed massive copper-plated towers, after the manner of the Kistine Church at Falun. Outside the city wall were promenading gentlemen, in kneebreeches and buckled shoes, who carried Bengal canes. A coach was seen driving out of the gateway of the town, in which were seated ladies in powdered wigs and wearing Watteau hats. Beyond the wall were trees, with a profusion of dark green foliage; and on the ground, between patches of tall, waving grass, ran little shimmering brooklets. At the bottom of the picture was painted in large, ornate letters: "This is God's Holy City Jerusalem."

The old canvas being hung like that, so close to the ceiling, it seldom attracted any notice. Most of the people who visited the Ingmar Farm did not even know of its being there.

But that day it was enframed in a wreath of green whortleberry twigs, so that it instantly caught the eye of the caller. Eva Gunnersdotter saw it at once, and remarked under her breath: "Aha! Now the folks on the Ingmar Farm know that we must perish. That's why they want us to turn our eyes toward the Heavenly City."

Karin and Halvor came forward to greet her, looking even more gloomy and low spirited than the other Hellgumists. "It's plain they know now that the end is near," she thought.

Eva Gunnersdotter, being the oldest person present, was placed at the head of the long table. In front of her lay an opened letter, with American stamps on the envelope.

"Another letter has come from our dear brother Hellgum," said Halvor. "This is why I have called the brothers and sisters together."

"I gather that you must think this a very important document, Halvor," said Bullet Gunner, thoughtfully.

"I do," replied Halvor. "Now we shall learn what Hellgum meant when he wrote in his last letter that a great trial of our faith was before us."

"I don't think that any of us will be afraid to suffer in the Lord's cause," Gunner assured him.

All the Hellgumists had not yet arrived, and there was a long wait before the last one finally made his appearance. Old Eva Gunnersdotter, with her far-sighted eyes, meanwhile sat gazing at Hellgum's letter. She was reminded of the letter with the seven seals, in Revelation, and fancied that the instant any human hand should touch that letter, the Angel of Destruction would come flying down from Heaven.

She raised her eyes and glanced up at the Jerusalem picture. "Yes, yes," she mumbled, "of course I want to go to that city whose gates are of gold and whose walls are of crystal!" And she began reading to herself: "'And the foundations of the wall of the city were garnished with all manner of precious stones. The first foundation was jasper; the second, sapphire; the third, a chalcedony; the fourth, an emerald; the fifth, sardonyx; the sixth, sardius; the seventh, chrysolite; the eighth, beryl; the ninth, a topaz; the tenth, a chrysoprasus; the eleventh, a jacinth; the twelfth, an amethyst.'"

The old woman was so deep in her precious Book of Revelation that she started as if she had been caught napping when Halvor went over to that end of the table where the letter lay.

"We will open our meeting with a hymn," Halvor announced. "Let us all join in singing number two hundred and forty-four." And the Hellgumists sang in unison, "Jerusalem, my happy home."

Eva Gunnersdotter heaved a sigh of relief because the dreaded moment had been put off for a little. "Alack-a-day! that a doddering old woman like me should be so afraid to die," she thought, half ashamed of her weakness.

At the close of the hymn Halvor took up the letter and began unfolding it. Whereupon the Spirit moved Eva Gunnersdotter to arise and offer up a lengthy prayer for grace to receive in a proper spirit the message contained therein. Halvor, with the letter in his hand, stood quietly waiting till she had finished. Then he began reading it in a tone he might have used had he been delivering a sermon:

"My dear brothers and sisters, peace be with you.

"Hitherto I had thought that I and you, who have embraced my teaching, were alone in this our faith. But, praise be to God! here in Chicago we have found brethren who are likeminded, who think and act in accordance with the principles.

"For be it known unto you that here, in Chicago, there lived in the early eighties a man by the name of Edward Gordon. He and his wife were God-fearing people. They were sorely grieved at seeing so much distress in the world, and prayed God that grace might be given them to help the sorrowing ones.

"It so happened that the wife of Edward Gordon had to make a long voyage across the sea, where she suffered shipwreck and was cast upon the waters. When she found herself in the most extreme peril, the Voice of God spoke to her. And the Voice of God commanded her to teach mankind to live in unity.

"And the woman was saved from the sea and the peril of death, and she returned to her husband and told him about the message from God. 'This is a great command our Lord hath given unto us—that we should live in unity—and we must follow it. So great is this message that in all the world there is but one spot worthy of receiving it. Let us, therefore, gather our friends together and go with them to Jerusalem, that we may proclaim God's holy commandment from the Mount of Zion.'

"Then Edward Gordon and his wife, together with thirty others who wanted to obey the Lord's last holy commandment, set out for Jerusalem, where all of them are now living in concord under one roof. They share with one another all their worldly goods, and serve one another, each protecting the other's welfare.

"And they have taken into their home the children of the poor, and they nurse the sick, they care for the aged, and succour all who appeal to them for aid, without expecting either money or gifts in return.

"But they do not preach in the churches or on street corners, for they say, 'It is our works that shall speak for us.'

"But the people who heard of their way of living said of them: 'They must be fools and fanatics.' And those who decried them the loudest were the Christians who had come to Palestine to convert Jews and Mohammedans, by preaching and teaching.

And they said: 'What sort of persons are these who do not preach? No doubt they have come hither to lead an evil life and to indulge their sinful lusts among the heathen.'

"And they raised a cry against these good people that travelled across the seas all the way to their own country. But amongst those who had settled in Jerusalem there was a rich widow, with her two half-grown children. She had left a brother in her native land, to whom every one was saying, 'How can you allow your sister to live among those dreadful people, who are so loose lived? They are nothing but idlers who live upon her bounty.' So the brother began legal proceedings against the sister, in order to compel her to send her children back to America to be reared there.

"And on account of these proceedings, the widow, with her children, returned to Chicago, accompanied by Edward Gordon and his wife. At that time they had been living in Jerusalem fourteen years.

"When they came back from that far country, the newspapers had much to say of them; and some called them lunatics and some said they were impostors."

When Halvor had read thus far, he paused a moment, and presently repeated the substance of what he had read in his own words, so that everybody would understand it. After which, he went on reading:

"But there is in Chicago a home of which you have heard. And the occupants of this home are people who try to serve God in spirit and in truth, who share all things in common, and watch over each other's lives.

"We who live in this home read something in a newspaper about these 'lunatics' who had come back from Jerusalem, and said among ourselves, 'These people are of our faith; they are banded together to work for righteousness, the same as ourselves. We would like to meet these persons who share our ideals.'

"And we wrote and asked them to come to see us, and those who had come back from Jerusalem accepted the invitation and called; and we compared our teachings with theirs, and found that our principles of faith were the same. 'It is by the grace of God that we have found each other,' we said.

"They told us of the glories of the Holy City, that city which lies resplendent on its white mountain, and we deemed them fortunate in that they had been privileged to tread the paths our Saviour had trod.

"Then one of our own brethren said: 'Why shouldn't we go along with you to Jerusalem?'

"They answered: 'You must not accompany us thither, for God's Holy City is full of strife and dissension, of want and sickness, of hate and poverty.'

"Instantly another of our brethren cried: 'Mayhap God has sent you to us because it is His meaning that we shall go with you to that far country, to help you fight all this?'

"Then one and all of us heard the voice of the Spirit in our hearts say, 'Yea, this is My will!'

"Then we asked them whether they would be willing to receive us into their fold, although we were poor and unlettered. And they answered that they would.

"Then we determined to become brethren in the fullest sense. And they accepted our faith, and we theirs—and all the while the Spirit was upon us, and we were filled with a great gladness. And we said: 'Now we know that God loves us, since He sends us to that land where once He sent His own Son. And now we know that our teaching is the right teaching, inasmuch as God wants it proclaimed from his holy mountain Zion.'

"And then a third member of our own household said: 'And there are our brothers and sisters at home in Sweden.' So we told the brethren from Jerusalem that there were more of us than they saw here; that we also had some brothers and sisters in Sweden. We said: 'They are being sorely tried in their fight for righteousness, many of them have fallen away, and the few who have remained steadfast are obliged to live among unbelievers.'

"Then the travellers from Jerusalem answered: 'Let your brothers and sisters in Sweden follow us to Jerusalem, and share our holy work.'

"At first we were pleased at the thought of your following us, and living with us at Jerusalem, in peace and harmony. But afterward we began to feel troubled, and said: 'They will never leave their fine farms and old occupations.'

"And the Jerusalem travellers answered: 'Fields and

meadows we cannot offer them, but they will be allowed to
wander along the pathways where Jesus' feet have trod.'

"But we were still doubtful and said to them, 'They will
never journey to a strange land where no one understands their
speech.'

"And the travellers from Jerusalem answered: 'They will
understand what the stones of Palestine have to tell them about
their Saviour.'

"We said: 'They will never divide their property with
strangers and become poor as beggars; nor will they renounce
their authority, for they are the leading people of their own
parish.'

"The travellers from Jerusalem answered: 'We have
neither power nor worldly possessions to offer them; but we
invite them to become participants in the sufferings of Christ
their Redeemer.'

"When that was said, we were again filled with gladness,
and felt that you would come. And now, my dear brothers and
sisters, when you have read this, do not talk it over among
yourselves, but be still and listen. And whatever the Spirit bids
you do, that do."

Halvor folded the letter, saying, "Now we must do as
Hellgum writes; we must be still, and listen."

There was a long silence in the living-room at the Ingmar
Farm.

Old Eva Gunnersdotter was as silent as were the others,
waiting for the Voice of God to speak to her. She interpreted it
all in her own way. "Why, of course," she thought, "Hellgum
wants us to go to Jerusalem so that we may escape the great
destruction. The Lord would save us from the flood of
brimstone, and preserve us from the rain of fire; and those of us
who are righteous will hear the Voice of God warning us to flee
the wrath to come."

It never for a moment occurred to the old woman that it
could be a sacrifice for any one to leave his home and his native
land, when it came to a question of this sort. It never entered her
mind that any one could doubt the wisdom of leaving his native
woodlands, his smiling river, and his fertile fields. Some of the
Hellgumists thought with fear and trepidation of their having to

change their manner of living, of renouncing fatherland, parents, friends, and relatives; but not she. To her it simply meant that God wanted to spare them as He had once spared Noah and Lot. Were they not being called to a life of supernal glory in God's Holy City? It was to her as if Hellgum had written that they would be bodily taken up into heaven, like the prophet Elijah.

They were all sitting with closed eyes, deep in meditation. Some were suffering such intense mental agony that cold sweat broke out on their foreheads. "Ah, this is indeed the trial which Hellgum foretold!" they sighed.

The sun was at the horizon, and shot its piercing rays into the room. The crimson glow from the setting sun cast a blood-red glare upon the many blanched faces. Finally Martha Ingmarsson, the wife of Ljung Björn Olofsson, slipped down from her chair on to her knees. Then, one after another, they all went down on their knees. All at once several of them drew a deep breath, and a smile lighted up their faces.

Then Karin, daughter of Ingmar, said in a tone of wonderment: "I hear God's voice calling me!"

Gunhild, the daughter of Councillor Clementsson, lifted up her hands in ecstasy, and tears streamed down her face. "I, too, am going," she cried. "God's voice calls me."

Whereupon Krister Larsson and his wife said, almost in the same breath: "It cries into my ear that I must go. I can hear God's voice calling me!"

The call came to one after another, and with it all anguish of mind and all feeling of regret vanished. A great sense of joy had come to them. They thought no more of their farms or their relatives; they were thinking only of how their little colony would branch out and blossom anew, and of the wonder of having been called to the Holy City.

The call had now come to most of them. But it had not yet reached Halvor Halvorsson; he was wrestling in anguished prayer, thinking God would not call him as He had called the others. "He sees that I love my fields and meadows more than His word," he said to himself. "I am unworthy."

Karin then went up to Halvor and laid her hand upon his brow. "You must be still, Halvor, and listen in silence."

Halvor wrung his hands so hard that the joints of his

fingers cracked. "Perhaps God does not deem me worthy to go," he said.

"Yes, Halvor, you will be let go, but you must be still," said Karin. She knelt down beside him and put her arm around him. "Now listen quietly, Halvor, and without fear."

In a few moments the tense look was gone from his face. "I hear I hear something far, far away," he whispered.

"It is the harps of angels announcing the presence of the Lord," said the wife. "Be quite still now, Halvor." Then she nestled very close to him—something she had never done before in the presence of others.

"Ah!" he exclaimed, clapping his hands. "Now I have heard it. It spoke so loudly that it was as thunder in my ears. 'You shall go to my Holy City, Jerusalem,' it said. Have you all heard it in the same way?"

"Yes, yes," they cried, "we have all heard it."

But now old Eva Gunnersdotter began to wail. "I have heard nothing. I can't go along with you. I'm like Lot's wife, and may not flee the wrath to come, but must be left behind. Here I must stay and be turned into a pillar of salt."

She wept from despair, and the Hellgumists all gathered round to pray with her. Still she heard nothing. And her despair became a thing of terror. "I can't hear anything!" she groaned. "But you've got to take me along. You shan't leave me to perish in the lake of fire!"

"You must wait, Eva," said the Hellgumists. "The call may come. It will surely come, either to-night or in the morning."

"You don't answer me," cried the old woman, "you don't tell what I want to know. Maybe you don't intend to take me along if no call comes to me!"

"It will come, it will come!" the Hellgumists shouted.

"You don't answer me!" screamed the old woman in a frenzy.

"Dear Eva, we can't take you along if God doesn't call you!" the Hellgumists protested. "But the call will come, never fear."

Then the old dame suddenly rose from her kneeling attitude, straightened her rickety old body, and brought her cane down on the floor with a thud. "You people mean to go away and leave me to perish!" she thundered. "Yes, yes, yes, you mean to go and let me perish!" She had become furiously angry, and once more they saw before them Eva Gunnersdotter as she had been in her younger days—strong and passionate and fiery.

"I want nothing more to do with you!" she shrieked. "I don't want to be saved by you. Fie upon you! You would abandon wife and children, father and mother, to save yourselves. Fie! You're a parcel of idiots to be leaving your good farms. You're a lot of misguided fools running after false prophets, that's what you are! It's upon you that fire and brimstone will rain. It is you who must perish. But we who remain at home, we shall live."

The Big Log

At dusk, on this same beautiful February day, two young lovers stood talking together in the road. The youth had just driven down from the forest with a big log, which was so heavy that the horse could hardly pull it. All the same he had driven in a roundabout way so that the log might be hauled through the village and past the big white schoolhouse.

The horse had been halted in front of the school, and a young woman had come out to have a look at the log. She couldn't seem to say enough in praise of it—how long and thick it was, and how straight, and what a lovely tan bark it had, and how firm the wood was, and how flawless!

The young man then told her very impressively that it had been grown on a moor far north of Olaf's Peak, and when he had felled it, and how long it had been lying in the forest to dry out. He told her exactly how many inches it measured, both in circumference and diameter.

"But, Ingmar," she said, "it is only the first!"

Pleased as she was, the thought that Ingmar had been five years getting down the first bit of timber toward the building of their new home made her feel uneasy. But Ingmar seemed to think that all difficulties had now been met.

"Just you wait, Gertrude!" he said. "If I can only get the timber hauled while the roads are passable, we'll soon have the house up."

It was turning bitterly cold. The horse stood there all of a shiver, shaking its head and stamping its hoofs, its mane and forelock white with hoar frost. But the youth and the maid did not feel the cold. They kept themselves warm by building their house, in imagination, from cellar to attic. When they had got the house done, they set about to furnish it.

"We'll put the sofa over against the long wall here in the living-room," Ingmar decided.

"But I don't know that we've got any sofa," said Gertrude.

The young man bit his lip. He had not meant to tell her, until some time later, that he had a sofa in readiness at the cabinetmaker's shop; but now he had unwittingly let out the secret.

Then Gertrude, too, came out with something which she had kept from him for five years. She told him that she had made up hair into ornaments and had woven fancy ribbons for sale, and with the money she had earned in this way she had bought all sorts of household things—pots and pans, platters and dishes, sheets and pillow slips, table covers and rugs.

Ingmar was so pleased over what Gertrude had accomplished that he could not seem to commend her enough. In the middle of his praises he broke off abruptly and gazed at her in speechless adoration. He thought it was too good to be true that anything so sweet and so beautiful would some day be his very own.

"Why do you look at me so strangely?" asked the girl.

"I'm just thinking that the best of it all is that you will be mine."

Gertrude could not say anything, but she ran her hand caressingly over the big log which was to form a portion of the wall of that house in which she and Ingmar were to live. She felt that protection and love were in store for her, for the man she was going to marry was good and wise, noble and faithful.

Just then an old woman passed by. She walked rapidly, muttering to herself, as if terribly incensed over something: "Aye, aye, their happiness shall last no longer than from daybreak to rosy dawn. When the trial comes, their faith will be broken as though it were a rope spun from moss, and their lives shall be as a long darkness."

"Surely she can't mean us!" said the young girl.

"How could that apply to us?" laughed the young man.

The Ingmar Farm

It was the day after the meeting of the Hellgumists, and a Saturday. A blizzard was raging. The pastor, who had been called to the bedside of a sick person who lived way up at the north end of the great forest, was driving homeward late in the evening under great difficulties. His horse sank deep in the snowdrifts, and the sledge was time after time on the point of being upset. Both the pastor and his hired man were continually getting out to kick away the snow for a path. Happily it was not very dark. The moon came rolling out from behind the snow clouds, big and full, shedding its silvery light upon the ground. Glancing upward, the pastor noticed that the air was thick with whirling and flying snowflakes.

In some places they made their way quite easily. There were short stretches of road where the flying snow had not settled, and others where the snow was deep, but loose and even. The really troublesome thing was trying to get over the ground where the drifts were piled so high that one could not even look over them, and where they were obliged to turn from the road, and to drive across fields and hedges, at the risk of being dumped into a ditch or having the horse spiked on a fence rail.

Both the pastor and his servant spoke with much concern of the drift which always, after a heavy snow, was banked against a high boarding close to the Ingmar Farm. "If we can only clear that we are as good as at home," they said.

The pastor remembered how often he had asked Big Ingmar to remove the high boarding that was the cause of so much snow drifting toward that particular spot. But nothing had ever been done about it. Even though everything else on the Ingmar Farm had undergone changes, certainly those old boards were never disturbed.

At last they were within sight of the farm. And, sure enough, there was the snowdrift in its usual place, as high as a wall and as hard as a rock! Here there was no possibility of their turning to one side; they had no choice but to drive right over it. The thing looked impossible, so the servant asked whether he hadn't better go down to the farm and get some help. But to this the pastor would not consent. He had not exchanged a word with either Karin or Halvor in upward of five years, and the thought of meeting old friends with whom one is no longer on speaking terms, was no more pleasant to him than it is to most people.

So up the drift the horse had to mount. The icy crust held until the animal had reached the top, then it gave way and the horse suddenly disappeared from sight, as if into a grave, while the two men sat gazing down helplessly. One of the traces had snapped; so they could not have gone farther even if they had been able to get the horse out of the drift.

A few minutes later the pastor stepped into the living-room at the Ingmar Farm. A blazing log fire was burning on the hearth. The housewife sat at one side of the fireplace spinning fine carded wool; behind her were the maids, seated in a long row, spinning flax. The men had taken possession of the other side of the fireplace. They had just come in from their work; some were resting, others, to pass the time, had taken up some light work, such as whittling sticks, sharpening rakes, and making axe handles.

When the pastor told of his mishap, they all bestirred themselves, and the menservants went out to dig the horse out of the drift. Halvor led the pastor up to the table, and asked him to sit down. Karin sent the maids into the kitchen to make fresh coffee and to prepare a special supper. Then she took the pastor's big fur coat and hung it in front of the fire to dry, lighted the hanging lamp, and moved her spinning wheel up to the table, so that she could talk with the menfolk.

"I couldn't have had a better welcome had Big Ingmar himself been alive," thought the pastor.

Halvor talked at length about the weather and the state of the roads, then he asked the clergyman if he had got a good price for his grain, and if he had succeeded in getting certain repairs made that he had been wanting for such a long time. Karin then asked after the pastor's wife, and hoped that there had been some improvement in her health of late.

At that point the pastor's man came in and reported that the horse had been dug out, the trace mended, and that all was in readiness to start. But Karin and Halvor pressed the pastor to stay to supper, and would not take no for an answer.

The coffee tray was brought in. On it were the large silver coffee urn and the precious old silver sugar bowl, which was never used save at such high functions as weddings and funerals, and there were three big silver cake baskets full of fresh rusks and cookies.

The pastor's small, round eyes grew big with astonishment; he sat as if in a trance, afraid of being awakened.

Halvor showed the pastor the skin of an elk, which had been shot in the woods on the Ingmar Farm. The skin was then spread out upon the floor. The pastor declared that he had never seen a larger or more beautiful hide. Then Karin went up to Halvor and whispered in his ear. Immediately Halvor turned to the clergyman, and asked him to accept the skin as a gift.

Karin bustled back and forth, between the table and the cupboard, and brought out some choice old silverware. She had spread a fine hemstitched cloth on the table, which she was dressing as if for a grand party. She poured milk and unfermented beer into huge silver jugs.

When they had finished supper, the pastor excused himself, and rose to go. Halvor Halvorsson and two of his hired men went with him to open a way through the drifts, steadying the sledge whenever it was about to upset, and never leaving him till he was safe within his own dooryard.

The parson was thinking how pleasant it was to renew old friendships, as he bade Halvor a hearty good-bye. Halvor stood feeling for something in his pocket. Presently he pulled out a slip of folded paper. He wondered whether the pastor would mind taking it now. It was an announcement which was to be read after the service in the morning. If the pastor would be good enough to take it, it would save him the bother of sending it to the church by a special messenger.

When the pastor had gone inside, he lighted the lamp, unfolded the paper, and read:

"In consequence of the owner's contemplated removal to Jerusalem, the Ingmar Farm is offered for sale—"

He read no farther. "Well, well, so now it has come upon us," he murmured, as if speaking of a storm. "This is what I've been expecting for many a long year!"

Hök Matts Ericsson

It was a beautiful day in spring. A peasant and his son were on their way to the great ironworks, which are situated close to the southern boundary of the parish. As they lived up at the north end, they had to traverse almost the entire length of the parish. They went past newly sown fields, where the grain was just beginning to spring up. They saw all the green rye fields and all the fine meadows, where the clover would soon be reddening and sending forth its sweet fragrance.

They also walked past a number of houses which were being repainted, and fitted up with new windows and glass-enclosed verandas, and past gardens where spading and planting were going on. All whom they met along the way had muddy shoes and grimy hands from working in fields and vegetable gardens, where they had been planting potatoes, setting out cabbages, and sowing turnips and carrots.

The peasant simply had to stop and ask them what kind of potatoes they were planting and just when they had sown their oats. At sight of a calf or a foal, he at once began to figure out how old it was. He calculated the number of cows they would be likely to keep at such and such a farm, and wondered how much this or that colt would fetch when broken.

The son tried time after time to turn his father's thought away from such things. "I'm thinking that you and I will soon be wandering through the valley of Sharon and the desert of Judea," he said.

The father smiled, and his face brightened for a moment.

"It will indeed be a blessed privilege to walk in the footsteps of
our dear Lord Jesus," he answered. But the next minute, on
seeing a couple of cartloads of quicklime, his thoughts were
diverted. "I say, Gabriel, who do you suppose is hauling lime?
Folks say that lime as a fertilizer makes a rich crop. That will be
something to feast your eyes on in the fall."

"In the fall, father!" said the son reprovingly.

"Yes, I know," returned the farmer, "that by fall I shall
be dwelling in the tents of Jacob and labouring in the Lord's
vineyard."

"Amen!" cried the son. "So be it. Amen!"

Then they walked on in silence for a space, watching the
signs of spring. Water trickled in the ditches, and the road itself
was badly broken up from the spring rains. Whichever way they
looked there was work to be done. Every one wanted to turn to
and help, even when crossing some field other than his own.

"To tell the truth," said the farmer thoughtfully, "I wish I
had sold my property some fall, when the work was over. It's
hard having to leave it all in the springtime, just when you'd like
to take hold with might and main."

The son only shrugged; he knew that he would have to
let the old man talk.

"It's just thirty-one years now since I, as a young man,
bought a piece of waste land on the north side of this parish,"
said the farmer. "The ground had never been touched by a spade.
Half of it was bog, the other half a mass of stones. It looked
pretty bad. On that very land I worked like a slave, digging up
stones until my back was ready to break. But I think I laboured
even harder with the swamp, before I finally got it drained and
filled in."

"Yes, you have certainly worked hard, father," the son
admitted. "This is why God thinks of you, and summons you to
His Holy Land."

"At first," the farmer went on, "I lived in a hovel that
wasn't much better than a charcoaler's hut. It was made of
unstripped logs, with only sod for a roof. I could never make that
but water tight; so the rains always came in. It was mighty
uncomfortable, especially at night. The cow and the horse fared
no better than I; the whole of the first winter they were housed in

a mud cave that was as dark as a cellar."

"Father, how can you be so attached to a place where you have suffered such hardships?"

"But only think of the joy of it when I was able to build a big barn for the animals, and when year by year my livestock increased so that I was always having to add new extensions for housing them. If I were not going to sell the place now, I should have to put a new roof on the barn. This would have been just the time to do it—as soon as I'd finished with the sowing."

"Father, you are to do your sowing in that land where some seeds fall among thorns, some on stony ground, some by the wayside, and some on good ground."

"And the old cottage," the farmer pursued, "which I built after the first hut, I had thought of pulling down this year, to put up a fine new dwelling house. What's to be done now with all the timber that we two hauled home in the winter? It was mighty tough work getting it down. The horses were hard driven, and so were we."

The son began to feel troubled. He thought his father was slipping away from him. He feared that the old man was not going to offer his property to the Lord in the right spirit. "Well," he argued, "but what are new houses and barns as compared with the blessed privilege of living a pure life among people who are of one mind?"

"Hallelujah!" cried the father. "Don't you suppose I know that a wonderful portion has been allotted to us? Am I not on my way to the works to sell my property to the Company? When I come back this way everything will be gone, and I shall have nothing I can call mine."

The son did not reply, but he was pleased to hear that his father still held to his decision.

Presently they came to a farm beautifully situated on a hill. There was a white-painted dwelling house, with a balcony and a veranda, and round the house were tall poplars whose pretty silvery stems were swollen with sap.

"Look!" said the farmer. "That was just the sort of house I meant to have—with a veranda and a balcony and a lot of ornamental woodwork, and with just such a well-mown lawn in front. Wouldn't that have been nice, Gabriel?"

As the son said nothing, the farmer concluded that he must be tired of hearing about the farm, so he, too, lapsed into silence although his thoughts were still upon his home. He wondered how the horses would fare with their new owners, and how things in general would be run on the place. "My goodness!" he muttered under his breath, "I'm surely doing a foolish thing in selling out to a corporation! They'll go and cut down all the trees, and let the farm go to waste. It would be just like them to allow the land to become marshy again, and to let the birch woods grow down into the fields."

They had at last reached the works, where the farmer's interest was again roused. There he saw ploughs and harrows of the latest pattern, and was suddenly reminded that for a long time he had been thinking of getting a new reaper. Gazing fondly at his good-looking son, he pictured him sitting on a fine, red-painted reaper, cracking his whip over the horses, and mowing down the thick, waving grass, as a war hero mows down his enemies. And as he stepped into the office he seemed to hear the clicking noise of the reaper, the soft swish of falling grass and the shrill chirp and light flutter of frightened birds and insects.

On the desk in there lay the deed. The negotiations had been concluded, and the price settled upon; all that was needed to complete the deal was his signature.

While the deed was being read to him he sat quietly listening. He heard that there were so and so many acres of woodland, and so and so many of arable land and meadow, so and so many head of cattle, and such and such household furnishings, all of which he must turn over. His features became set.

"No," he said to himself, "it mustn't happen."

After the reading he was about to say that he had changed his mind, when his son bent down and whispered to him:

"Father, it's a choice between me and the farm, for I'm going anyway no matter what you do."

The peasant had been so completely taken up with thoughts of his farm that it had not occurred to him that his son would leave him. So Gabriel would go in any case! He could not quite make this out. He would never have thought of leaving had his son decided to remain at home. But, naturally, wherever his son went, he, too, must go.

He stepped up to the desk, where the deed was now spread out for him to sign. The manager himself handed him the pen, and pointed to the place where he was to write his name.

"Here," he said, "here's where you write your name in full—'Hök Matts Ericsson.'"

When he took the pen it flashed across his mind how, thirty-one years back, he had signed a deed whereby he had acquired a bit of barren land. He remembered that after writing his name, he had gone out to inspect his new property. Then this thought had come to him: "See what God has given you! Here you have work to keep you going a lifetime."

The manager, thinking his hesitancy was due to uncertainty as to where he should write his name, again pointed to the place.

"The name must be written there. Now write 'Hök Matts Ericsson.'"

He put the pen to the paper. "This," he mused, "I write for the sake of my faith and my soul's salvation; for the sake of my dear friends the Hellgumists, that I may be allowed to live with them in the unity of the spirit, and so as not to be left alone here when they all go."

And he wrote his first name.

"And this," he went on thinking, "I write for the sake of my son Gabriel, so I shan't have to lose the dear, good lad who has always been so kind to his old father, and to let him see that after all he is dearer to me than aught else."

And then he wrote his middle name.

"But this," he thought as he moved the pen for the third time, "why do I write this?" Then, all at once, his hand began to move, as of itself, up and down the page, leaving great black streaks upon the hateful document. "This I do because I'm an old man and must go on tilling the soil—go on plowing and sowing in the place where I have always worked and slaved."

Hök Matts Ericsson looked rather sheepish when he turned to the manager and showed him the paper.

"You'll have to excuse me, sir," he said. "It really was

my intention to part with my property, but when it came to the scratch, I couldn't do it."

The Auction

One day in May there was an auction sale at the Ingmar Farm, and what a perfect day it was!—quite as warm as in the summertime. The men had all discarded their long white sheepskin coats and were wearing their short jackets; the women already went about in the loose-sleeved white blouses which belonged with their summer dress.

The schoolmaster's wife was getting ready to attend the auction. Gertrude did not care to go, and Storm was too busy with his class work. When Mother Stina was all ready to start, she opened the door to the schoolroom, and nodded a good-bye to her husband. Storm was then telling the children the story of the destruction of the great city of Nineveh, and the look on his face was so stern and threatening that the poor youngsters were almost frightened to death.

Mother Stina, on her way to the Ingmar Farm, stopped whenever she came to a hawthorn in bloom, or a hillock decked with white, sweet-scented lilies of the valley.

"Where could you find anything lovelier than this," she thought, "even if you were to go as far away as Jerusalem?"

The schoolmaster's wife, like many others, had come to love the old parish more than ever since the Hellgumists had called it a second Sodom and wanted to abandon it. She plucked a few of the tiny wild flowers that grew by the roadside, and gazed at them almost tenderly. "If we were as bad as they try to make us out," she mused, "it would be an easy matter for God to destroy us. He need only let the cold continue and keep the ground covered with snow. But when our Lord allows the spring and the flowers to return, He must at least think us fit to live."

When Mother Stina finally reached the Ingmar Farm she halted and glanced round timidly. "I think I'll go back," she said to herself. "I could never standby and see this dear old home broken up." But all the same she was far too curious to find out what was to be done with the farm to turn back.

As soon as it became known that the farm was for sale, Ingmar put in a bid for it. But Ingmar had only about six thousand kroner, and Halvor had already been offered twenty-five thousand by the management of the big Bergsana sawmills and ironworks. Ingmar succeeded in borrowing enough money to enable him to offer an equally large sum. The Company then raised its bid to thirty thousand, which was more than Ingmar dared offer; for he could not think of assuming so heavy a debt. The worst of it was, that not only would the homestead by this means pass out of the hands of the Ingmars for all time—for the Company was never known to part with anything once it became its property—but moreover it was not likely that it would allow Ingmar to run the sawmill at Langfors Falls, in which case he would be deprived of his living. Then he would have to give up all thought of marrying Gertrude in the fall, as had been planned. It might even be necessary for him to go elsewhere, to seek employment.

When Mother Stina thought of this, she did not feel very pleasantly disposed toward Karin and Halvor. "I hope to goodness that Karin won't come up and speak to me!" she muttered to herself. "For if she does, I'll just have to let her know what I think of her treatment of Ingmar. After all, it's her fault that the farm does not already belong to him. I've been told that they'll need a lot of money for the journey. Just the same it seems mighty strange that Karin can have the heart to sell the old place to a corporation that would cut down all the timber and let the fields go to waste."

There was some one outside the corporation who wished to buy the place; it was the rich district judge, Berger Sven Persson. Mother Stina felt that such an arrangement would be better for Ingmar, as Sven Persson was a generous man, who would surely let him keep the sawmill. "Sven Persson will not forget that he was once a poor goose boy on this farm," she reflected; "and that it was Big Ingmar who first took him in hand and gave him a start in life."

Mother Stina did not go into the house, but remained in the yard, as did most of the people who had come to attend the sale. She sat down on a pile of boards, and began to glance about her very carefully, as one is wont to do when taking a last look at some beloved spot.

Surrounding the farmyard on three sides were ranges of outbuildings, and in the centre was a little storehouse propped on four posts. Nothing looked particularly old, with the exception of the porch with the carved moulding at the entrance to the dwelling-house, and another one, still older, with stout twisted pillars, at the entrance of the washhouse.

Mother Stina thought of all the old Ingmarssons whose feet had trod the yard. She seemed to see them coming home from their work in the evening, and gathering around the hearth, tall and somewhat bent, always afraid of intruding themselves, or of accepting more than they felt was their due.

And she thought of the industry and honesty which had always been practised on this farm. "It ought never to be allowed!" was her thought as regards the auction. "The king should be told of it!" Mother Stina took it more to heart than if it had been a question of parting with her own home.

The sale had not yet begun, but a good many people had arrived. Some had gone into the barns to look over the live stock; others remained out in the yard examining the farm implements placed there for inspection. Mother Stina on seeing a couple of peasant women come out of a cowshed grew indignant. "Just look at Mother Inga and Mother Stava!" she muttered. "Now they've been in and picked out a cow apiece. Think how they'll be going around bragging that they've got a cow of the old breed from the Ingmar Farm!"

When she saw old Crofter Nils trying to choose a plow she smiled a little scornfully.

"Crofter Nils will think himself a real farmer when he can drive a plough that Big Ingmar himself has used."

More and more people kept gathering round the things to be auctioned off. The men looked wonderingly at many of the farming tools, which were of such old-time make that it was difficult to guess what they had been used for. A few spectators had the temerity to laugh at the old sleighs some of which were from ancient times and were gorgeously painted in red and green; and the harnesses that went with them were studded with white shells, and fringed with tassels of many colours.

Mother Stina seemed to see the old Ingmarssons driving slowly in these old sleighs, going to a party or coming home from a church wedding, with a bride seated beside them. "Many good people are leaving the parish," she sighed. For to her it was as if all the old Ingmars had gone on living at the farm up to that very day, when their implements and their old carts and sleds were being hawked about.

"I wonder where Ingmar is keeping himself, and how he feels? When it seems so dreadful to me, what must it be for him?"

The weather being so fine, the auctioneer proposed that they carry out all the things that were to go under the hammer, so as to avoid any overcrowding of the rooms. So maids and farm hands carried out boxes and chests, all painted in tulips and roses, Some of them had been standing in the attic, undisturbed, for centuries. They also brought out silver jugs and old-fashioned copper kettles, spinning-wheels and carders, and all kinds of odd-looking weaving appliances. The peasant women gathered around all these old treasures, picking them up and turning them over.

Mother Stina had not intended to buy anything, when she remembered that there was supposed to be a loom here on which could be woven the finest damask, and went up to look for it. Just then a maid came out with a huge Bible, which, with its thick leather bindings and its brass clasps and mountings, was so heavy that she could hardly carry it.

Mother Stina was as astounded as if some one had struck her in the face; and went back to her seat. She knew, of course, that no one nowadays reads these old Bibles, with their obsolete and antiquated language, but just the same it seemed strange that Karin would want to sell it.

It was perhaps the very Bible the old housewife was reading when they came and told her that her husband, the great-

grandfather of young Ingmar, had been killed by a bear.
Everything that Mother Stina saw had something to tell her. The
old silver buckles lying on the table had been taken from the
trolls in Mount Klack by an Ingmar Ingmarsson. In the rickety
chaise over yonder the Ingmar Ingmarsson who had lived during
her childhood had driven to church. She remembered that every
time he had passed by her and her mother on their way to
church, the mother had nudged her and said: "Now you must
curtsy, Stina, fox here comes Ingmar Ingmarsson."

She used to wonder why it was that her mother always
wanted her to curtsy to Ingmar Ingmarsson; she had never been
so particular when it came to the judge or the bailiff.

Afterward she was told that when her mother was a little
girl and went to church with her mother, the latter had always
nudged her and said: 'Now you must curtsy, Stina, for here
comes Ingmar Ingmarsson."

"God knows," sighed Mother Stina, "it's not only
because I had expected that Gertrude would some day have been
mistress here that I grieve, but it seems to me as if the whole
parish were done for."

Just then the pastor came along, looking solemn and
depressed. He did not stop an instant, but went straight to the
house. Mother Stina surmised that he had come to plead
Ingmar's cause with Karin and Halvor.

Shortly after, the manager of the sawmills at Bergsåna
arrived, and also judge Persson. The manager, who was there in
the interest of the corporation, straightway went inside, but Sven
Persson walked about in the yard for a while and looked at the
things. Presently he stopped in front of a little old man with a big
beard, who was sitting on the same pile of boards as Mother
Stina.

"I don't suppose you happen to know, Strong Ingmar,
whether Ingmar Ingmarsson has decided to buy the timber I
offered him?"

"He says no," the old man answered, "but I shouldn't be
surprised if he were to change his mind soon." At the same time
he winked and jerked his thumb in the direction of Mother Stina,
thus cautioning Sven Persson not to let her hear what they were
talking about.

"I should think he'd be satisfied to accept my terms," said the Judge. "I don't make these offers everyday; but this I'm doing for Big Ingmar's sake."

"You're right about its being a good offer," the old man agreed, "but he says that he has already made a deal else where."

"I wonder if he has really considered what it is that he's losing?" said Sven Persson, and walked on.

Thus far none of the Ingmarsson family had been seen about the yard; but presently young Ingmar was discovered standing leaning against a wall, quite motionless, and with his eyes half closed. Now a number of people got up to go over and shake hands with him, but when they were quite close, they bethought themselves and went back to their seats.

Ingmar was deathly pale, and every one who looked at him could see that he was suffering keenly; therefore, no one ventured to speak to him. He stood so quietly that many had not even noticed that he was there. But those who had could think of nothing else. Here there was none of the merriment which usually prevails at auctions. With Ingmar standing there, hugging the wall of the old home he was about to lose, they felt no inclination to laugh or to joke.

Then came a moment for the opening of the auction. The auctioneer mounted a chair, and began to offer the first lot—an old plow.

Ingmar never moved. He was more like a statue than a human being.

"Good heavens! why can't he go away?" said the people. "He doesn't have to stay here and witness this miserable business. But the Ingmarssons never behave like other folks."

The hammer then fell for the first sale. Ingmar started as if it had caught him; but in a moment he again became motionless. But at every ring of the hammer a shudder went through him.

Two peasant women passed just in front of Mother Stina; they were talking about Ingmar.

"Think! If he had only proposed to some rich farmer's daughter he might have had enough money to buy the farm; but of course he's going to marry the schoolmaster's Gertrude," said one.

"They say that a rich and influential man has offered to give him the Ingmar Farm as a wedding present, if he will marry his daughter," said the other. "You see, they don't mind his being poor, because he belongs to such a good family."

"Anyway, there's some advantage in being the son of Big Ingmar."

"It would indeed have been a good thing if Gertrude had had a little, so that she could have given him a lift," thought Mother Stina.

When all the farming implements had been sold, the auctioneer moved over to another part of the yard, where the household linens were piled. He then bean to offer for sale home-woven fabrics—table cloths, bed linen, and hangings, holding them up so that the embroidered tulips and the various fancy weaves could be seen all over the yard.

Ingmar must have noticed the light flutter of the linen pieces as they were being held aloft, for he involuntarily glanced up. For a moment his tired eyes looked out upon the desecration, then he turned away.

"I've never seen the like of that," said a young peasant girl. "The poor boy looks as if he were dying. If he'd only go away instead of standing here tormenting himself!"

Mother Stina suddenly jumped to her feet as if to cry out that this thing must be stopped; then she sat down again. "I mustn't forget that I'm only a poor old woman," she sighed.

All at once there was a dead silence, which made Mother Stina look up. The silence was due to the sudden appearance of Karin, who had just come out from the house. Now it was quite plain what they all thought of Karin and her dealings, for as she went across the yard every one drew back. No one put out a hand to greet her, no one spoke to her; they simply stared disapprovingly.

Karin looked tired and worn, and stooped more than usual. A bright red spot appeared on both cheeks, and she looked as miserable as in the days when she had had her struggles with Elof. She had come out to find Mother Stina and ask her to go inside. "I didn't know till just now that you were here, Mother Storm," she said.

Mother Stina at first declined, but was finally persuaded.

"We want all the old antagonisms to be forgotten now that we are going away," said Karin.

While they were going toward the house Mother Stina ventured: "This must be a trying day for you, Karin."

Karin's only response was a sigh.

"I don't see how you can have the heart to sell all these old things, Karin."

"It is what one loves most that one must first and foremost sacrifice to the Lord," said Karin.

"Folks think it strange—" Mother Stina began, but Karin cut her short.

"The Lord, too, would think it strange if we held back anything we had offered in His Name."

Mother Stina bit her lip. She could not bring herself to say anything further. All the reproaches which she had meant to heap upon Karin stuck in her throat. There was an air of lofty dignity about Karin that disarmed people; therefore, no one had the courage to upbraid her. When they were on the broad step in front of the porch, Mother Stina tapped Karin on the shoulder.

"Have you noticed who is standing over there?" she asked, and pointed to Ingmar.

Karin winced a little, but was careful not to look over at her brother. "The Lord will find a way out for him," she murmured. "The Lord will surely find away out."

To all appearances the living-room was not much changed by reason of the auction, for in there the seats and cupboards and bedsteads were stationary. But shining copper utensils no longer adorned the walls, the built-in bedsteads looked bare, stripped of their coverings and hangings, and the doors of the blue-painted cupboards, which in the old days were always left standing half open, to let visitors see the great silver jugs and beakers that filled its shelves, were now closed; which meant that there was nothing inside worth showing. The only wall decoration the room boasted was the Jerusalem canvas, which on that day had a fresh wreath around it.

The large room was thronged with relatives and coreligionists of Halvor and Karin. One after another, they were conducted with much ceremony to a large, well-spread table, for refreshments.

The door to the inside room was closed. In there
negotiations for the sale of the farm itself were pending. The
talking was loud and heated, especially on the part of the pastor.

In the living-room, on the other hand, the people were
very quiet, and when any one spoke, it was in hushed tones; for
every one's thoughts were in the little room where the fate of the
farm was being settled.

Mother Stina turned to Gabriel, saying: "I suppose
there's no chance of Ingmar getting the farm?"

"The bidding has gone far beyond his figure by now,"
Gabriel replied. "The innkeeper from Karmsund is said to have
offered thirty-two thousand, and the Company's bid has been
raised to thirty-five. The pastor is now trying to persuade Karin
and Halvor to let it go to the innkeeper rather than to the
Company."

"But what about Berger Sven Persson?"

"It seems that he has not made any bid to-day."

The pastor was still talking. He was evidently pleading
with some one. They could not hear what he said, but they knew
that no decision had been reached or the pastor would not have
gone on talking.

Then came a moment of silence, after which the
innkeeper was heard to say, not exactly loudly, but with a
clearness that made every word carry: "I bid thirty-six thousand,
not that I think the place is worth that much, but I can't bear the
thought of its becoming a corporation property."

Immediately after there was a noise as of some one
striking a table with his fist, and the manager of the Company
was heard to shout: "I bid forty thousand, and more than that
Karin and Halvor are not likely to get."

Mother Stina, who had turned as white as a sheet, got up
and went back to the yard. It was dreary enough out there, but
not as insufferable as sitting in the close room listening to the
haggling.

The sale of linen was over; the auctioneer had again
changed his place, and was about to cry out the old family
silverware—the heavy silver jugs inlaid with gold coin, and the
beakers bearing inscriptions from the seventeenth century. When
he held up the first jug, Ingmar started forward as if to stop the

sale, but restrained himself at once, and went back to his place.

A few minutes later an old peasant came bearing the silver jug, which he respectfully deposited at Ingmar's feet. "You must keep this as a souvenir of all that by right should have been yours," he said.

Again a tremor passed through Ingmar's body; his lips quivered, and he tried to say something.

"You needn't say anything now," said the old peasant. "That will keep till another time." He withdrew a few paces, then suddenly turned back. "I hear that folks are saying you could take over the farm if you cared to. It would be the greatest service you could render this parish."

There were a number of old servants living at the farm, who had been there from early youth. Now that old age had overtaken them they still stayed on, and over these hung a pall of uncertainty such as had not touched the others. They feared that under a new master they would be turned out of their old home to become beggars. Or, whatever happened, they knew in their hearts that no stranger would care for them as their old master and mistress had done. These poor old pensioners wandered restlessly about the farmyard all day long. Seeing them shrink past, frail and helpless, with a look of hopeless appeal in their weak, watery eyes, every one felt sorry for them.

Finally one old man, who was nearly a hundred, hobbled up to Ingmar, and sat down on the ground quite close to him. It seemed to be the only place where he could be at ease, for there he remained quietly, resting his shaky old hands on the crook of his cane. And as soon as old Lisa and Cowhouse Martha saw where Pickaxe Bengt had taken refuge, they, too, came tottering up, and sat down at Ingmar's feet. They did not speak to him, but somehow they must have had a vague idea that he would be able to protect them—he who was now Ingmar Ingmarsson.

Ingmar no longer kept his eyes closed. He stood looking down at them, as if he were counting up all the years and all the trials through which they had lived, serving his people; and it seemed to him that his first duty was to see that they be allowed to live out their days in their old home. He glanced out over the yard, caught the eye of Strong Ingmar, and nodded to him, significantly.

Whereupon Strong Ingmar, without a word, went straight to the house. He passed through the living-room to the inner room, and stationed himself by the door, where he waited for an opportunity to deliver his message.

The pastor was standing in the middle of the room talking to Karin and Halvor, who were sitting as stiff and motionless as a pair of mummies. The manager from Bergsåna was at the table looking confident, for he knew that he was in a position to outbid all the others. The innkeeper from Karmsund was standing at the window, in such a fever of agitation that great beads of sweat came out on his forehead, and his hands shook. Berger Sven Persson sat on the sofa at the far end of the room, twiddling his thumbs, his hands clasped over his stomach, his big commanding face impassive.

The pastor was done talking, and Halvor glanced over at Karin for advice; but she sat as if in a trance, staring blankly at the floor.

Then Halvor turned to the pastor, and said: "Karin and I have got to consider that we are going to a strange land, and that we and the brethren must live on the money we can get for the farm. We've been told that the fare alone to Jerusalem will cost us fifteen thousand kroner. And then, afterward, we must get a house and keep ourselves in food and clothes. So we can hardly afford to give anything away."

"It's unreasonable of you people to expect Karin and Halvor to sell the farm for a mere song, just because you don't want the Company to have it!" said the manager. "It seems to me that it would be well to accept my offer at once, if for no other reason than to put an end to all these useless arguments."

"Yes," Karin spoke up, "we'd better take the highest bid."

But the parson was not so easily beaten! When it came to a question of handling a worldly matter he always knew just what to say. Now he was the man, and not the preacher.

"I'm sure that Karin and Halvor care enough about this old farm to want to sell to some person who would keep up the property, even if they have to take a couple of thousand kroner less," he said.

Then he proceeded to tell—for Karin's special benefit—

of various farms that had gone to waste after falling into the hands of corporations.

Once or twice Karin glanced up at the pastor. He wondered whether he had finally succeeded in making some impression upon her. "There must surely be a little of the pride of the old peasant matron still left in her," he thought as he went on telling of tumbledown farmhouses and underfed cattle.

He finally ended with these words: "I know perfectly well that if the corporation is fully determined to buy the Ingmar Farm, it can go on bidding against the farmers until they are forced to give up; but if Karin and Halvor want to prevent this old place from becoming a ruined corporation property, they will have to settle on a price, so that the farmers may know what to be guided by."

When the pastor made that proposition, Halvor, uneasy, glanced over at Karin, who slowly raised her eyelids.

"Certainly Halvor and I would rather sell the place to some one of our own kind. Then we could go away from here knowing that everything would continue in the old way."

"If some person outside the Company wants to give forty thousand for the property, we will be satisfied to accept that sum for it," said Halvor, knowing at last what his wife's wishes were.

When that was said, Strong Ingmar walked over to Sven Persson and whispered to him.

Judge Persson immediately arose and went up to Halvor. "Since you say you are willing to take forty thousand kroner for the farm, I'll buy it at that figure," he said.

Halvor's face began to twitch, and a lump seemed to rise in his throat; he had to swallow before he could speak. "Thank you, judge," he finally stammered. "I'm glad that I can leave the farm in such good hands!"

Judge Persson then shook hands with Karin, who was so moved that she could hardly keep back the tears.

"You may be sure, Karin, that everything here will be as of old," he said.

"Are you going to live at the farm yourself?" Karin inquired.

"No," said he, then added with great solemnity: "My youngest daughter is to be married in the summer, and she and

her husband are to have the farm as a gift from me." He then
turned to the pastor and thanked him.

"Well, Parson, you'll have it your own way," he said. "I
never dreamed in the days when I was a poor goose boy on this
place that some time it would be in my power to arrange for an
Ingmar Ingmarsson to come back to the Ingmar Farm!"

The pastor and the other men all stood staring at the
judge in dumb amazement, not grasping at first what was meant.

Karin left the room at once. While passing through the
living-room to the yard, she drew herself up, retied her
headkerchief, and smoothed out her apron. Then, with an air of
solemn dignity, she went straight up to Ingmar and grasped his
hand.

"Let me congratulate you, Ingmar," she said, her voice
shaking with joy. "You and I have been strongly opposed to
each other of late in matters of religion; but since God does not
grant me the solace of having you with us, I thank Him for
allowing you to become master of the old farm."

Ingmar did not speak. His hand lay limp in Karin's, and
when she let it drop, he stood there looking just as unhappy as he
had looked all day.

The men who had been inside at the final settlement
came out now, and shook hands with Ingmar, offering their
congratulations. "Good luck to you, Ingmar Ingmarsson of the
Ingmar Farm!" they said.

At that a glimmer of happiness crossed Ingmar's face,
and he murmured softly to himself: "Ingmar Ingmarsson of the
Ingmar Farm." He was like a child that has just received a gift it
has long been wishing for. But the next moment his expression
changed to one of intense revolt and repugnance, as if he would
have thrust the coveted prize from him.

In a flash the news had spread .all over the farm. People
talked loudly and questioned eagerly; some were so pleased they
wept for joy. No one listened now to the cries of the auctioneer,
but everybody crowded around Ingmar to wish him happiness—
peasants and gentlefolk, friends and strangers, alike.

Ingmar, standing there, surrounded by all these happy
people, suddenly looked up. He then saw Mother Stina, standing
a little apart from the others, her eyes fixed on him. She was

very pale, and looked old and poor. As he met her gaze, she turned and walked away.

Ingmar hastily left the others and hurried after her. Then bending down to her, every muscle of his face aquiver with grief, he said in a husky voice:

"Go home to Gertrude, Mother Stina, and tell her that I have betrayed her, that I've sold myself for the farm. Tell her never to think more of such a miserable wretch as I."

Gertrude

Something strange had come over Gertrude that she could neither stay nor control—something that grew and grew until it finally threatened to take complete possession of her.

It began at the moment when she learned that Ingmar had failed her. It was really a boundless fear of seeing Ingmar again—of suddenly meeting him on the road, or at church, or elsewhere. Why that would be such a terrible thing she hardly knew, but she felt that she could never endure it.

Gertrude would have preferred shutting herself in, day and night, so as to be sure of not meeting Ingmar; but that was not possible for a poor girl like her. She had to go out and work in the garden, and every morning and evening she was obliged to tramp the long distance from the house to the pasture to milk the cows, and she was often sent to the village store to buy sugar and meal and whatever else was needed in the house.

When Gertrude went out on the road she would always draw her kerchief far down over her face, keep her eyes lowered, and rush on as if fiends were pursuing her. As soon as she could, she would turn from the highroad, and take the narrow bypaths alongside the ditches and drains, where she felt there was less likelihood of her meeting Ingmar.

Never for a moment did she feel free from fear; for there was not a single place in all the parish where she could feel certain of not running across him. If she went rowing on the river, he might be there floating his timber, or if she ventured into the depths of the forest, he might cross her path on his way to work.

When weeding in the garden, she would often glance down the road, so that she might see if he were approaching, and make her escape. Ingmar was so well known about the place that her dog would not have barked at sight of him, and her pigeons, that strutted about the gravel walk, would not have flown up and warned her of his approach with the rustle of their flapping wings.

Gertrude's haunting dread did not diminish, but rather increased from day to day. All her grief had turned to fear, and her strength to combat it grew less and less. "Soon I shall not dare venture outside the door," she thought. "I may get to be a bit queer and morose, even if I don't become quite insane. God, God, take this awful fear away from me!" she prayed. "I can see that my mother and father think I'm not right in my head; and every one else must think the same. Oh, dear Lord God, help me!" she cried.

When this fear condition was at its worst, it happened one night that Gertrude had an extraordinary dream. She dreamed that she had gone out, with her milk pail on her arm, to do the milking. The cows were grazing in an enclosed meadow near the skirt of the forest, a long way from home. She went by the narrow paths, alongside the ditches and field drains. She had great difficulty in walking, for she felt so weak and weary that she could hardly lift her feet. "What can be the matter with me?" she asked herself, in the dream. "Why is it so hard for me to walk?" And she also answered herself. "You are tired because you carry about with you this heavy burden of sorrow."

When she finally got to the pasturage, there were no cows in sight. She became uneasy, and began to look for them in their usual haunts—behind the brushwood, over by the brook, and under the birches—but there was not a sign of them. While searching for the cows she discovered a gap in the hedge, on the side fronting the forest. She grew terribly alarmed, and stood wringing her hands. It suddenly occurred to her that the cows must have cleared this opening. "Tired as I am, must I now tramp the whole forest to find them!" she whimpered, in her dream.

But she went straight on into the woods, slowly pushing her way through fir brush and prickly juniper bushes. Presently she found herself walking on a smooth and even road without knowing how she had got there. The road was soft and rather slippery from the brown fir needles that covered it. On either side stood great towering pines, and on the yellow moss under the trees sunbeams were playing. Here it was so lovely and so peaceful that she almost forgot her fears.

Of a sudden, she caught sight of an old woman moving about in among the trees. It was Finne-Marit, she who was famed as a witch. "How dreadful that that wicked old woman is still alive," thought Gertrude, "and that I should come upon her here in the forest!" She tried to slip along very cautiously, so as not to be seen by the witch. But before Gertrude could get past, the old woman looked up.

"Hi, there!" the old woman shouted. "Wait a bit, and you'll see something!" In a twinkling, Finne-Marit was in the road and on her knees almost in front of Gertrude. Then, with her forefinger, she drew a circle in the carpet of fir needles, at the centre of which she placed a shallow brass bowl.

"Now she's going to do some conjuring," thought Gertrude. "Why, then it must be true that she is a witch!"

"Look down into the bowl!" said Finne-Marit, "and maybe you'll see something." When Gertrude glanced down, she gave a start. Mirrored in the bowl, she saw plainly the face of Ingmar. Immediately the old woman handed her a long needle. "See here," she said; "take this and pierce his eyes. Do this to him because he has played you false." Gertrude hesitated a little, but felt strongly tempted. "Why should he fare well, and be rich and happy, while you suffer?" said the old dame. With that Gertrude was seized by an uncontrollable desire to do the ogre's bidding, and lowered the needle. "Mind you stick him right in the eye!" said the witch. Whereupon Gertrude quickly drove the needle, first into one and then into the other of Ingmar's eyes. In so doing, she noticed that the needle went far down-not as though it had come into contact with metal, but rather as if it had penetrated some soft substance. When she drew it out, there was blood on it.

Gertrude, seeing blood on the needle, thought she had really put out Ingmar's eyes. Then she was so overcome by remorse for what she had done, and so frightened, that she woke up.

She lay for a long while, trembling and weeping, before she was able to convince herself that it was only a dream. "May God preserve me from any thought of vengeance!" she moaned.

She had barely quieted down and dropped off to sleep again, when the dream recurred.

Once more she wandered along the narrow paths toward the grazing ground. This time, too, the cows had strayed, and she went into the forest to look for them. Again she came to the beautiful road, and saw the sunbeams playing on the moss. Then she suddenly recalled all that had just happened to her in a dream, and grew terribly frightened lest she should meet the old witch again. Seeing nothing of her, she felt greatly relieved.

All at once she seemed to see the earth between a couple of moss tufts open. Suddenly a head appeared. Then she saw the body of a tiny little man work its way up out of the earth, and all the while the little man was making a buzzing and humming noise. By that she knew whom she had encountered. It was Humming Pete, of course, who was said to be a bit queer in his head. Sometimes he used to stay down in the village, but during the summer he always lived in a mud cave in the forest.

Then Gertrude recalled to memory what she had heard folks say of Pete: "Any one wanting to injure an enemy without risking discovery could avail himself of his services." He was suspected of having started a number of incendiary fires at the instigation of others.

Gertrude then went up to the man and asked him, half in fun, if he wouldn't like to set fire to the Ingmar Farm. She wished it done, she said, because Ingmar Ingmarsson thought more of the farm than of her.

To her horror, the half-witted dwarf was ready to act on her suggestion. Nodding gleefully, he started on a run toward the settlement. She hurried after, but could not seem to overtake him. Her dress caught in the brushwood, her feet sank in the marsh, and she stumbled over stony ground. When she was almost out of the forest, what should she see through the trees but the glow from a fire. "He has done it, he has set fire to the farm!" she shrieked, again awakening from the horror of the dream.

Now Gertrude sat up in bed; tears ran down her cheeks. She dared not sink back on her pillow again for fear of dreaming further. "Oh, Lord help me, Lord help me!" she cried. "I don't know how much evil there may be hidden in my heart, but God knows that never once during all this time have I thought of revenging myself on Ingmar. O God, let me not fall into this sin!" she prayed. Wringing her hands in an agony of despair, she cried out:

"Grief is a menace, grief is a menace, grief is a menace!"

It was not very clear to her just what she meant by that; but she felt somehow that her poor heart was like a ravaged garden, in which all the flowers had been uprooted, and now Grief, as a gardener, moved about in there, planting thistles and poisonous herbs.

The whole forenoon of the following day, Gertrude thought that she was still dreaming. Her dream had seemed so real that she could not get it out of her mind. Remembering with what satisfaction she had plunged the needle into Ingmar's eyes, she shuddered. "How dreadful that I should have become so cruel and resentful! What shall I do to rid myself of this? I'm really getting to be a very wicked person!"

After dinner Gertrude went out to milk the cows. She drew her kerchief down over her face, as usual, and kept her eyes on the ground. Walking along the narrow paths where she had wandered in the dream, even the flowers by the wayside looked the same as in the dream. In her strange state of semi-wakefulness, she could hardly distinguish between what she actually saw and what she only seemed to see in fancy.

When she reached the pasturage, there were no cows to be seen. And she began to search for them, as she had done in the dream—looking down by the brook, under the birches, and behind the brushwood. She could not find them, yet she felt quite certain that they must be thereabout, and that she would probably see them were she only wide awake. Presently she came upon an opening in the hedge, and knew at once that the cows had made their escape through this.

Gertrude straightway started in search of the strayed cattle, following the track which their hoofs had made in the soft earth of the forest. It was plain that they had turned in on a road leading to a remote Säter. "Ah!" she said, "now I know where they are. I remember that the folks down at Luck Farm were going to drive their cattle to the Säter this morning. Our cows, on hearing the tinkle of their cowbells, must have broken loose and followed the others."

Gertrude's anxiety had for the moment made her wide awake. So she determined to go up to the Säter, and fetch the cows herself; otherwise there was no telling when they would come back. Now she walked briskly along the steep and rocky road.

After going uphill for a time there was an abrupt turn in the road, and she suddenly came upon smooth and even ground that was thick with pine needles. She recognized it as the road of her dream. There stood the selfsame towering pines, and on the moss were the selfsame yellow sun spots.

At sight of the road Gertrude lapsed into the dreamy state in which she had been most of the day. She moved along, half expecting that something wonderful would happen to her. She looked under the fir trees to see if any of the mysterious beings who wander about in the depths of the forest would suddenly appear to her. However, none appeared. But in her mind new thoughts were awakened. "What if I should really take revenge on Ingmar, would that still my fears? Would I then escape the horrors of insanity? If he were to suffer what I am suffering, would that be any relief to me?"

The beautiful road seemed interminably long. She walked there a whole hour, astonished that nothing unusual had happened. The road finally ended in a forest meadow. It was a lovely spot, covered with fresh green grass and many wild flowers. On one side rose a steep mountain; the other sides were covered with high trees—mostly mountain ash, with thick clusters of white blossoms, and here and there was a group of birches and alders. A rather broad stream gushed down the mountainside and wound its way through the meadow, then went hurling down into a gap that was covered with dwarfed trees and bushes.

Gertrude stood stock still; she knew the place at once. That stream was Blackwater Brook, and strange tales were told of it. Sometimes, when crossing this stream, people had clear visions of events that were taking place elsewhere. A little lad, in crossing, once saw a bridal procession which happened just then to be moving toward the church far down in the village, and a charcoal burner once saw a king, with crown and sceptre, ride to his coronation.

Gertrude's heart was in her mouth "God have mercy on me for what I may see here!" she gasped, half tempted to turn back. "Poor little me!" she wailed, feeling sorry for herself. "But I must—I must cross here to fetch my cows."

"Dear Lord, don't let me see anything dreadful or bad!" she prayed, her hands tightly clasped, and shaking from fright. "And don't let me fall into temptation."

There was no doubt in her mind that she would see something; she was so sure of it, in fact, that she hardly dared venture out upon the stones that led across the brook. Yet something made her do it. When halfway over, all at once she saw something moving in among the trees on the other side of the brook. It was no bridal procession, however, but a solitary man, who was slowly coming toward the meadow.

The man was tall and young, and was dressed in a long black garment that came to his feet. His head was uncovered, and his hair hung in long black locks over his shoulders. He had a slender and very beautiful face. He was coming straight toward Gertrude. In his eyes, which were clear and radiant, there was a wonderful light; and when his gaze fell upon Gertrude, she felt that he could read all her sorrowful thoughts, and she saw that he pitied her whose mind was haunted by fears of the paltry things of earth, whose soul had become darkened by thoughts of revenge, and whose heart had been sown with the thistles and poison flowers of Grief.

As he drew nigh, there came over Gertrude such a blissful sense of ever growing peace and serenity! And when he had passed by, there was no longer any fear or resentment in her thought. All that was not good had vanished like a sickness of which one has been healed.

Gertrude stood rapt for a long while. The vision faded away, but she was still held by the beauty of it, and the impression of what she had seen stayed with her. Clasping her hands she raised them in ecstasy.

"I have seen the Christ!" she cried out with joy. "I have seen the Christ! He has freed me from my sorrow, and I love Him. Now I can never again love anyone else in the world."

The trials of life had suddenly dwindled into mere nothings, and life's long years appeared as but a moment in the Glass of Time, while earthly joys seemed trivial and shallow and meaningless. All at once it became clear to Gertrude how she was to order her life; so that she might never again sink down into the darkness of fear, nor be tempted into doing anything mean or hateful, she would go with the Hellgumists to Jerusalem. This thought had come to her when the Christ passed by. She felt that it had come from Him; she had read it in His eyes.

* * * * *

On the beautiful June day when the daughter of Berger Sven Persson was given in marriage to Ingmar Ingmarsson, a tall, slender young woman stopped at the Ingmar Farm early in the morning, and asked if she might speak to the bridegroom. She wore her kerchief so far down over her face that nothing could be seen of it save a creamy cheek and a pair of rosy lips. On her arm was a basket that held little bundles of handmade trimmings, a few hair chains, and hair bracelets.

She gave her message to an old maidservant, whom she met in the yard, and who went in and told the housewife. The housewife answered sharply:

"Go straight back and tell her that Ingmar Ingmarsson is just going to drive to church; he has no time to talk with her."

As soon as the young woman received this curt dismissal, she went her way. When the bridal party had returned from the church, she came back, and again asked if she might speak to Ingmar Ingmarsson. This time she approached one of the menservants who was hanging round the stable door; he went in and told the master.

"Tell her that Ingmar Ingmarsson is about to sit down to the wedding feast," said the master. "He has no time to talk to her."

On receiving this answer, she sighed and went her way.

When she came again it was late in the evening, as the sun was setting. This time she gave her message to a child that was swinging on the gate. The child ran straight to the house and told the bride.

"Tell her that Ingmar Ingmarsson is dancing with his wife," said the bride. "He has no time to talk to anyone else."

When the child came back and repeated what had been told her, the young woman smiled indulgently, and said: "Now you are telling something that isn't true. Ingmar Ingmarsson is not dancing with his bride."

This time she did not go away, but remained standing at the gate.

The bride, meanwhile, thought to herself: "I have told a lie on my wedding day!" Sorry for what she had done, she went up to Ingmar, and told him that there was a stranger outside who wished to speak with him. Ingmar went out, and found Gertrude standing at the gate, waiting.

When Gertrude saw him coming, she started down the road, Ingmar following. They walked along in silence till they were some distance away from the house.

As to Ingmar, it could be truthfully said of him that he had aged in the short time of a few weeks. At any rate, there was something about his face that showed added shrewdness and caution. He also stooped more, and looked more subdued, now that he had acquired riches, than was the case when he had nothing.

Indeed, he was anything but glad to see Gertrude! Every day since the auction he had been trying to persuade himself into the belief that he was satisfied with his bargain. "In fact, we Ingmarssons care for little else than to plow and to sow the fields on the Ingmar Farm," was what he had said to himself.

But there was something that troubled him even more than the loss of Gertrude—the thought that now there was one human being who could say of him that he had not lived up to his word. Keeping a little behind Gertrude all the while, he went over in his mind all the scornful things which she had a right to say to him.

Presently Gertrude sat down on a stone at the roadside, and put her basket on the ground; then she drew her kerchief still farther over her face.

"Sit down," she said to Ingmar, pointing to another stone. "I have many things to talk over with you."

Ingmar sat down, and was glad that he felt quite calm. "This will be easier than I had expected," he said to himself. "I thought it was going to be much harder on me to see Gertrude again, and to hear her speak. I was afraid that my love for her would get the better of me."

"I should never have come like this, and disturbed you on your wedding day, had I not been compelled to do so," said Gertrude. "I shall soon be leaving this part of the world, never to return. I was ready to start a week ago, when something came up that made it necessary for me to put off going, that I might speak with you to-day."

Ingmar sat all huddled up, with his shoulders hunched and his head drawn in, as if he were expecting a tempest, saying to himself, meanwhile: "Whatever Gertrude may think about it, I'm sure I did the right thing in choosing the farm. I should have been lost without it."

"Ingmar," said Gertrude, blushing so that the little corner of her cheek that could be seen behind the kerchief showed crimson. "You remember, of course, that five years ago I was ready to join the Hellgumists. At that time I had given my heart to Christ. But I took it back, to give it to you. In so doing, I acted wrongly, and that's why I've had to suffer all this. As I once forsook Christ, even so have I been forsaken by the one I loved."

When Ingmar perceived that Gertrude was about to tell him that she was going with the Hellgumists, he at once showed signs of disapproval. "I can't bear to have her join these Jerusalem people, and go away to a strange land," he thought. And he opposed her plan as vehemently as he would have done had he still been engaged to her. "You mustn't think like that, Gertrude," he protested. "God never meant this as a punishment to you."

"No, no, Ingmar, not as a punishment, indeed not! but only to show me how badly I had chosen the second time. Ah, this is no punishment! I feel so happy, and lack for nothing. All my sorrow has been turned into joy. You will understand this, Ingmar, when I tell you that the Lord Himself has chosen me, and called me."

Ingmar was silent; a look of weariness came into his eyes. "Don't be a fool!" he said to himself. "Let Gertrude go. To put sea and land between you and her would be the best thing that could happen—sea and land, yes, sea and land!"

And yet that something within him which did not want to let Gertrude go was, nevertheless, stronger than himself. So he said: "I can't conceive of your parents allowing you to leave them."

"That they'll never do!" Gertrude replied. "And I know it so well that I wouldn't even dare ask them. Father would never give his consent. He would use force, if necessary, to prevent my going. The hard part of it is that I shall have to sneak away. They think now that I'm going about the country selling my handiwork; so they won't know about it until I have joined the Jerusalem pilgrims at Gothenburg and am well out of Sweden."

Ingmar was very much distressed to think that Gertrude would be willing to cause her parents such heavy sorrow. "Can it be that she realizes how badly she is behaving?" he wondered. He was about to remonstrate with her, then checked himself. "You're hardly the proper person to reproach Gertrude for anything that she may do," he remarked to himself.

"Indeed, I know it will be hard on father and mother," said Gertrude, "but I must follow Jesus." And she smiled as she named the name of the Saviour. "He has saved me from destruction. He has healed my sick soul!" she said feelingly.

And as if she had only now found courage to do so, she pushed back her kerchief, and looked Ingmar straight in the eyes. It struck Ingmar that she was drawing comparisons between him and some one whose image she carried in her heart, and he felt that she found him small and insignificant.

"It will be very hard for father and mother," she reiterated. "Father is an old man now, and must soon give up his school; so they will have even less to live upon than before. When he has no work to take up his mind, he will become restless and irritable. Mother won't have an easy time with him. They'll be very unhappy, both of them. Of course it would have been quite different could I have stayed at home to cheer them."

Gertrude paused, as if afraid to come out with what she

wanted to say. Ingmar's throat tightened, and his eyes began to
fill. He divined that Gertrude wanted to ask him to look after her
old parents.

"And I fancied that she had come here to-day only to
abuse and threaten me! And instead she opens her heart to me."

"You won't have to ask me, Gertrude," he said. "This is
a great honour for you to confer upon one who has behaved so
badly to you. Be assured that I shall treat your old parents better
than I have treated you."

When Ingmar said this, his voice trembled, and the wary
look was gone from his face. "How kind Gertrude is to me!" he
thought. "She does not ask this of me only out of consideration
for her parents, but she wants to show me that she has forgiven
me."

"I knew, Ingmar, that you wouldn't say no to this. And I
have something more to tell you." She spoke now in a brighter
and more confident tone. "I've got a great surprise for you!"

"How charmingly Gertrude speaks!" Ingmar was
thinking. "She has the sweetest, the cheeriest, and most tuneful
voice I have ever heard!"

"About a week ago," Gertrude continued, "I left home
intending to go straight on to Gothenburg, so as to be there when
the Hellgumists arrive. The first night I stopped over at Bergsåna
with a poor widow whose name it Marie Boving. That name I
want you to remember Ingmar—*Marie Boving*. If she should
ever come to want, you must help her."

"How pretty Gertrude is!" he thought, as he nodded and
promised to remember Marie Boving's name. "How pretty she
is! What will become of me when she goes? God forgive me if I
did wrong in giving her up for an old farm! Fields and meadows
can never be the same to you as a human being; they can't laugh
with you when you're happy, nor comfort you when you're sad!
Nothing on earth can make up for the loss of one who has loved
you."

"Marie Boving," Gertrude went on, "has a little room off
her kitchen, which she let me have for the night. 'You'll surely
sleep well to-night,' she said to me, 'as you are to lie on the
bedding which I bought at the sale on the Ingmar Farm.' But as
soon as I laid down, I felt a hard lump in the pillow under my

head. After all, it wasn't such extra good bedding Marie had bought for herself, I thought; but I was so tired out from tramping around all day, that I finally dropped off to sleep. In the middle of the night I awoke and turned the pillow, so I shouldn't feel that hard lump. While smoothing out the pillow, I discovered that the ticking had been cut and clumsily basted together. Inside there was something hard that crackled like paper. 'I don't have to lie on rocks,' I said to myself; then I ripped open a corner of the pillow, and pulled out a small parcel, which was done up in wrapping paper and tied with string."

Gertrude paused and glanced at Ingmar, to see whether his curiosity was aroused; but apparently he had not listened very closely to what she was telling.

"How prettily Gertrude uses her hands when she talks!" he thought. "I don't think I've ever seen any one as graceful as she is. There's an old saying that man loves mankind above everything. However, I believe that I did the right thing, for it wasn't only the farm that needed me, but the whole parish." Just the same, he felt to his discomfort that now it was not so easy to persuade himself that he loved his old home more than he loved Gertrude.

"I put the parcel down beside the bed, thinking that in the morning I would give it to Marie. But at daybreak I saw that your name was written on the wrapper. On closer examination I decided to take it along, and turn it over to you without saying anything about it, either to Marie or to any one else." Then taking a little parcel from the bottom of her basket, she said: "Here it is, Ingmar. Take it; it's your property." She supposed, of course, that he would be happily surprised.

Ingmar took the parcel, without much thought as to what he was receiving. He was struggling to ward off the bitter regrets that were stealing in on him.

"If Gertrude only knew how bewitching she is when she's so sweet and gentle! It would have been better for me had she come to upbraid me. I suppose I ought to be glad that she is as she is," he thought, "but I'm not. It seems as if she were grateful to me for having failed her."

"Ingmar," said Gertrude, in a tone that finally made him understand that she had something very important to tell him.

"When Elof lay sick at the Ingmar Farm, he must have used that very pillow."

She took the parcel from Ingmar and opened it. Then she counted out twenty crisp, new bank notes, each of which was a thousand-krona bill. Holding the money in front of his eyes, she said:

"Look, Ingmar! here's every krona of your inheritance money. It was Elof, of course, who hid it in the pillow!"

Ingmar heard what she said, and he saw the bank notes—but he saw and heard as in a daze. Gertrude placed the money in his hand, but his fingers would not close over it, and it fell to the ground. Then Gertrude picked it up and stuffed it into his pocket. Ingmar stood there, reeling like a drunken man. Suddenly he raised his arm, clenched his fist tight, and shook it, just as a drunken man might have done. "My God! My God!" he groaned.

Indeed, he wished that he could have had a word with our Lord, could have asked Him why this money had not been found sooner, and why it should have turned up now when it was not needed, and when Gertrude was already lost to him. The next moment his hand dropped heavily on Gertrude's shoulder.

"You certainly know how to take your revenge!"

"Do you call this revenge, Ingmar?" asked Gertrude, in dismay.

"What else should I call it? Why didn't you bring me this money at once?"

"I wanted to wait until the day of your wedding."

"If you had only come before, I'm sure I could have bought back the farm from Berger Sven Persson, and then I would have married you."

"Yes, I knew that."

"And yet you come on my wedding day, when it's too late!"

"It would have been too late in any case, Ingmar. It was too late a week ago, it is too late now, and it will be too late forever."

Ingmar had again sunk down on the stone. He covered his face with his hands and wailed:

"And I thought there was no help for it! I believed that

no power on earth could have altered this; but now I find that there was a way out, that we might all have been happy."

"Understand one thing, Ingmar: when I found the money, I knew at once that it would be the kind of help to us that you say. But it was no temptation to me—no, not for a second; for I belong to another."

"You should have kept it yourself!" cried Ingmar. "I feel as if a wolf were gnawing at my heart. So long as I believed there was no other course open to me, it wasn't so bad; but now that I know you could have been mine, I can't—"

"Why Ingmar! I came here to bring you happiness."

* * * * *

Meanwhile, the folks at the house had become impatient, and had gone out on the porch, where they were calling: "Ingmar! Ingmar!"

"Yes, and there's the bride, too, waiting for me!" he said mournfully. "And to think that you, Gertrude, should have brought all this about! When I had to give you up, circumstances forced me to do so, while you have spoiled everything simply to make me unhappy. Now I know how my father felt when my mother killed the child!"

Then he broke into violent sobs. "Never have I felt toward you as I do now!" he cried passionately. "I've never loved you half so much as I do now. Little did I think that love could be so cruelly bitter!"

Gertrude gently placed her hand on his head. "Ingmar," she said very quietly, "it was never, never my meaning to take revenge on you. But so long as your heart is wedded to the things of this earth, it is wedded to sorrow."

For a long while Ingmar sat motionless, his head bowed. When he at last looked up, Gertrude was gone. People now came running from the farm to find him. He struck his clenched fist against the stone upon which he sat, and a look of determination came into his face.

"Gertrude and I will surely meet again," he said. "Then maybe it will be altogether different. We Ingmarssons are known to win what we yearn for."

The Dean's Widow

Everybody tried to dissuade the Hellgumists from going to Jerusalem. And toward the last, it seemed as though the very hills and vales echoed the plea, "Do not go! Do not go!"

Even the country gentlemen did their best to get the peasants to abandon the idea. The bailiff, the judge, and the councilmen gave them no peace; they asked them how they could feel sure that these Americans were not imposters; for they had no way of knowing what sort of folk they would be getting in with. In that far Eastern country there was neither law nor order; there one was always in danger of falling into the hands of brigands. Besides, there were no decent roads in that land—all their goods would have to be transported by means of pack-horses, as in the wild forests up North.

The doctor told them they would never be able to stand the climate; that Jerusalem was full of smallpox and malignant fevers; they were going away only to die.

The Hellgumists answered that they knew all this, and it was for that very reason they were going. They were going there in order to fight the smallpox and the fevers, to build roads and to till the soil. God's country should no longer lie waste; they would transform it into a paradise. And no one was able to turn them from their purpose.

Down in the village lived an old lady, the widow of the Dean. She was very, very old! She occupied a large chamber above the post office, just across the street from the church, where she had lived since the death of her husband.

Some of the more well-to-do peasant women had always made it a rule to drop in to see the old lady on Sundays, before the service, and bring her some freshly baked bread, a pat of butter, or a can of milk. On these occasions she would always have the coffee pot put on the fire the moment they came in, and the one who could shout the loudest always talked with her, for she was frightfully deaf. Of course they would try to tell her about everything that had happened during the week, but they could never be certain as to how much she heard of what was told her.

She never left her room, and there were times when it seemed as if people had forgotten her entirely. Then some one, in passing, would see her old face back of the draped white curtains at the window, and think: "I must not forget her in her loneliness; to-morrow when we have killed the calf, I'll run in to see her, and take her a bit of fresh meat."

No one could find out just how much she knew or did not know of what went on in the parish. With the advancing years, she became more and more detached, and apparently lost all interest in the things of this world. Now she just sat reading all the while in an old Postil, which she seemed to know by heart.

Living with her was a faithful old servant, who helped her dress, and prepared her meals. The two of them were in mortal fear of robbers and mice, and they were so afraid of fire that they would sit in the dark the whole evening rather than light the lamp.

Several among those who had lately become followers of Hellgum, used to call on the Dean's widow in the old days, and bring her little gifts; but since their conversion they had separated themselves from all who were not of their faith; so they no longer went to see her. No one knew whether she understood why they did not come. Nor did anybody know whether she had heard anything about their proposed emigration to Jerusalem.

But one day the old lady took it into her head to go for a drive, and ordered the servant to get her a carriage and pair. Imagine the astonishment of the old servant! But when she attempted to remonstrate, the old lady suddenly became stone deaf. Raising her right hand, her forefinger poised in the air, she said:

"I wish to go for a drive, Sara Lena, you must find me a carriage and a pair of horses."

There was nothing for Sara Lena but to do as she was told. So she went over to the pastor's to ask for the loan of his rig, which was a fairly decent-looking turnout. That done, she was put to the bother of airing and brushing an old fur cape and an old velvet bonnet that had been lying in camphor twenty consecutive years. And it was no small task getting the old lady down the stairs and into the wagon! She was so feeble that it seemed as if her life could have been as easily snuffed out as a candle flame in a storm.

When the Dean's widow was at last safely seated in the carriage, she ordered the driver to take her to the Ingmar Farm.

Maybe the folks up at the farm were not surprised when they saw who was coming! The housefolk came running out, and lifted her down from the carriage, and ushered her into the living-room. Seated at the table in there were quite a number of Hellgumists. Of late they had been in the habit of coming together and having their frugal meals in common—meals which consisted of rice and tea and other light things; this was to prepare them for the coming journey across the desert.

The Dean's widow glanced around the room. Several persons tried to speak to her, but that day she heard nothing whatever. Suddenly she put up her hand, and said in that hard, dry voice in which deaf people are wont to speak: "You do not come to see *me* any more; therefore, I have come to *you*, to warn you not to go to Jerusalem. It is a wicked city. It was there they crucified our Saviour."

Karin attempted to answer the old lady, who apparently did not hear, for she went right on:

"It is a wicked city," she repeated. "Bad people live there. 'Twas there they crucified Christ. I have come here to-day," she added, "because this has been a good house. Ingmarsson has been a good name; it has always been a good name. Therefore, you must remain in our parish,"

Then she turned and walked out of the house. Now she had done her part, and could die in peace. This was the last service that life demanded of her.

After the old lady had gone, Karin broke into tears. "Perhaps it isn't right for us to go," she sighed. But she was pleased that the Dean's widow had said that Ingmarsson was a good name—that it had always been a good name.

It was the first and only time Karin had been known to waver, or to express any doubt as to the advisability of the great undertaking.

The Departure Of The Pilgrims

One beautiful morning in July, a long train of carts and wagons set out from the Ingmar Farm. The Hellgumists had at last completed their arrangements, and were now leaving for Jerusalem—the first stage of their journey being the long drive to the railway station.

The procession, in moving toward the village, had to pass a wretched hovel which was called Mucklemire. The people who lived there were a disreputable lot—the kind of scum of the earth which must have sprung into being when our Lord's eyes were turned, or when he had been busy elsewhere.

There was a whole horde of dirty, ragged youngsters on the place, who were in the habit of running loose all day, shrieking after passing vehicles, and calling the occupants bad names; there was an old crone, who usually sat by the roadside, tipsy; and there were a husband and wife who were always quarrelling and fighting, and who had never been known to do any honest work. No one could say whether they begged more than they stole, or stole more than they begged.

When the Jerusalem-farers came alongside this wretched hovel, which was about as tumbledown as a place can become where wind and storm have, for many years, been allowed to work havoc, they saw the old crone standing erect and sober at the roadside, on the same spot where she usually sat in a drunken stupor, lurching to and fro, and babbling incoherently, and with her were four of the children. All five were now washed and combed, and as decently dressed as was possible for them to be.

When the persons seated in the first cart caught sight of them, they slackened their speed and drove by very slowly; the others did likewise, walking their horses.

All the Jerusalem-farers suddenly burst into tears, the grown-ups crying softly, while the children broke into loud sobs and wails.

Nothing had so moved them as the sight of Beggar Lina standing at the roadside clean and sober. Even to this day their eyes fill when they think of her; of how on that morning she had denied herself the drink, and had come forth sober, with the grandchildren washed and combed, to do honour to their departure.

When they had all passed by, Beggar Lina also began to weep.

"Those people are going to Heaven to meet Jesus," she told the children. "All those people are going to Heaven but we are left standing by the wayside."

* * * * *

When the procession of carts and wagons had driven halfway through the parish, it came to the long floating bridge that lies rocking on the river.

This is a difficult bridge to cross. The first part of it is a steep incline all the way down to the edge of the stream; then come two rather abrupt elevations, under which boats and timber rafts can pass; and at the other end the up grade is so heavy that both man and beast dread to climb it.

That bridge has always been a source of annoyance. The planks keep rotting, and have to be replaced continually. In the spring, when the ice breaks, it has to be watched day and night to prevent its being knocked to pieces by drifting ice floes; and when the spring rains cause a rise in the river, large portions of the bridge are washed away.

But the people of the parish are proud of their bridge, and glad to have it, rickety as it is. But for that blessed bridge they would have to use a rowboat or a ferry every time they wanted to cross from one side of the parish to the other.

The bridge groaned and swayed as the Jerusalem-farers

passed over it, and the water came up through the cracks in the planks and splashed the horses' legs.

They felt sad at having to leave their dear old bridge, for they knew it was something which belonged to all of them. Houses and farms, groves and meadows, were owned by different persons, but the bridge was their common property.

But was there nothing else that they had in common? Had they not the church in among the birches on the other side of the bridge? Had they not the pretty white schoolhouse, and the parsonage?

And they had something more in common. Theirs was the beauty which they saw from the bridge: the lovely view of the broad and mighty river flowing peacefully on between its tree-clad banks, and all a-sparkle in the summer light; the wide view across the valley clear over to the blue hills. All this was theirs! It was as if burned into their eyes. And now they would never see it again.

When the Hellgumists came to the middle of the bridge, they began to sing one of Sankey's hymns. "We shall meet once again," they sang, "we shall meet in that Eden above."

There was no one on the bridge to hear them. They were singing to the blue hills of their homeland, to the silvery waters of the river, to the waving trees. And from throats tightened by sobs and tears came the song of farewell:

"O beautiful homeland, with thy peaceful farms with their red and white tree-sheltered houses; with thy fertile fields and green meadows; thy groves and orchards; thy long valley, divided by the shining river, hear us! Pray God that we may meet again, that we may see thee again in Paradise!"

* * * * *

When the long procession of carts and wagons had crossed the bridge, it came to the churchyard. In the churchyard there was a large flat gravestone that was crumbling from age. It bore neither name nor date, but according to tradition, the bones of an ancestor of the Ljung family rested under it.

When Ljung Björn Olafsson, who was now going to Jerusalem, and his brother Pehr were children, they had once sat on that stone and talked. At first they were as chummy as could be; then all at once they got to quarrelling about something, became very much excited, and raised their voices. What they quarrelled about they had long since forgotten, but what they never could forget was, that while they were quarreling the hardest, they heard several distinct and deliberate rappings on the stone where they were seated. They broke off instantly. Then they took each other by the hand, and stole quietly away. Afterward, they could never see that stone without thinking of this incident.

And now, when Ljung Björn was driving past the churchyard, who should he see but his brother Pehr, sitting on that selfsame stone, with his head resting on his hands. Ljung Björn reined in his horse, and signalled to the others to wait for him. He got down from the cart, climbed over the cemetery wall, and went and sat on the stone beside his brother.

Pehr Olafsson immediately said: "So you sold the farm, Björn!"

"Yes," answered Björn. "I have given all I owned to God."

"But the farm was not yours," the brother mildly protested.

"Not mine?"

"No, it belonged to the family."

Ljung Björn did not reply, but sat quietly waiting. He knew that when his brother had seated himself on that stone, it was for the purpose of speaking words of peace. Therefore, he was not afraid of what Pehr might say.

"I have bought back the farm," said the brother.

Ljung Björn gave a start. "Couldn't you bear to have it go out of the family?" he asked.

"I'm hardly rich enough to do such things for that reason."

Björn looked at his brother inquiringly.

"I did it that you might have something to come back to."

Björn was overwhelmed, and could hardly keep the tears back.

"And that your children may have a place to come back to—"

Björn put his arm around his brother's neck.

"—and for the sake of my dear sister-in-law," said Pehr. "It will be good for her to know that she has a house and home waiting for her. The old home will always be open to any of you who may want to come back."

"Pehr, take my place in the cart and go to Jerusalem, and I'll stay at home. You are far more worthy to enter the Promised Land than I am."

"No, no!" said the brother smilingly. "I understand how you mean it, but I guess I fit in better at home."

"I think you're more fit for Heaven," said Björn, laying his head on his brother's shoulder. "Now you must forgive me everything," he said.

Then they got up and clasped hands in farewell.

"This time there were no rappings," Pehr remarked.

"Strange you should have thought of coming here," said Björn.

"We brothers have had some difficulty in maintaining peace, when we've met of late."

"Did you think that I would want to quarrel to-day?"

"No, but I become angry when I think of having to lose you!"

They walked together down to the road. Presently Pehr went up to Björn's wife, and gave her a hearty handclasp.

"I've bought the Ljung Farm," he said. "I tell you this now so that you may know you've always got a place to come to." Then he took the eldest of the children by the hand, and said: "Remember, now, that you have a house and land to come back to, should you want to return to the old country." He went from one child to the other, even to little Eric, who was only two years old and couldn't understand what it all meant. "The rest of you youngsters must not forget to tell little Eric that he has a home to return to whenever he wants to come back."

And the Jerusalem-farers went on.

* * * * *

When the long line of carts and wagons had passed the churchyard, the travellers came upon a large crowd of friends

and relatives who had come out to bid them goodbye. They had
a long halt here, for everybody wanted to shake hands with
them, and say a few parting words.

And later, when they drove through the village, the road
was lined with people who wished to witness their departure.
There were people standing on every doorstep and leaning out of
every window; they sat upon the low stone hedges all along the
way, and those who lived farther off stood on mounds and hills
waving a last farewell.

The long procession moved slowly past all these people
until it came to the home of Councilman Lars Clementsson,
where it halted. Here Gunhild got down to say good-bye to her
folks.

Gunhild had been staying at the Ingmar Farm since
deciding to go with the others to Jerusalem. She had felt that this
was preferable to living at home in constant strife with her
parents, who could not become reconciled to the thought of her
going.

As Gunhild stepped down from the cart she noticed that
the place looked quite deserted. There was not a soul to be seen,
either outside or at the windows. When she reached the gate she
found it locked. She stepped over the stile into the yard. Even
the front door of the house was fastened. Then Gunhild went
round to the kitchen door; it was hooked on the inside! She
knocked several times, but as no one came she pulled the door
toward her, inserted a stick in the crack, and lifted the hook. So
she finally got in. There was no one in the kitchen, nor was there
any one in the living-room, nor yet in the inner room.

Gunhild did not want to go away without letting her
parents know that she had been to say good-bye to them. She
went over to the big combination desk and bureau, where her
father always kept his writing materials, and drew down the lid.
She could not at first find the ink, so looked for it in drawers and
pigeonholes. While searching, she came upon a small casket
which she remembered well. It was her mother's—she had
received it from her husband as a wedding present. When
Gunhild was a little girl her mother had often shown it to her.
The casket was enamelled in white, with a garland of hand-
painted flowers. On the inside of the lid was a picture of a

shepherd piping to a flock of white lambs. Gunhild now opened the box to take a last peep at the shepherd.

In this casket Gunhild's mother had always kept her most cherished keepsakes-the worn-down wedding ring which had belonged to her mother, the old-fashioned watch which had been her father's, and her own gold earrings. But when Gunhild opened the box, she found that all these things had been taken out, and in their place lay a letter. It was a letter that she herself had written. A year or two before, she had made a trip to Mora by boat across Lake Siljan. The boat had capsized. Some of her fellow-passengers were drowned, and her parents had been told that she, too, had perished. It flashed upon Gunhild that her mother must have been made so happy on receiving a letter from her daughter telling of her safety, that she had taken everything else out of the casket, and placed the letter there as her most priceless treasure.

Gunhild turned as pale as death; her heart was being wrung. "Now I know that I'm killing my mother," she said, She no longer thought of writing anything, but hurried away. She got up into the cart, taking no notice of the many questions as to whether she had seen her parents. During the remainder of the drive she sat motionless, with her hands in her lap, and staring straight ahead. "I'm killing my mother," she was saying to herself. "I know that I'm killing my mother. I know that mother will die. I can never be happy again. I may go to the Holy Land, but I am killing my own mother."

* * * * *

When the long line of carts and wagons had passed through the village, it turned in on a forest road. Here the Jerusalem-farers noticed for the first time that they were being shadowed by two persons whom they did not seem to know. While still in the village, they had been so engrossed in their leave-takings that they had not seen the strange vehicle in which the two unknown people sat; but in the wood their attention was drawn to it.

Sometimes it would drive past all the other carts and lead the procession; then again it would take the side of the road and let the other teams go by. It was an ordinary wagon, the kind commonly used for carting; therefore, it was impossible to tell to whom it belonged. Nor did any one recognize the horse.

It was driven by an old man, who was much bent, and had wrinkled hands and a long white beard. Certainly none of them knew who he was. But by his side sat a woman whom they somehow felt they knew. No one could see her face, for her head was covered with a black shawl, both sides of which she held together so closely that not even her eyes were seen. Many tried to guess from her figure and size who she was, but no two guessed alike.

Gunhild said at once, "It's my mother," and Israel Tomasson's wife declared that it was her sister. There was scarcely a person among them but had his or her own notion as to who it was. Tims Halvor thought it was old Eva Gunnersdotter.

The strange cart accompanied them all the way, but not once did the woman draw the shawl back from her face. To some of the Hellgumists she became a person they loved, to others one they feared, but to most of them she was some one whom they had deserted.

Wherever the road was wide enough to allow of it, the strange cart would drive past the whole line of wagons, and then pull to one side until they had all gone by. At such times the unknown woman would turn toward the travellers, and watch them from behind her drawn shawl; but she made no sign to any of them, so that no one could really say for certain who she was. She followed all the way to the railway station. There they expected to see her face; but when they got down and began to look around for her—she was gone.

* * * * *

When the procession of carts and wagons passed along the countryside, no one was seen cutting grass, or raking hay, or stacking hay. That morning all work had been suspended, and every one was either standing at the roadside in their Sunday clothes or driving to see the travellers off; some went with them six miles, some twelve, a few accompanied them all the way to the railway station.

Throughout the entire length and breadth of the parish only one man was seen at work. That man was Hök Matts Ericsson. Nor was he mowing grass-that he regarded as only child's play. He was clearing away stones from his land, just as he had done in his youth, when preparing his newly acquired acres for cultivation.

Gabriel, as he drove along, could see his father from the road. Hök Matts was out in the grove prying up stones with his crowbar, and piling them on to a stone hedge. He never once looked up from his work, but went right on digging and lugging stones, some of which were so big that Gabriel thought they were enough to break his back—and afterward throwing them up on to the hedge with a force that caused them to splinter, and made sparks fly. Gabriel, who was driving one of the goods wagons, let his horse look out for itself for a long time while his eyes were turned toward his father.

Old Hök Matts worked on' and on, toiling and slaving exactly as he had done when his son was a little lad, and he strove to develop his property. Grief had taken a firm hold on Hök Matts; yet he went on digging and prying up larger and larger stones, and piling them on the hedge.

Soon after the procession had passed, a violent thunderstorm came up. Everybody ran for cover, and Hök Matts, too, thought of doing the same; then he changed his mind. He dared not leave off working.

At noon his daughter came to the door and called to him to come to dinner. Hök Matts was not very hungry; still, he felt that he might need a bite to eat. He did not go in, however, for he was afraid to stop his work.

His wife had gone with Gabriel to the railway station. On her return, late in the evening, she stopped to tell her husband that now their son had gone, but he would not leave off an instant to hear what she had to say. The neighbours noticed how Hök Matts worked that day. They came out to watch him, and after looking on a while, they went in and reported that he was still there, that he had been at it the whole day without a break.

Evening came, but the light lingered a while, and Hök Matts kept right on working. He felt that if he were to leave off while still able to drag a foot, his grief would overpower him.

By and by his wife came back again, and stood watching him. The grove was now almost clear of stones, and the hedge quite high enough, but still the little old man went on lugging stones that were more fit for a giant to handle. Now and then a neighbour would come over to see if he was still at it; but no one spoke to him.

Then darkness fell. They could no longer see him, but they could hear him—could hear the dull thud of stone against stone as he went on building the wall.

Then at last as he raised the crowbar it slipped from his hands, and when he stooped to pick it up he fell; and before he could think, he was asleep.

Some time afterward he roused himself sufficiently to get to the house. He said nothing, he did not even attempt to undress, but simply threw himself down on a wooden bench and dropped off to sleep.

* * * * *

The Jerusalem-farers had at last reached the railway station which was newly built in a big clearing in the middle of the forest. There was no town, nor were there any fields or gardens, but everything had been planned on a grand scale in the expectation that an important railway community would some day spring up in this wilderness.

Round the station itself the ground was levelled; there was a broad stone platform, with roomy baggage sheds and no end of gravel drives. A couple of stores and workshops, a photographic studio, and a hotel had already been put up around the gravelled square, but the remainder of the clearing was nothing but unbroken stubble land.

The Dal River also flowed past here. It came with a wild and angry rush from the dark woods, and dashed foamingly onward in a cascade of falls. The Jerusalem-farers could hardly credit that this was a part of the broad, majestic river they had crossed in the morning. Here no smiling valley met their gaze; on all sides the view was obstructed by dark fir-clad heights.

When the little children who were going with their

parents to Jerusalem were lifted out of the carts in this desolate-looking place, they became uneasy and began to cry. Before, they had been very happy in the thought of travelling to Jerusalem. Of course they had cried a good deal when leaving their homes, but down at the station they became quite disconsolate.

Their elders were busy unloading their goods from the wagons and stowing them away in a baggage car. They all helped, so that no one had any time to look after the children, and see what they were up to.

The youngsters meanwhile got together, and held council as to what they should do.

After a bit the older children took the little ones by the hand and walked away from the station, two by two-a big child and a little child. They went the same way they had come across the sea of sand, through the stubble ground, over the river and into the dark forest.

Suddenly, one of the women happened to think of the children, and opened a food basket to give them something to eat. She called to them, but got no answer. They had disappeared from sight. Two of the men went to look for them. Following the tracks which the many little feet had left in the sand, they went on into the woods, where they caught sight of the youngsters, marching along in line, two by two, a big child and a little child. When the men called to them they did not stop, but kept right on.

The men ran to overtake them. Then the children tried to run away, but the smaller ones could not keep up; they stumbled and fell. Then all of them stood still—wretchedly unhappy, and crying as if their little hearts would break.

"But, children, where are you going?" asked one of the men. Whereupon the littlest ones set up a loud wail, and the eldest boy answered:

"We don't want to go to Jerusalem; we want to go home."

And for a long time, even after the children had been brought back to the station, and were seated in the railway carriage, they still went on whimpering and crying: "We don't want to go to Jerusalem; we want to go home."

9 781934 648476